MEAN
TOWN
BLUES

MEAN TOWN BLUES

SAM REAVES

PEGASUS BOOKS
NEW YORK

All events and characters depicted in this story are fictional. There is no Chicago suburb named Maywood Park, and nothing depicted in this story should be construed as an allegation against any existing municipality or police department.

———◄◦►———

MEAN TOWN BLUES

Pegasus Books LLC
45 Wall Street, Suite 1021
New York, NY 10005

First Pegasus Books edition 2008

Interior design by Maria Fernandez

Library of Congress Cataloging-in-Publication Data is available.

ISBN: 978-1-60598-003-4

10 9 8 7 8 6 5 4 3 2 1

Printed in the United States of America
Distributed by W. W. Norton & Company, Inc.
www.pegasusbooks.us

Thanks are due to Dave Salter and Frank Cappitelli for their advice on practical matters beyond the author's experience. Neither of them should be held responsible for the author's flights of fancy.

This book is dedicated to the infantryman,
Army or Marine Corps, wherever he serves.

MEAN
TOWN
BLUES

1

For Staff Sergeant Thomas McLain the war ended on MSR Tampa a few kilometers east of Baghdad International Airport and a few days shy of his twenty-seventh birthday. It was a busy day.

In the morning Tommy and his Quick Reaction Force had escorted an investigator and his interpreter out to look at an IED third platoon had found. The platoon had scooped up a suspect too, but after a lot of back-and-forth through the interpreter the investigator said cut him loose: he had nothing to do with it. He was just the usual dickless vagrant kicking around the landscape. Iraq was full of them. The third platoon guys were not happy, having seen three men dusted off in a Blackhawk after an IED took out their Hummer three days before, but the investigator wasn't buying it. However these guys made their judgments, he had made his. Tommy left the platoon waiting for EOD to come and make that little stretch of freeway safe for democracy while he escorted the investigator back to base.

Things got exciting after lunch when the radio started squawking. Second platoon had been ambushed on Route Tampa and had managed to shoot their way out of it, but they had used up all their ammunition doing it. Tommy and company ran a resupply mission out to them at a safe place on Route Tampa. The platoon had been lucky and hadn't taken any serious casualties. Tommy was half expecting to be told to go find the bad guys, but everybody was ordered back to ECP7 for refit.

Approaching the base they passed a convoy of civilian tankers full of diesel fuel, heading for the highway. Tommy flagged them down. "Y'all might want to think twice," he told the lead driver. "These guys just hit an ambush about three kilometers north on the highway."

The burly driver chewed on his mustache for a few seconds, giving Tommy the eye. "North?" he said finally. "We're going south. I think we'll take our chances."

Tommy shrugged and gave him a wave. "Drive fast," he said.

Ten minutes later Tommy was standing with his battalion commander just inside Entrance Check Point 7, looking at a column of thick black smoke to the north, about three kilometers up the highway. "God damn it," said Tommy. "Permission requested to go and rescue those dumb sons of bitches."

Permission granted, Tommy and the QRF jumped back in

the Hummers and hauled ass. When they got to the ambush site, sure enough it was the same convoy they had passed, stopped dead on the highway and taking fire from both sides. The smoke was coming from a tanker in the middle of the convoy that had taken a hit from something, maybe a mortar, and was going to be burning for a good long while. "What kind of a dumbass can't tell north from south?" Tommy shouted over the noise of the engine and the tearing sound of small arms fire as his driver steered past two tankers that were nearly blocking the road, slewed around with their tires shot out.

Mortar rounds were landing here and there, going wham but not doing any major damage, not yet. Tommy knew it was a matter of time before another lucky hit sent up another big column of smoke, and he truly did not want to see that close up. He started shouting into his radio and in a couple of minutes his guys had set up a base of fire and were pouring rounds into the tall grass behind a berm a couple of hundred meters to the west and into some trees and houses to the east. They had M2s, M240 Bs, M249s and Mark 19s to work with, and it all made a hell of a noise.

Somebody who was on the ball had already called in a Medevac, and the pilot set it down in the middle of the chaos as gentle as could be in a clear space between two tankers. Tommy was running from truck to truck, jumping up on the cab to see who was alive and who was not. Fuel was pouring out of holes in the sides of the tankers and the road was covered with it; small arms fire was kicking up sparks and that made Tommy nervous as hell. Most of the drivers were just cowering, keeping their heads down and praying or crying or shouting, but some of them were hurt. Tommy and the other men he had detailed started pulling the wounded out and dragging them toward the chopper.

The incoming fire was lessening a little. Tommy thought maybe the bad guys were starting to withdraw. The U.S. Army could put out a lot of firepower in a hurry. All he had to do was get the wounded out of these trucks and get everybody turned around and heading back toward the base before the whole thing went up. The smell of diesel fuel was starting to bother Tommy McLain a whole lot.

When it happened, he truly did not know for a second what had hit him: it was a lot like the time in Little League when he got an aluminum bat in the back of the head trying to throw out the runner. For a moment he was just dazed, wondering what had happened to make everything so strange, so confusing.

The first thing he really knew for certain after that was that he was being dragged toward the chopper, just like the drivers he had pulled out of the cabs. Somebody was shouting that the sergeant was hit. He didn't know where he had been hit but he believed it: he had a general deep-seated feeling of awful bodily distress. He had time to think that he couldn't be dying if he could think so clearly and then knew immediately that that didn't mean jack shit, and then somebody opened the oven door and a great wave of heat washed over them all and the last thing Tommy heard before he passed out, faint and high beneath the roar of the fire and the throb of the chopper, was the sound of grown men screaming, burning to death.

2

Chicago, why not? People had been going up Interstate 65 to Chicago as long as Tommy could remember. His Uncle Pete had worked in Chicago for a few years before coming back and buying the gas station in Lexington. Some people only made it to Louisville or Cincinnati, but the go-getters pushed on up to the Big Town on the lake. Chicago was where the jobs were.

There wasn't much left for him in Kentucky, that was for sure. Tommy drove by the house and sat looking at it for a moment, at other people's lawn furniture, at the porch swing and the old oak and the peeling paint, and then wondered why he had come. There was nothing there but sad memories. Then he called the Holmeses' and found out Mrs. Holmes had died the year before, dropped dead one day in her garden. Bill Holmes told Tommy to come on by and gave him a beer and told him how his wife had always said that he was her favorite student of all time. Bill looked old and worn out and Tommy got the impression he was just waiting to go join his wife. It made Tommy sad, more than he'd thought it would, maybe because Mrs. Holmes had been a substitute for the mother he could barely remember.

The McLain family was history now in this town. There were plenty of people still around who knew him, had known his dad: on Main Street he got a lot of slaps on the back and a couple of free drinks and a lot of well-meaning horseshit about being a hero, but he could tell there was nothing here for him anymore. The last thing he did on his way out of town was to go visit the graves. Nothing had changed. His mother and father and sister still lay side by side in the old cemetery in the hollow, under the sun and the rain and the stars. He jumped in the car and went.

Brian Dawson had gone off to UK in Lexington and then wound up in Chicago. If Tommy had ever had a best friend it was Brian, though he'd had his doubts for a few years there as Brian got gentrified and Tommy got hammered into shape by the army. There had been a couple of awkward meetings. But Brian had turned up out of the blue at Tommy's dad's funeral and told him if he ever wanted to check out Chicago he had a place to stay. Tommy had called him from Fort Hood when he got out of the hospital and told Brian to look for him in a week or two.

He crossed the Ohio at Louisville and wheeled north. Southern Indiana was pretty much like Kentucky, just the other bank of the big winding river that had brought everybody's ancestors west a couple of hundred years before. But as he went north the woods thinned out and the vistas got flatter and farther, and when he stopped for gas somewhere north of Indianapolis the people already sounded different and there was a chill in the air: he had gone from South to North in half a day.

He had second thoughts about the whole thing, riding the brake through the bottleneck on I-80 in the crowded northwest corner of Indiana and then charging up the gut through the South Side of Chicago on 90-94, night falling and the skyline of the Loop twinkling ahead. He wasn't sure if he could take a steady diet of this shit. Swinging out onto Lake Shore Drive with the lake shimmering on his right and the wall of skyscrapers to the left made him feel a little better: bright lights and good times ahead. Tommy was ready for some fun. The last year or so had been gruesome.

Brian lived in a place called Lincoln Park, on the North Side, and full of high brick houses all jammed together. The narrow streets under the trees were pretty but the Park part of it evidently did not refer to a place to leave your car. After he spotted Brian's address Tommy cruised for half an hour before he found a legal spot to drop the worn-out Chevy he'd bought off an Iraq-bound E-4 at Fort Hood. He humped his duffel bag the three blocks back to Brian's place and rang the bell.

"Jesus, Tom. You look like you been through the ringer," Brian said, stepping back from a quick hug with a couple of hard backslaps thrown in. "You all healed now?"

"Pretty much." Tommy dropped his bag on the floor,

looking around the place. High windows, bare wood floor with a rug over it, nice furniture: a real grown-up's place instead of the college-boy dump Brian had lived in down in Lexington.

"Damn, it's good to see you. You want a beer?"

"Wouldn't fight one off." Tommy was having doubts again. Brian was different: he had put on weight, cut his hair. Here it was a Sunday night and he was wearing corduroys and a sweater. He looked like a banker, which was what he was. He had a job in the Loop and was making tons of money, to hear him tell it. It showed.

Brian wanted to know all about Iraq, and Tommy gave him the canned rap he had worked up to tell people about it, which didn't even come close.

"You should write a book about it, man."

Brian was serious, apparently. Tommy looked at him for a second and snorted a little. "It'd be a short one. 'Everything sucked and a lot of people got hurt. The End.' "

Brian just nodded, giving him a long look. "Well, you made it. You out for good now?"

"I guess so. My hitch ran out while I was in the hospital. I wanted to re-up but the doc wouldn't clear me. He said it was time to go join the VFW and fatten up on potato salad, let my insides heal."

"So what are you planning to do?"

Tommy looked around the room for a moment, then back at Brian. "Damned if I know."

They drank a little more and got caught up on mutual acquaintances, which took about a minute. Tommy didn't really care about any of them. With the second beer, Tommy tossed Brian a couple of war stories after all, and then Brian had to go to bed because he had to work in the morning. He fixed Tommy up with a spare key and a spare pillow, and at ten-thirty Tommy was standing at a window in a dark room looking out at a strange city and wondering what the rest of his life was going to be like. He wasn't sure about Brian, but if he had learned one thing, it was that you needed friends in this life, and all the rest of Tommy's friends were still in Iraq, the ones that were still alive, anyway.

3

Tommy could do cities. He'd gone into the service with hay behind his ears but eight years in the army had taken him around the block a few times. If it wasn't for the low clouds and the badass wind coming off the lake Chicago would have been one of the nicer towns he'd seen. It was big, unbelievably big, but he found lots of corners he liked. He spent a day just driving around, covering the whole city from north to south, and then he said hell with the car and spent another day poking around on the trains and the buses, just figuring things out. Tommy like to reconnoiter wherever he went. It was the infantryman in him: he didn't like surprises.

It didn't take him long to get the basic geography down. The Loop sat on the lakefront and everything funneled into it. West of the Loop things looked pretty grim: Tommy didn't see anything in that direction to tempt him. North of the river was nightlife, then neighborhoods, mostly prosperous except for Uptown, which was touch and go. Tommy heard people talking on Wilson Avenue who sounded like they'd come from back home. The South Side went on forever and was mostly black, though the southwest was white, like the northwest. In between were the Mexicans, lots of them, which surprised Tommy. Texas was one thing, but this far north? The black areas were a mixed bag, like black areas everywhere. Tommy saw streets that looked pretty nice and streets that looked like hell. Nobody bothered him anywhere. Tommy didn't have a problem with black people, not since the army.

He was going to need a job, and he realized he didn't have a very good idea how to get one. Other than the part-time lumberyard gig he'd had in high school, the army was the only job he'd ever had. He bought the paper one day and looked at the want ads, and Brian showed him how to use his computer to search for jobs online, but the real problem became apparent right away: Tommy didn't have any idea of what he wanted to do.

"You probably need to go back to school," Brian said, looking like he wasn't sure how Tommy was going to take it. "It's a new economy, man. The education premium is higher than ever. You're gonna need a degree."

Tommy nodded. "No doubt." He wasn't worried yet. He had money saved up from the army, enough to live on for a while, maybe even enough to pay for a little schooling. He just needed an idea. On his fourth day in town he got a job, just by walking into a restaurant on Irving Park that had a sign in the window. The Greek who owned the place needed a janitor and he hired Tommy on the spot. It was a dogshit job for part-time money, working at night after the place closed, but it was work. Tommy wasn't the type of guy who liked to sit around. He started that night.

"You're shitting me," said Brian. "You can do better than that."

Tommy shrugged. "I ain't planning to make it a career."

The next item on the agenda was a place to live. Brian told him there was no hurry, but one thing Tommy had looked forward to about getting out of the service was having his own place. Living with other guys was getting old. But he couldn't believe how high rents were in this town. He actually had enough money to get his own place right away, but if he didn't get more work soon, an apartment was just going to drain his savings. He decided to hang with Brian until he had a better job or until things started to get uncomfortable.

Which wouldn't be for a while, he hoped. Brian was gone all day, came in tired and seemed to consider Tommy's bunkhouse cooking an improvement over whatever he'd been eating before. They'd have a couple of beers with the pork chops and shoot the shit or watch some TV. A couple of times Brian took him out to a bar on Halsted Street a few blocks away. He introduced Tommy to some guys he knew who seemed okay. There were women there, too, another thing Tommy had promised himself about life after the army. But these women wouldn't even look at him. Tommy knew he'd have to be patient.

He and Brian were catching up on things, little by little. Tommy had to admire what Brian had done, gotten an education and made something of himself. Tommy had never really considered college, despite all Mrs. Holmes's quiet pleading. At the time, his father had been in the process of drinking himself to death and there hadn't been a lot of support on the home front. "It's never too late," Brian said. "You got the brains."

Tommy didn't doubt that. He just didn't know what the hell he wanted. He thought about it late at night, swabbing the floors in the restaurant, but nothing came to him. He figured he had time; he'd been in town a little more than a week.

The restaurant was on the southern fringe of Uptown, near the Sheridan El stop. Tommy finished up at the restaurant about three in the morning and took the train back down to Fullerton to get to Brian's place. He never felt unsafe until the night a Mexican-looking punk with multiple earrings who had looked half asleep as Tommy came up onto the platform revived all of a sudden and pulled a gun out from under his Phat Farm sweatshirt. "Gimme your wallet, jag-off," the kid said, aiming at Tommy's face from six feet away. He looked wide-awake now.

Tommy looked him in the eye and decided he was serious. He said, "Okay, don't get excited," and reached slowly for his hip pocket. He thought about just ducking and running, knowing most people couldn't hit shit with a handgun, but the kid was between him and the stairs and there wasn't anywhere else to run to. Besides, the range was a little too close for comfort. He pulled out his wallet and threw it down on the platform at the kid's feet.

Sure enough the kid bent over to pick it up without keeping the gun trained on Tommy, and Tommy punted his face like a football, hard. It would have had a hang time of four seconds, easy. As it was the kid just collapsed and started to bleed onto the planks.

Tommy picked up his wallet and put it back in his pocket. He looked at the gun for a second, just lying there. It was a Browning .25 automatic, not a big gun but capable of doing damage. The kid was making moaning, bubbling noises through his flattened nose, starting to get in touch with his feelings as the fog cleared. Tommy picked up the gun and put it on safety, took out the clip, racked the slide. The round that had been in the chamber kicked out onto the platform. "You little shit," said Tommy. He picked up the ejected round and put it in his jacket pocket along with the gun and the clip. He thought for about two seconds about calling the police, spending the rest of the night explaining.

"Fuck that," he said out loud. He could hear the train coming down from Wilson, slowing for the curve. He grabbed the kid by his sweatshirt and dragged him to the head of the stairs. He gave him a shove and watched him go ass-over-teakettle down to the landing, squawking all the way, leaving a few drops of blood on the steps. Then Tommy went and stood in the cold wind with his hands in his jacket pockets as the train pulled into the station. His instep hurt a little where he'd kicked the kid but he had his work boots on and that had helped. He flexed the foot and nothing was broken.

4

On Saturday night Brian took him to a party. "Long story," he said. "This chick I knew at UK wound up here and we went out a couple of times. Nothing much happened but she was friends with this Mary, whose house this is we're going to, and Mary and I kept running into each other on the El and stuff, so then we kind of got to know each other."

They drove to Mary's in Brian's bright red Mustang, an extravagance he was a little sheepish about. "I always wanted one, and now that I can afford it I actually don't drive it that much. It's more trouble than it's worth, because of the parking situation. But it sure is pretty."

"And it turns the ladies' heads as you go by."

Brian laughed. "It's tough, man. All these great-looking women in this city, but it's hard to get to know people. I haven't exactly been racking up notches on the bedpost, you know what I mean?"

Tommy knew what he meant. He'd lost his virginity in more ways than one in the army, but there had never been anybody waving good-bye with a tear in her eye when he moved on to the next post. The longest run he'd ever had was with a divorced barmaid in a Killeen, Texas, roadhouse, and that had flamed out in a couple of months. Tommy still shook his head at the memories.

It seemed to Tommy that they walked farther from where Brian parked than they would have from his house. Tramping through a chilly fall evening, leaves and trash swirling in the wind, Brian said, "Mary has this friend, too. She's pretty nice. Wait'll you see her."

It wasn't a big party, maybe fifteen people in an apartment at the back of a big courtyard building. There was a balcony that looked onto the courtyard and a couple of people were out there smoking in the cold, but most of the action was in the big living room, music not quite loud enough to make you shout and lights not quite dim enough to make you stumble over the furniture. Brian got them beers and made introductions all around and Tommy forgot the names instantly, except for Mary. She was small and perky, the type of woman who was always organizing things. She had a pleasant face with kind brown eyes but not the kind of looks you'd write home about. She was friendly and Tommy appreciated that, but she lost him when she told him, "Wow, and I thought *Brian* had an accent."

Brian started telling people Tommy was just back from Iraq,

and all of a sudden he had a little audience in front of him. Tommy knew Brian was only trying to make him interesting, to get people to talk to him, but he would just as soon not have gone into all that. "It wasn't a whole lot of fun," he said, waving it away with a beer in his hand.

"You see any action?" a guy said, peering at him like he was a zoo animal.

Tommy just blinked at him. "Enough to last me awhile."

He went and got himself another beer. He figured it was about time for Brian to abandon him and go after Mary's friend, which was fine with him. Nothing was going to happen with him at this party anyway: he had to go to work at midnight, more or less sober. When he got back to the living room, sure enough, Brian had hooked up with a dark-haired woman in a corner. Tommy was going to leave him to it but Brian looked up and waved to him to come over.

The friend's name was Lisa and he could see why Brian liked her: she had a nice complexion, big dark eyes, a nice figure in a tight sweater. She was pretty but not Tommy's type. Tommy liked women who looked as if they might enjoy an open-pit barbecue or a ride on a motorcycle late at night. Lisa looked too well-tended for that, the kind of woman who spent a lot of time on her makeup. She looked a little snooty, to tell the truth. But at least she didn't tell him he had an accent.

"Tom here just got back from Iraq," Brian said.

Lisa's eyes got wide at that. "Oh my God," she said. Tommy shrugged. It sounded to him like Brian had just killed the conversation. "Welcome home," Lisa said.

Tommy raised his beer. "'Preciate it."

Lisa surprised him then: she reached out and put her hand

on his forearm. "I'm really glad you made it." She sounded like she meant it. Nobody had said that to him yet, not even Brian.

"Me, too," Tommy said. "I can't even begin to tell you." He grinned at her and she smiled back. All of a sudden he could see what Brian saw in this girl. She had some warmth to her.

He did his best for a while, making small talk, but he wasn't much good at it, never had been. He figured he needed to let Brian have his shot at Lisa, so after a while he excused himself and moved on. He went out onto the balcony and stood there looking down at the courtyard, beer in hand, getting cold but not minding. After a while he came back inside.

He was ready to go. It was early still but he'd had enough. He didn't belong here, with all these people who had gone to college and were familiar with so many things he didn't know anything about and who didn't have any idea, not the faintest, of how he'd spent the last year and a half of his life. He wanted to go get a quiet bite to eat somewhere and then get on the El and go to work.

He found Brian in the kitchen with Lisa and Mary. When he walked in he got a brief impression he was interrupting something serious, from the expressions they had, and he stopped in the doorway, ready to back out. But Mary flashed him a smile and beckoned him in, and he figured he must have imagined it. When he said he was leaving, Mary put on a disappointed face. "You just got here. We haven't even done any dancing yet."

"Not much of a dancer, I'm afraid. Besides, I got to go to work."

Then he had to explain that, and he could see her estimation of him sinking even lower than where his accent had put it. "That's no fun," she said, trying to make a joke of it, batting her eyelids at him. She was trying to be nice but writing him off, he could see.

"Hey," said Brian. "Maybe we could walk you home."

He was talking to Lisa. Lisa stood with her arms folded, not a party pose exactly and maybe the reason Tommy had gotten the feeling something serious was going on; her face had a grave look, too. She looked at Brian for a moment and said, "Maybe that's not a bad idea. Would you mind?"

"You kidding? No problem." Brian turned to Tommy. "Can we give Lisa a little escort home? She's, uh . . ." Brian shot a quick look at Lisa, who was looking at the floor.

"She's being stalked," said Mary.

"Maybe." Lisa was looking at Tommy now. "There's been a guy hanging around sometimes. I don't know what he wants. But it's a little creepy."

"Well hel-*lo*," said Mary. "What do you mean, you don't know what he wants? He's a creep."

"The thing is, I'm not sure. He talked to me once, I told him to go away. Then he was sitting in his car outside my house the other night. Just sitting there."

Tommy said, "Anybody you know?"

Lisa shook her head. "No. I talked to him once, that's all. At a bar, casual like, you know, hi how's it going, and nothing happened. I thought it was just one of those things where a guy says hi, you hold up the 'not interested' sign, and that's it. I mean, I was with a bunch of people from work and he was just there, by himself. He like catches my eye, says hi, I say hi back and smile at him and turn my back. That was it. Then he shows up a couple of days later on the El platform, at the Merchandise Mart, as I'm coming home from work, out of the blue, just pops up in front of me, and

19

says remember me and asks me out, just like that. I was like, wow, this is a weird coincidence, and I said no thanks, and he kept insisting, not aggressive but just kind of pathetic like, and I finally said look, please don't bother me and I moved on down the platform, and I thought that was it. And then the other night he's sitting in his car outside my house. He rolled down the window and called to me. Now *that* freaked me out. I ran inside and locked the door. And then when I looked out the window he was gone."

There was a brief silence. "Lisa," said Mary. "What's not to be sure about? He's stalking you."

"Oh, *shit*. I know, I guess you're right."

"Did you call the cops?"

Lisa shook her head. "Maybe I should have."

Brian said, "I'd say that's a no-brainer."

"What am I going to tell them? I have no idea who this guy is."

"You give them a description, anyway. What's he look like?"

"I don't know, ordinary-looking. Glasses. Starting to lose his hair. Maybe in his thirties. Just a guy."

"What about his car? What was he driving?"

"Oh, I don't know. A car is a car to me. I wasn't looking at the car."

Brian and Mary looked at each other and then at Tommy. What the hell do you want me to say? Tommy thought. He shrugged.

"Okay," said Brian. "I think here's what we do. Tom and I'll walk you home. If he's there, we'll at least get a license number. That's something you can take to the police. That goes for whenever you see him next. Get the license number and make of the car if you can. And tell the cops about it."

Lisa nodded. She looked thoughtful, not helpless or frantic. Tommy said, "When he called to you, did he call you by name?"

She just stared at him for a second. "Yeah. He did." Her eyes widened a little. "God, I didn't even think about that."

"How did he know?" said Mary.

"He probably heard it in the bar. He was sitting near us."

"You might ask the people you were with if anyone knows him," said Brian.

Mary nodded. "Or go back to the bar and ask the bartender. Maybe he's a regular."

"I think you let the cops do that," said Brian.

"Yeah, that's the first step. Call the police."

Lisa took them all in with a look. "If I see him again. I will. First thing."

"Even if you don't see him again," said Mary.

"Maybe." Lisa took a deep breath. "Let's see what happens right now."

Brian and Tommy walked on either side of her. She took them down quiet streets lined with houses and a few two- and three-story apartment buildings, with cars parked bumper-to-bumper along both curbs. The trees had lost most of their leaves and the sidewalks were brightly lit. Brian and Lisa talked some at first but fell silent as they turned down Lisa's block. Tommy was looking at cars. One of the things he had most appreciated about being home from Iraq was not having to worry about cars on the street blowing up or sprouting automatic weapons all of a sudden, and now here he was scanning for danger again.

Lisa lived on the top floor of a narrow brick three-flat with bay windows in front. They pulled up at the steps and Lisa thanked them. Her eyes were straying toward the cars at the curb but she didn't seem too ill at ease. "You guys want to come up for a while?" she said.

Brian looked at Tommy, who said, "I gotta get to work. Some other time maybe." Brian looked like he was about to fumble his big chance, so Tommy helped him out by giving him a slap on the shoulder and saying, "See you around." He smiled at Lisa and said, "Nice meeting you. Take care and keep your eyes open."

"I'll do that. Thanks." To Brian she said, "You want to come up?"

Brian looked a little panicked, but he said, "Maybe just for a bit."

Tommy was moving away as she unlocked her front door. He walked slowly, still looking at cars. The light reflected on the windshields made it hard to see if there was anyone inside until you were right on top of them. Halfway down the block he slipped between two cars and crossed the street. On the opposite sidewalk he turned and came back toward Lisa's building, just dawdling. He'd spotted one car he wanted a second look at.

He was fifty feet behind it when the ignition came on, twenty feet from it when the car peeled out of the parking spot and tore off down the street, headlights coming on only as it picked up speed. Tommy hustled out into the street but not fast enough to get a reading on the license plate. It was a dark-colored Lexus, and that was about all he could say for sure. Before it pulled out he had just gotten a glimpse of a face in the driver's side mirror, glasses shining faintly in the dark, looking, he was pretty sure, at him.

"Nervous, huh?" Tommy said to the disappearing Lexus. "You piece of shit."

5

The Greek liked Tommy's work. "You wouldn't believe the guys I've had to put up with," he said. "I had a guy used to come in here and sleep all the time instead of doing the work."

Tommy wasn't surprised. At the lumberyard back home and in the army he'd learned that most of the time if you just did what you were supposed to do with a reasonable amount of attention, you stood out from the crowd. A whole lot of people were basically fuckups. It made Tommy pessimistic about the state of the world sometimes.

The upshot was that the Greek gave Tommy a quarter-an-hour raise and offered him more work. He had an apartment building up the street on Kenmore Avenue with a janitor who was having problems with the bottle. "I been thinking about canning the guy anyway. You want his job, it's yours." Tommy didn't especially want to put anyone out of work, but after the business with his father he didn't have any patience for drunks, either. He said sure. It was a few hours of work per week, taking the trash down and doing simple maintenance. The main thing was, he had to be available for emergencies, so he had to go out and get a cell phone. It put a dent in his budget, wiping out some of his gains. He was still working part time and not really making a living, but it was early days yet. Brian had told him not to sweat it about getting his own place. Tommy figured he had a month or so before he had to get serious. He figured he could always drive a cab if he had to. There was a test to take, a license you had to get. He'd look into it eventually.

He still didn't know what the hell he wanted to do with his life. He felt like a big part of him was still over in Iraq. He had used Brian's computer to e-mail a couple of friends over there and found out they'd had some more people hurt and one KIA, a guy Tommy had liked pretty well. It hurt to hear about it. Tommy was glad to be out but at the same time he wished he was over there, sharing the load. He felt guilty. He wasn't sure he was ready for civilian life. He wondered if he ever would be.

"We been invited to dinner," Brian told him one evening. "Lisa's having us over. Along with Mary and some other people."

"She likes you, man."

"I don't know about that."

Nothing had happened the night Brian went upstairs

with Lisa. "We had a cup of tea and talked about movies," Brian had said. "There wasn't a lot of what you'd call erotic tension in the air."

Now he said, "My theory is, this dinner thing is Mary's idea. I think she's angling for you."

Tommy snorted. "She thinks I'm a dumb cracker."

"Well, you are. What the hell? Some women go for that."

Tommy smiled a little. Brian could get away with that, being from back home. Anybody else, he'd have decked him. Around Uptown he was starting to get the impression that half the population of Appalachia had relocated there. Tommy hated conforming to stereotypes, and here he was, another Kentucky boy sweeping floors in Uptown.

The night of the dinner party it was cold out, winter in the air for real. Brian had bought a bottle of wine to bring along. "You can drink that stuff?" Tommy said. He had a six-pack under his arm.

"You ever heard of class? Besides, Lisa's Italian. That's what they drink."

"The Italian guys I knew in the army drank beer."

"I got news for you, man. The army's not exactly the standard for sophisticated living."

Tommy laughed, but he also knew it was true: he had a lot to learn.

Lisa's apartment was nice, with furniture that matched and prints on the walls. There were flowers in a vase on the table and good smells coming from the kitchen. Besides Lisa and Mary there was another couple there that had been at the party, Jason and Diane, friends of Mary's. It looked like a setup to Tommy, everybody paired off neatly, and he started to think

SAM REAVES

Brian was right. Mary was being awfully friendly. Tommy didn't mind too much. She wasn't all that bad-looking and the attention was nice. Mostly he kept his mouth shut and just listened. It wasn't that he felt dumb: Tommy knew he was as smart as anybody else at the table. But there were holes in his education you could drive a truck through. He was starting to get an impression of the dimensions of the world outside the army.

The doorbell rang. For a few seconds they all just sat there looking at each other, and then Lisa got up from the table with a frown on her face and went down the hall to the front door of the apartment. From where he was sitting Tommy could see her lean close to the speaker phone and press the button. "Who is it?" she said.

A tinny voice came out of the speaker. "It's me, Lisa. Your dream date."

Tommy saw Lisa stiffen "Go away," she said.

"That's not very friendly. Why can't you be nice to me?"

There was shock on people's faces now. Mary gasped and put a hand to her mouth.

Tommy pushed away from the table. As he headed for the kitchen he heard Lisa say, her voice rising with tension, "Please . . . leave me . . . alone."

Tommy was out the back door, across the porch and on the stairs in a heartbeat. He took the steps three at a time, swinging around the landings with a hand on the post to steady himself. At the bottom he had to open a gate to get into the gangway at the side of the building, and it creaked a little, but he didn't think it would give him away. The guy had to be inside the front door, talking into the speakerphone. He trotted up the gangway, moving as quietly as he could.

It took Tommy no more than thirty seconds to get from the kitchen to the sidewalk out front, but when he got there, the front door was slowly swinging shut on its automatic closer and there was nobody in the foyer. Tommy could hear people thumping down the steps inside, making a lot of noise. He ran back down to the sidewalk and looked up and down the block, but he didn't see anybody moving. Behind him the door came open and Brian and Jason burst out. "You scared him off," Tommy said, still scanning, as they came down the steps to join him.

"Where the hell did he go?" said Brian, breathless.

"Not very far away, that's for sure. Look for a dark-colored Lexus."

Brian was peering at him. "How do you know he's driving a Lexus?"

"I think I saw him the other night, when we walked Lisa home. I didn't say anything because I wasn't sure."

Jason spoke up. "You guys want to look for the car? I'll check the gangways."

"Hang on," said Tommy. "The girls are up there by themselves and the back door's open."

Jason gaped at him. "Shit."

"You two go back up. I'll just hang out down here for a while. Make sure you lock that kitchen door."

They traded a look but they deferred to Tommy and went back inside. Tommy thought about timing and what he had heard and seen coming up the gangway, or more exactly hadn't. He walked south past the building next door and saw that the gangway went through to the alley behind. He thought about the door he'd left open and was glad he'd sent the other two back upstairs. He went down the gangway and took a long look up and down the alley, but he didn't see anybody. He went back up front and started walking down the block. He was pretty sure the guy wasn't parked anywhere nearby this time, but he had to take a look. He walked down to the end of the block and back up on the other side, finally around again to Lisa's door. He had seen two Lexuses parked, but they were both the wrong color.

Tommy hadn't grabbed his jacket and he was getting seriously cold. He stood for a moment on Lisa's steps just watching, and as he was standing there the squad car pulled up.

"There's not a lot we can do until we know who he is."

Cops in the living room were like hogs in the chicken run: they stood out. There was an older cop and a younger one, and in their black leather jackets with all the equipment on their belts and their casual way of taking over a room, they were hard to miss. The older cop signed the form he'd filled out and handed a copy to Lisa. "I mean, I sympathize, but there's nothing we can do till we have something to go on."

Everyone was sitting around the living room with gloom in their eyes, the food getting cold on the table. "You've got a description," said Jason. "Can't you try tracking him down through that bar or something?"

The cop gave him a blank look. "What's he done, that the detective supervisor's gonna sic the dicks on him?"

"Isn't stalking a crime?"

"Sure it is. Is that what we have here?"

"He's following her around."

"That's one element. But also he has to have threatened her with bodily harm, confinement or restraint. Has he done that?"

"Not yet. You mean we have to wait for him to attack her before you can do anything?"

"We don't have preventive detention in this country, I'm afraid."

Nobody could think of anything to say to that. Finally Mary said, "Can't she get a restraining order or something?"

"She can get an order of protection if she has had a relationship with this gentleman. That's the way the law is written."

"I don't even know who he is," Lisa said.

"Then right now there's nothing we can do except pass the report on to the dicks. There's a Special Victims unit that handles stalking cases. If you're lucky and they're not too busy, somebody should get in touch with you before too long."

"I understand," said Lisa quietly, folding the report. "So what do I do in the meantime?"

The cop sighed and said, "You keep the doors locked. You try to have somebody walk you home. You give us something to go on, like a license number for that car, we can try and find out who he is. Till then . . ." He shrugged, leaving it hanging.

After the cops left, Lisa made an attempt to salvage the meal, but nobody seemed to be hungry. Lisa was working hard to be cheerful but it wasn't working. "It makes me so mad," said Mary, close to tears. "There's got to be something they can do."

"They've got limited resources," said Brian. "There's a lot of crime."

"The way the system works," said Jason, "something bad has to happen before they'll sit up and take notice. You just have to be supercareful. Look, we can help out. I can be available to walk you home and stuff."

"Me, too," said Brian. He looked at Tommy.

Tommy shrugged. "Sure." He hadn't said much since the cops showed up, but he had been thinking hard.

"All of us," said Mary. "We can work out a schedule or something. We'll make sure somebody's always around."

"Terrific," Lisa said. "I mean, thanks, but am I supposed to never be alone again?"

"Till we get a lead on this guy. Sooner or later we'll get a license number or something."

Tommy said, "Has he ever rung the doorbell before?"

Lisa shook her head. "No. He's approached me in public and called to me from his car. He's never rung before."

"So he's escalating."

They all looked at that one for a little while. "This is creepy," said Diane.

"It is *real* creepy," said Mary. "Maybe you should move out temporarily or something. You could come stay with me."

"Maybe," said Lisa. "I don't know if it's that serious yet."

"Oh, come *on*. Who knows what a guy like that is going to do?"

Jason said, "I agree, Lisa. Why take chances?"

"So I have to move because of this guy? Wonderful." Lisa looked grave but she sounded calm.

Jason said, "Hopefully not, but I think you have to look at the possibility. I mean, frankly, I don't know how helpful the cops are gonna be on something like this. You heard the guy. 'He hasn't committed any crime.' If they have to wait for this creep to attack you before they can do something, what good are they?"

"So what do we do?" said Brian. "Get some guys together and beat this asshole up?"

"I wouldn't mind," said Jason.

"Oh, right." Diane rolled her eyes. "Give me a break."

"You think I wouldn't?"

"Please. You're thinking with testosterone again."

"Well, I'm a guy. That's what we do."

"You got a better idea?" said Brian.

Diane waved a hand in disgust. Brian looked at Tommy. "What do you think, Tom?"

Tommy waited until everyone was looking at him. He didn't know why the hell anybody expected him to have any ideas. "Me, I'd shoot him like a dog," he said.

Now they looked shocked. "But then that would probably be a little extreme," Tommy added.

6

Tommy was settling into a routine: he spent a couple of hours every morning at the apartment house on Kenmore, had the afternoon and evening off, and went in to do his restaurant gig at midnight. He'd arranged with the Greek to have Tuesday off both jobs. He took his sleep in two stretches, a few hours in the afternoon at Brian's place and then a nap in the wee hours on a cot the drunk had left in the basement of the apartment building. He threw out the blanket the drunk had left and replaced it with a new one he bought at the Army-Navy store up the street on Broadway. His jacket made a good pillow. It was living a little rough, but compared to Iraq it was a picnic. And it kept him out of Brian's hair, which was convenient: he didn't want to wear out his welcome there before he had gotten his finances in a little better shape. He and Brian hung out some in the evening, Tommy still doing a lot of the cooking.

Nothing much was happening with Brian and Lisa. He had asked her out and they had gone to a movie, but Brian said there was no spark there. He was pessimistic. At least she hadn't seen the creep hanging around since the night of the dinner party. Brian was hoping the guy had been scared off. Tommy said that would be good, but he tended to be pessimistic about that kind of thing.

Brian shook his head over Tommy's lifestyle, and Tommy left the want ads lying around sometimes to show Brian he was looking for something more permanent. The truth was he still didn't have a clue what to do with his life.

Moving around at night, he was getting a strange view of the city. There was an all-night coffee shop on Wilson where he liked to eat sometimes after he finished up the restaurant job, and he was starting to get to know some of the other night-riders: cops and cabbies and a couple of women he figured were hookers. Tommy was amazed sometimes at how much went on at night in a big city.

One night he was just leaving Brian's place on his way to the restaurant when Brian came up the stairs looking like hell. He had a fat lip and a couple of wads of bloody cotton stuffed up his nose. He stopped on the landing and looked up at Tommy like he was waiting for a smartass remark. "What the hell happened to you?" Tommy said.

"I ran into that guy." Brian came on up the stairs. "He showed up again."

"What, the guy that's been after Lisa?" Tommy followed Brian back into the apartment.

"Yeah. At the Red Lion. I was supposed to meet Lisa there for a drink. When I got there, she was at the bar and there he was, in her face. Lisa was trying to get the bartender to call the cops but it was busy and she couldn't get his attention. I just told the guy to get lost and he said basically fuck you, make me. So I tried to make him."

Tommy followed Brian to the bathroom door and watched him take out the cotton, examine his face in the mirror. "What happened?"

"He left." Brian shot him a grin, doing his best, but just looking at him Tommy could tell he was shaky; he was looking at a man who had gotten his ass kicked. "But he smacked me pretty good a couple of times first," Brian said.

"You land any on him?"

"Nothing too solid. Shit, he's bigger than me. Got the bartender's attention, though, finally."

"You talk to the cops?"

Brian made a noise of disgust. "When they finally showed up. And guess what? There's nothing they can do." Brian looked up from the sink again and now he looked ashamed, like a whipped dog. "One of them said they got better things to do than hold a guy's hand when he loses a fight in a bar."

Tommy watched his friend wash his face, gingerly. He said, "But you earned points with Lisa, I bet. Big time."

Brian dried his face and pushed past him. "She's freaked out, man. I mean, that girl is scared shitless."

"You take her home?"

"I took her to Mary's place. She's gonna spend the night

there. I don't know what she's gonna do about this. What's she supposed to do, go into hiding till this asshole dies? I can't believe the cops won't do anything." He pulled a beer out of the fridge.

"I don't suppose anyone thought to follow the guy, get a plate number or something?"

Brian shook his head. "All anybody saw was a bar fight. It was just a bar fight over a chick. And I lost." He held the cold can of beer to his fat lip for a moment, looking at Tommy.

Tommy felt bad for him. "Shake it off, man. I can't count the number of times I got my ass kicked in my life. What counts is the last round, not the first. Just be ready next time."

"Fuck, man. We gotta do something."

Tommy stood and watched him drink for a moment. "You got Mary's number?"

"It's on the pad by the phone."

Tommy went over and found the number and dialed it. It rang four times and he could picture the two women a few blocks away staring at the phone, afraid to pick it up. He figured he could leave them a message. Then Mary's voice said, "Hello?"

"Hey, Mary. It's Tom. Brian's friend?"

"Yeah, hey. Hi."

"Brian told me what happened."

"Oh, God. Can you believe it?"

"Lisa okay?"

"Well, she's a little shook up. We're going through a bottle of wine over here. But she's tough, she'll be okay. How's Brian?"

"He's fine. I actually think his looks are improved a bit." Brian gave him the finger from the kitchen table and Tommy figured he was starting to recover. "Can I talk to Lisa for a second?" he said.

35

When Lisa came on the line she sounded subdued and far away. "How you doin'?" Tommy said.

"I'll live. Is Brian okay?"

"Brian's happy as a pig in shit. He's just been telling me how he laid the guy out cold."

"God damn it." Brian slammed the beer down on the table. "I did not say that!" he shouted loud enough for Lisa to hear him.

"I'm bullshitting you," Tommy said into the phone. "He told me what happened. Listen, the reason I'm calling is, I probably got more free time than anybody else you know right now. So I'm available to walk you home, watch your place, whatever."

"I appreciate that. I'm not sure actually what to do next."

"Right now you just need somebody to be around. You got any brothers, by any chance?"

"One. He's in Seattle."

"Well, you need people. You need somebody to make things harder for this guy, just by being there. You need a deterrent."

"Yeah . . ." Tommy could hear the doubt in her voice, and he knew what she was thinking: was this new guy now going to try to use the situation as an excuse to make a move on her?

"I'm gonna give you my cell phone number," he said. "Call me if you need anything. Just somebody to walk you to the El or whatever. And if this guy shows up again, I don't care when or where, call me. Call the cops if you want, but call me first."

Tommy could hear her thinking hard at the other end of the line. Her level of trust in men had to be fairly low at this point. All he could do was offer, he figured.

"Thanks, Tom. I just might do that," Lisa said. "What's the number?"

Tommy was depressed when he finished up at the restaurant at two in the morning. He locked the back door, stowed the key and stood there in the alley listening to the soft night roar of the city, looking up into the yellow sky. He went out onto Sheridan and started walking north. There was light traffic on the streets, a few hookers in doorways. One of them called to him and he shook his head. She was young and it made him sad to see her there. He wondered if she had any brothers and what the hell they were doing letting her stand out here night after night.

Asking Lisa if she had any brothers had set off a chain of thoughts that had wound up bringing him way down. He was thinking about his sister Beth for the first time in a long time. A hell of a lot of good it had done her to have a brother. Tommy knew this was not a good line of thinking. He had been through all that and he knew he had to get past it, get past the guilt and the fruitless what-ifs. He had to stop dwelling on it or he was going to wind up like his father, which was nowhere.

He had a cup of coffee and a piece of pie in the coffee shop on Wilson and shot the shit with the fry cook and listened to a couple of El trains rumble overhead. He sat and drank coffee and thought about what he would do if he was obsessed with a woman. It was time to start anticipating.

7

Tommy figured the evening was prime time. The time the guy had cornered Lisa on the El seemed to be an exception so far, though that was obviously a danger zone, too. But the guy probably had a job somewhere, and how it probably went was, he had a drink or two after work and then started prowling for Lisa. A little booze always greased the skids for a thing like that.

Tommy didn't like the progression from bar to El platform to parked car to ringing the doorbell. The guy was getting bolder. And then tonight. How had he known Lisa was going to be there? Had he followed her from work again? From home? He was devoting a lot of effort to tracking Lisa. Lisa was his new hobby.

Tommy still hadn't gotten a real look at the guy. Everyone else had, it seemed like. Tommy wanted to talk to this son of a bitch, in the worst way.

He figured that tactically the best thing he could do was to stalk Lisa himself, just follow her around and wait for the guy to jump out of the bushes. But he didn't want to do it without telling her he was going to, and he was hesitant to suggest it because he didn't want her to think he was just one more guy to worry about. He decided he would wait and see if she called him.

Which she did, the next afternoon.

"I was wondering if you could walk me home." Lisa sounded hesitant. "I came straight here to Mary's from work and she's not around. I need to check in at home, and I'm a little nervous about it."

"I'll be there in a couple of minutes." Tommy had been lying awake on the couch after his nap, thinking about what to do with his evening.

"I hate to bother you."

"It's no bother." He reached for his shoes with his free hand. "I'm not doing anything else."

"I really appreciate this," she said over the noise of the traffic, walking beside him up Halsted in the fading light. "I thought maybe the guy had given up, and then he shows up again last night. I couldn't believe it."

"What'd he do, follow you there?"

"I don't know. I was sitting there at the bar waiting for Brian, watching the door, you know, and instead of Brian, who walks in but this guy?"

"Was he surprised to see you? Did he just happen to bump into you, or did he know you'd be there?"

"That's a good question." Lisa frowned, marching along with a hand on the strap of her shoulder bag, as Tommy watched her profile. "He didn't look particularly surprised. He came in and I just sat there, like shocked. He smiled. He's got this . . ." She shook her head, groping for a word. ". . . this cocky little grin. God, do I hate that grin. Maybe he did follow me, I don't know. I went to the bar from the El, so he could have been on the train again and I just didn't see him. But he's starting to get *seriously* on my nerves."

"I never got a look at him. Can you give me a real good description? All I remember is, he wears glasses."

Lisa shrugged. "He's just a guy, I don't know. Kinda big, I guess, over six feet tall, not very good-looking or anything, just kind of ordinary, brown hair, the glasses. Kind of a sharp nose, pointy chin, a little like, jowly. Going a little bald. He wears a brown leather jacket."

"What'd he say to you last night?"

She walked along with her lips pressed tight for a few seconds before answering. "The usual. How he loved me the first time he laid eyes on me. How we'd be so good together. Yuck, he makes me want to puke."

"I'm assuming you're way past being polite to the guy. I mean, he can't claim you're leading him on or anything."

"Oh, no. I was polite the first time, in the bar. Since then, he knows. I haven't screamed at him yet, but I did actually use the words 'fuck off' last night."

"Did he get mad?"

"He just laughed."

"Sounds like the man doesn't know how to take a hint."

She laughed. "No. I think it'll take more than a hint."

They turned down the street Lisa lived on and that was it for the conversation. Tommy scanned: parked cars, people on the sidewalks. He didn't see anything suspicious and then they were at Lisa's place. Tommy was hoping she'd ask him to come upstairs because he really didn't like the thought of the guy waiting for her up there if he'd escalated to the next stage, but he didn't know if he should bring it up. "You mind coming upstairs with me?" Lisa said, reading his mind. "Maybe I'm paranoid, but you never know."

"Sometimes paranoid is what keeps you healthy," Tommy said.

Once they were upstairs Tommy took the initiative and walked through every room in the apartment, just looking. There was nobody in the kitchen, nobody in the dining room, nobody in the front room. He felt like he was invading her privacy going into her bedroom, but her look told him she expected him to. The bedroom was just like he would have expected, just like her: neat, cared-for, nothing out of place, the bed made and the clothes put away, a paperback novel on a table by the bed. He checked the closet, and the clothes in there were all hung neatly as well. In the bathroom there was a faint perfumy smell. All Lisa's cosmetics and fancy soaps and things were on a shelf, and there was nobody hiding in the tub behind the drawn shower curtain.

"Whew," she said when he was finished. "Thanks. I was more nervous than I thought. Am I being paranoid? I mean, he can't really get in here, can he? I have good locks and burglar bars and everything. Can I come home by myself without worrying about finding him in here?"

41

Tommy didn't know what to tell her. She was in a bad situation. What she really needed was a man to stay with her. Either that, or move. "Probably. But there's no guarantee. You need to find out who this guy is, so the cops can do something. Has he ever called you, on the phone?"

"Yeah. Till I started hanging up on him."

"You got caller ID?"

"I just ordered it. Though it's probably closing the barn door after the horse is out." She stood for a moment looking at him, just looking. "Want some tea or something?"

Tommy didn't drink much tea, but he could see she wanted company. It couldn't be any fun sitting up here by herself, wondering when the doorbell was going to ring. "Sure."

"A detective called me," Lisa said, sitting across the kitchen table from him as the kettle heated up. "He was very sympathetic, but he told me basically the same thing. Nothing he can do until we know who he is. They could put a trap on my phone, he said, whatever that is, but I told him I was getting caller ID and he seemed to think that was good enough. He said if the stalker establishes a pattern they can put a special attention notice on my place and hope the district personnel can make a street stop. I told him what the pattern was so far, but I didn't get the impression he was ready to call out the troops just yet. He said keep him up-to-date."

"It's a start, I guess."

"Yeah. I've been trying to read up on this. There's lots of stuff on the Internet about stalking. It's a pretty common thing, unfortunately."

"I know."

"Most stalkers are former boyfriends, rejected lovers or

husbands. Stranger stalking is the least common kind. Just my luck to draw the weirdest type."

Tommy didn't say anything. He figured his thoughts about stalkers were best kept to himself.

"There's a whole list of things you're supposed to do," Lisa said. "First you make sure to tell him in no uncertain terms that he's not welcome." She laughed. "I think I've taken care of that. Then you have to document everything. For the police. You have to write down every time you see him, every time he calls, dates and times, what happened, any witnesses, all that stuff. So I started a notebook. I put your name and number in it as a witness. I hope that's okay."

"Sure, except I didn't actually see him."

Lisa nodded and he could see the strain in her eyes. "The way my luck is going," she said, "you probably will."

"If I do, I'll have a little talk with him."

She smiled a little at that, and then suddenly she put her hands to her face. When she took them away she blew out a deep breath and the corners of her eyes were glistening a little. "It's really getting to me. What am I supposed to do? Hire armed guards? Move? I read about a woman who moved to get away from a stalker and he tracked her down through the Internet and killed her."

Tommy didn't have anything to say that would make her feel better. "Staying at Mary's for a while is a good idea."

"Till he tracks me down there. How do I know he's not watching every time I leave the building, following me wherever I go?"

You don't, Tommy thought. He said, "You got parents in the area?"

43

"They're in Florida. That's a little far to commute to my job. I have a sister in Schaumburg. That's a little closer, but still a lot of disruption. And how long do I have to put up with it?"

Tommy nodded. "Only thing I can say, I'll see what I can do about spotting the guy, getting a license number, finding out who he is. Then you can take it to the cops again."

The kettle boiled, and Lisa went and made the tea. Tommy watched her move around. She was nice to look at, trim and petite, and he could see why Brian liked her.

While they sat and waited for the tea in their mugs to cool, Lisa just stared at him for a while. "Brian said you were the type of guy who would always help somebody in trouble, back home."

"Brian talks a lot of shit."

"I think he kind of hero-worships you."

"I don't know why."

She sipped tea. "Why'd you go into the army?" Tommy was used to the question, but it usually came in the form of a challenge. Lisa had a look on her face as if she really wanted to know.

"Didn't know what else to do with myself."

"Did you like the military?"

"It was okay. Iraq was kind of rough."

"Brian said you were wounded?"

"Yeah, I got my insides rearranged a little. But the army's got pretty good surgeons. I'm down to one kidney and missing some intestines, but I should be good for a few years yet."

"What are you going to do now?"

Tommy had to smile. "If I knew that, I'd be doing it."

Lisa took a sip of tea and her eyes strayed to the pile of letters she had taken out of her mailbox and brought upstairs.

She froze. Tommy didn't quite know what was going on as she put down her mug and said, "What the hell is that?"

"What?"

Lisa reached slowly for the pile of letters and pulled out a single sheet of paper, folded lengthwise and a little crumpled, maybe from being stuffed through the mail slot. She unfolded it. From where he sat, Tommy could see writing on it, and what looked like a drawing. Lisa's face took on a horrified look and after a second or two she cried out, "Oh, *God!*" and threw the paper down on the table.

Tommy reached for it. It was a plain white sheet of notepaper, and on it somebody had written *I LOVE YOU AND WILL NEVER NEVER GIVE UP TILL YOU LOVE ME.* Below that was a drawing, very crude, of two cartoonish figures, one with long hair and one with glasses. The long-haired figure was labeled YOU and the other one ME. Running from the neck of one to the neck of the other was a line of overlapping circles, clearly depicting a chain.

Tommy looked up from the paper and said, "Let's go talk to your detective."

8

'd be upset, too," the detective said. "If my wife or my daughter got something like this, I'd be real upset. All's I'm saying is, we don't have a lot to go on. Till you can tell us who he is." The detective had a photo ID on a lanyard and a badge hanging on his jacket pocket. The ID said his name was Hays. He was a gray-haired man about fifty years old, with a mustache and a sympathetic expression that looked to Tommy as if the man practiced it in a mirror. They were in the detectives' office up on the second floor of a big sprawling brick building at Belmont and Western that housed one of the Branch Courts as well as the police department's Area Three headquarters.

"Can you get fingerprints off the paper or something? We were real careful about handling it." Lisa sat on the edge of her chair, very calm, but Tommy could see she was working to keep the lid on. "Or analyze the writing or something? I don't know."

The cop shrugged. "Maybe. I know they can work miracles on TV, but it's a little harder in real life. It looks like he disguised the writing, maybe used his left hand or something, and these block capitals aren't going to tell us much. The paper could have come from anywhere. Fingerprints, maybe but don't hold your breath. This isn't going to lead us to anybody. The best we can hope for is this might corroborate, if we can find out who he is some other way. We need a name, a plate number or something. But there's a file now, a case, and we'll do what we can. The important thing is for you to keep your eyes open, be careful, and call us the second he shows up again."

That was all they were going to get, Tommy could tell. Lisa looked at him as if she wanted him to step in and tell the detective how to do his job, but he just shrugged and stood up to go. They all shook hands and then Tommy and Lisa left.

Driving back east, Tommy tried to think of something to say that would raise Lisa's spirits, but he couldn't come up with anything. "Can you move in with Mary? Like tonight? I think maybe it's time."

"I'll call her." Tommy could barely hear her. She was starting to get demoralized, he could tell. Tommy wished he could promise her it was going to be all right, but he couldn't. "I don't know what I did to attract this guy," she said. "I didn't lead him on or anything. I mean, I never even *noticed* him. He came like, out of the blue. How come he picked me? What did I do wrong?"

"You didn't have to do anything wrong. He's a head case. He's a sick fuck, excuse my language. You just happened to be there where his eye lit. The cops will take care of him."

Tommy scowled out the windshield. He hated lying to people, and he knew damn well what he had just said was nothing more than wishful thinking.

Tommy escorted her back upstairs, being careful. Mary came over to talk about Lisa moving in with her temporarily. Tommy stayed for a while after Mary got there and then left. He had time on his hands, and he couldn't think of anything better to do with it than hunt for the guy. He had asked Lisa where the bar was where he had first approached her, and he had looked at the list of incidents in her notebook. With the exception of the one time on the El outside the Merchandise Mart, he'd always shown up late in the evening, outside her house, or in the two bars. It was early yet and Tommy decided to try the bars. He figured the guy probably lived in the neighborhood and hung out in certain places. An obvious one to try was the place where she'd first seen him.

The bar was on Webster, near DePaul University. It had a big shamrock painted on the side of the building and it was full of people, not a hard-hat-and-lunch-pail type of crowd. Tommy had a beer and sat at the end of the bar and watched for anyone who fit the description Lisa had given him. He saw one guy who could have matched, but he was wearing a parka instead of a leather jacket and he didn't look like the type of guy who would take a swing at anybody. Tommy left.

The other bar was on Lincoln Avenue and was an imitation English pub. Tommy was a little hungry, and he had a burger and fries while he sat with another beer and kept one eye on the TV and the other on the crowd. Everyone here seemed to know each other. Tommy still felt like an outsider after nearly a month in town. For a moment he missed the army, badly. He missed his friends, he missed the dogass bars around Killeen where they didn't have fancy beers on tap but people were glad to see him when he walked in. Here nobody gave a damn about Tommy McLain.

His cell phone rang. "Tom? It's Lisa."

Tommy was already sliding off the bar stool. "Hey, what's up?"

"He's back."

"Where? You at home?"

"Yeah. Mary's still with me. He rang the doorbell. I didn't say anything after he said who it was, but he didn't go away. He's still down there ringing the bell. Just standing there ringing it, every few seconds."

"You call the cops?"

"Yeah."

Tommy was out the door. "It might take them a while to get there. Sit tight."

It was four blocks to where Lisa lived, and Tommy ran. By the time he got there he was hurting, out of shape and his guts still tender after all the trauma and surgery, but he was ready. He slowed to a walk when he hit Lisa's block and got his breath back coming up the other side of the street from her place. He pulled up even and looked.

He could see the guy in there in the lighted foyer. He had the brown leather jacket on, the glasses, just as advertised. Tommy watched him put his finger to the bell again, for a full five seconds, then release.

Tommy made a quick decision. Part of him wanted to cross the street, go in there and grab the guy, knock him around a little. He wasn't going to get sucker-punched like Brian. But he knew the important thing was to find out who the hell he was dealing with, and that meant patience. He moved into the shadows at the side of a porch and waited. The guy had been there ringing the bell for at least ten minutes by this time, and he had to get tired eventually.

It took a couple of minutes. The guy finally gave up and came out onto the porch and stood there for a second. Lisa's description had been pretty good. He looked to be in his thirties, big but not in terrific shape, with a bit of a gut, the kind of guy that walked with a swagger but would fold if he ever came up against somebody who really knew how to fight. He stood on the porch for a second with a sour look on his face, like he was pissed off at Lisa for not opening the door, and then he took off north up the block.

Tommy followed, on the other side of the street. When they got to the end of the block the guy turned left and went out of sight. Tommy hurried across the street and took a look around the corner in time to see him getting into the Lexus, which was parked fifty feet away on the near side of the street.

Tommy crossed the sidewalk and went out into the street. As the ignition of the Lexus came on he pulled his keys out of his pocket and started thumbing through them like he was looking for a car key, walking along the line of cars toward the Lexus. When it started to pull out of the spot Tommy looked up and got a clear look at the front plate. He veered out into the street like he was trying to get out of the guy's way, but really he was blocking him. The guy jammed on the brakes and laid on the horn.

Tommy stepped to the driver's window and rapped on the glass with his key. He could see the guy mouthing shit at him inside. The window came down and the guy said, "What the fuck, this look like a sidewalk to you?"

Tommy leaned down to the window and said, "Don't bother Lisa again."

The guy stared at him and then laughed. "Who the fuck are you? Big brother?"

"She don't want to see you no more, I don't want to see you no more."

"Listen, Jethro, like I give a shit what you want. Lisa's my business, not yours."

"Not anymore."

"What, you fuckin' her? That why you're playing hero here?"

"If I am or I'm not, that's none of your business. You just make sure she never sees you or hears from you again."

"Oh, well, shit. Now you got me scared. What are you gonna do, pound your little fists on my chest? Like that dick-head last night? You a friend of his, maybe?"

Tommy gave it a couple of seconds, just looking at him, and said, "Lisa lays eyes on you again, you won't see me coming, I promise you."

The guy's eyebrows went up. "You call that a threat?"

"Call it what you want. Just don't let Lisa see you again. Even by accident."

"That's not a threat. *This* is a threat, cracker." He leveled a finger at Tommy. "Fuck with me and I'll kill you. That clear enough for you?"

Tommy looked into the pale eyes behind the glasses. "I think we both made ourselves clear."

"Terrific. Now get your hands off my car and go fuck a sheep."

Tommy stepped away and the guy peeled out of the space in a hurry, just giving Tommy a chance to look at the rear plate and confirm the number. He walked back toward Lisa's, repeating the figures in his head.

"There you go," Tommy said, writing the number on a piece of paper Lisa had given him. "Give that to the cops. If they ever get here." He handed her the paper. Lisa just stared at it for a moment, then looked up at Tommy. "You're awesome," she said. She had a look on her face like she couldn't believe what was happening.

"You *are* awesome," said Mary. She was practically squeaking, she was so excited.

"Make sure you tell the cops you've talked to Hays about this. Give them the case number."

Lisa didn't answer for a second, looking at the paper. Finally she looked up and said, "Tom, I can't thank you enough for this."

"Thank me when he's off the street," Tommy said.

9

Tommy had asked Lisa to keep him posted. He didn't hear from her until two days later, when his cell phone went off in the Starbucks where he was reading about Iraq in the newspaper and thinking about absent friends.

"I have good news and bad news," said Lisa when he answered.

"Which one do I get first?"

"The good news is, the police identified the guy from the license number you got. His name is Joe Salerno."

"Man, that is good. So what's the bad news?"

"They talked to him and he says all he did was ask me out a couple of times and that's no crime. He denied writing the note, and they can't prove he did. So they can't arrest him. He hasn't committed any crime. He's free to go on doing what he's doing. I can apply for an order of protection, but it's not sure I'll get one. And it takes time. Meanwhile, there's nothing they can do. The detective said, and I quote, 'Unfortunately it's not a crime to be a pathetic asshole.' They can't do anything until he threatens me with bodily harm."

Tommy heard the note of desperation in Lisa's voice. "I didn't think they could arrest him. But if they knew what they were doing they should have put the fear of God into him. Hopefully he'll think twice about bothering you now."

"You think? I don't know if people like that back off just because a cop tells them they're being naughty. I'm afraid this will just make him mad."

Tommy didn't say anything for a moment because he was thinking exactly the same thing. He knew it was just whistling in the dark to think the cops could scare the guy off, but he didn't want to tell Lisa that. "Did the detective give you any advice? He tell you how you're supposed to live with this?"

"He basically advised me to move and not leave a forwarding address."

Tommy listened to the faint static in his ear for a few seconds. "You okay with Mary for a few days?"

"Until he finds me."

"He'd have to be lucky to do that, but you never know. Just keep your eyes open. You might want to stay out of the bars for a while. Meanwhile . . ." Tommy let it hang there: he really didn't have any idea how to finish the sentence.

"Meanwhile what?"

"I don't know, Lisa. Let me think about it. I don't suppose the cop told you where this guy lives?"

"He gave me all the guy's information, yeah. I need it if I want to apply for the order of protection. Why?"

"It would just be good to be able to find him. In case I have to talk to him again."

"Oh, Jesus, Tom. Be careful."

"I will. Where does the guy live?"

There was a pause. Finally Lisa said, "Maywood Park."

"Where's that?"

"Out on the West Side. West of Harlem."

"What's the address?"

"Tom, don't do anything dangerous, okay? I mean it. Don't get in trouble. You've been unbelievable, but leave it to the police now, please."

Tommy just sat there. Finally he said, "I won't do anything unless I have to. But give me the address, just in case."

The pause was shorter this time. "Okay. Twenty-eight-oh-three Seventy-third Avenue."

Tommy wrote it down. "All right. Hopefully I won't have to do anything with it. Call me if you need any help, okay?"

There was a second or two of silence. "I will," she said.

Tommy figured Joe Salerno would be back in the neighborhood soon enough, but he was tired of waiting around. He wanted to find the son of a bitch. He wasn't sure what he was going to do when he found him, but he thought it was time to take the initiative.

Tommy had an address, but he figured he could use more.

He sat down at Brian's computer. He knew you could find out a lot about a person on the Internet. He had no idea how to go about it, but he had some time to fool around with it.

He found a site where for $39.95 you could practically undress a person: addresses, phone, birth date, what property they owned, tax liens out on them, all kinds of things. All you needed was a credit card, and Tommy had one of those, although he hadn't used it much over the past year and a half. For an extra ten bucks you could get a guy's criminal record. Tommy said what the hell: it was money well spent.

The search engine kicked up a whole bunch of Joe Salernos. Fortunately their ages were listed, so Tommy could do a little weeding out. It didn't take long to find the one in Maywood Park. Tommy typed in his credit card number and punched the button.

It took a while, but finally the report came up. If you could believe the computer, the Joe Salerno who lived on 73rd Avenue in Maywood Park had a few possible relatives in the same town, owned his house, and had been married and divorced. Another interesting thing was, he seemed to own a bar, at least some kind of establishment that had a liquor license. The address given was also in Maywood Park. Salerno had owned it since 1996.

And down at the bottom was the good stuff. In 1998 this Joe Salerno had pleaded guilty to domestic battery, a Class 4 felony because it had violated an order of protection. Amazingly, he had been given a suspended sentence.

"You worthless piece of shit," Tommy said out loud, and clicked on PRINT.

Maywood Park was due west of Lincoln Park, but it was a long hard eight-mile slog out Fullerton Avenue to get there, the neighborhoods changing as Tommy went. For a while all the signs were in Spanish, then there was a lot of Polish, all of it a long way from the upscale yuppie-nightlife feel of Lincoln Park. He went by Riis Park, a huge expanse of bare trees on his right, and then in another mile he hit Harlem Avenue, which his map told him was the Chicago city limits. There were signs welcoming him to Maywood Park, but there was no sudden change to ranch houses and big yards. This suburb looked pretty much the same as the big city across the street. It looked like a workingman's town.

There were railroad tracks slicing across the town that complicated the street pattern a little, but after some wrong turns and a little confusion between 73rd Avenue and 73rd Court, Tommy found the place he was looking for, an ordinary-looking brick house sitting with a lot of similar ones on a quiet block with a few trees. He checked the address and cruised on by, looking for the Lexus. It wasn't there, which didn't surprise him. Tommy didn't know what exactly he was doing here, besides reconnoitering.

He found the car at the bar. It was a little neighborhood bar on a quiet street, with neon and Christmas lights in the front window, just like a million others Tommy had seen. They were all over Chicago. The Lexus was sitting in a parking lot at the side. Tommy slowed enough to check the license number as he passed and then pulled over half a block down and just sat for a while, looking at the place in the mirror. He sat there wondering if it was time to go in and have another talk with Salerno. He decided it wasn't, finally. If the cops had talked to him, then the ball was in his court. Tommy didn't have high hopes that a visit from the law would get Salerno to leave Lisa alone, but you never knew. Getting in his face now would put Tommy in the wrong. He had to wait and see. At least now he knew where to look for the guy.

Tommy put the Chevy in gear. He wasn't sure which he was hoping for: whether Salerno would give it up, or whether he would give Tommy an excuse to talk to him again, something Tommy thought he might enjoy.

Two days later he had just gotten up from a nap on Brian's sofa and was poking around in the kitchen when the doorbell rang. He pressed the button to open the street door and then went out into the hall to see who it was coming up the stairs. To his surprise it was Lisa. "Hey," Tommy said.

"Hi." She stopped at the foot of the last flight of steps and looked up at him like she was waiting for permission to proceed.

Tommy said, "Brian's not home yet. He usually gets in around six."

She just stood there for a second and then said, "Are you busy?"

"I was about to make some coffee. Once I get that under control I'll have all kinds of time on my hands."

"Can I have some?"

"Come on up." Something in Lisa's face told him she wasn't here just to pass the time of day. Inside the apartment she took off her coat and laid it over the back of the sofa, then stood in the doorway of the kitchen watching Tommy pour boiling water over the coffee. "What's up?" Tommy said.

"He's been inside my apartment."

Tommy's head snapped up. Lisa was looking in his direction

but not really at him. If it wasn't quite a thousand-yard stare yet, it was at least a few hundred. "How do you know?"

"I went back over there to get some things. I took a chance, I know, going by myself, but I was tired of bothering other people. And I was careful. I went up the back and everything. And then when I got inside, things just weren't right."

"What do you mean?"

She took a deep breath and let it out. "He went through my clothes." She pursed her lips, a bitter look on her face. "My underwear drawer. It was all messed up. And my dirty laundry was all over the floor of my closet."

Tommy didn't need her to spell it out. "That's serious. That's home invasion."

"I know."

"How'd he get in?"

Lisa walked to the table and sat down. "I did something really stupid, just like you're not supposed to do. I kept an extra key hidden by the back door in case I ever lost my keys and got locked out. To tell you the truth, I'd forgotten all about it. He must have found it, because when I looked, it wasn't there anymore."

Tommy looked into her eyes for a little while. He could tell she was aware how dumb that was and knew there was nothing useful he could say. "You tell the cops?"

"What good would it do? I can't even prove he's been in there."

They were silent while Tommy poured two cups of coffee. "He might have left fingerprints or something."

"You think they're going to bother to look for them? I think all I would get would be a lecture. Which I deserve, I know. Right now I don't care. I'm just . . . I'm ready to just take off, abandon everything in the place. I mean, he was in there, in my private space, just . . . rooting around. I mean, *yuck.* I want to burn it all. I, like, freaked when I realized what had happened and ran out of there. I don't want to go back. I want . . ."

Lisa put her hands to her face and for a few seconds nothing happened. Then she started to shake, and after a few shakes she took a couple of sharp rasping breaths and Tommy realized she was sobbing. "I just want him to leave me alone," she said, squeezing the words out. "I want him to go away." After that she sat there and cried for a while, as Tommy sat there paralyzed. He wanted to reach out and touch her, but he couldn't. He wanted to kill somebody.

After a while Lisa took her hands away from her face. She sniffed and wiped her eyes with her fingers. She looked miserable, eyes red and her makeup starting to run. She said, "I'm sorry," and got up and practically ran out of the kitchen. Tommy listened as water ran in the bathroom. In a few minutes she was back, looking pale. She sat down and looked at Tommy with her big dark eyes. "What am I going to do?" she said.

Tommy said, "I'll go talk to him."

"Talk to him? What are you going to say?"

"I don't know. I'll just try to make it clear to him that if he doesn't leave you alone, he's going to have to face some consequences."

Lisa just stared at him for a while. "Shouldn't we just let the police handle it?"

"How long do you want to give them?"

"But he's dangerous."

"I know." Tommy took a sip of coffee. "I don't mean to brag, but I spent the last year and a half dealing with people that make him look pretty tame."

She blinked at him a few times and said, "Don't get hurt. Please don't get hurt."

"Don't worry. Once was enough. I'm through getting hurt, believe me."

Tommy lay on the couch with the lights off, listening to the soft rumble of the city outside. Brian had come home, had dinner, watched a little TV and hit the sack, leaving Tommy alone with his thoughts. Tommy hadn't said anything to Brian about Lisa's visit because he had a feeling he was moving into territory where the fewer people knew about what he was thinking, the better.

Tommy hadn't beaten anybody up since his sophomore year in high school, when he'd had to be pulled off a senior he had overheard making a thoughtless crack about his sister, a few months after she died. He'd dodged expulsion and maybe a court date only because there had been a lot of sympathy for him in the wake of what happened to Beth.

Tommy was thinking about her again tonight, lying there in the dark. It made him sad that so much of her life had faded away in his mind; he had a few key memories he liked to hold on to, but too much of her was gone forever, like the memories of his mother. Beth had done a lot of mothering herself, taking care of a little brother while going through her own struggles to grow up. And then she was gone.

Tommy was fervently grateful for one thing in his life: he hadn't had to find his sister's body. That had fallen on his dad, who had tried to shield Tommy from the whole thing and borne it all in silence while he drank himself into the grave.

It was all too much to think about. Beneath the sadness Tommy could feel a stirring of the blistering anger he had worked so hard to bury. He had figured out early on that the rage would burn him alive if he let it, and he had learned how to keep the fires banked. He knew he couldn't let them flare up too often.

There were occasions, however. Tommy thought this might be one of them.

10

Tommy tried to look at it as a technical problem. That approach had gotten him through some rough patches in Iraq. He figured this was no different. He had to find the man, make him see the light, and get away clean. He didn't want to have to deal with cops or with any friends the guy might have. Tommy believed in striking fast and hard, just like they had taught him in the infantry.

Tommy was going to make Joe Salerno think twice about ever coming within a mile of Lisa again. He was going to make Joe Salerno afraid, afraid to set eyes on Lisa even by accident again. Tommy had seen more than once in his life how a competent beating could serve as a very effective deterrent. He wasn't worried about Joe Salerno being able to defend himself. Tommy had looked at the guy. He gave Salerno a couple of inches and at least thirty pounds, but Tommy knew that didn't matter nearly as much as the fact that Tommy knew what it was to fight for keeps. Nobody who hadn't ever had to do that was going to whip somebody who had.

The hardest thing, just like in the army, was target acquisition. But there Tommy had an edge. And he figured there was no time like the present.

Before he left, Tommy went and dug the .25 automatic he'd taken off the punk at the El stop out of his bag. He stood looking at it in the palm of his hand, thinking it might bring him more trouble than it was worth. On the other hand, he didn't know how likely Joe Salerno was to pull something of his own out of a pocket.

Tommy shoved in the magazine but didn't rack the slide. He made sure it was on safety and stowed it in a pocket of his jacket. If everything went well it would stay there.

Instead of taking the El he drove up to the restaurant and parked on Broadway. He made sure to chew the fat some with the kitchen staff while they were finishing up, to let everyone know he was there. He didn't think alibis were going to come into play but you never knew. When everyone but him was gone he rushed through his routine, hustling more than usual and cutting a few corners so he could get out of there. By one-thirty he was through.

He jumped in the car and went. He wanted to be out in Maywood Park by two. It was all guesswork, but most bars closed at two, and Tommy figured that was a good time to try picking up Joe Salerno. He tried not to think too much on the way. It was a technical problem, that was all. Thinking too much about the rest of it would mean getting cold feet, and then he would let Lisa down the way he'd let his sister down.

Tommy knew he couldn't let the Chevy be noticed anywhere near the action. With Texas plates it would stick out. He wound up parking it on Armitage on the Chicago side of Harlem and walking east, then doubling back around the block to cross over into Maywood Park. There was nobody out on the streets. It was cold, with a sharp wind, but Tommy could handle cold. He walked all the way up quiet residential streets to Salerno's bar and made a pass.

The Lexus was parked in the little lot at the side of the building, along with one other car, a Taurus. Tommy went on by. It was past two by this time and he knew Salerno might be leaving soon, but he tried to be patient. If it didn't happen here and now there would be other chances. At the end of the block he turned right and looked for the alley. It led him straight back to the lot at the side of the bar.

The two cars were still there. Tommy stopped to scope things out: There was a single light on a pole at the corner of the lot, but he spotted another light on the side of the bar above where the cars were parked that was probably motion-sensitive. The Lexus was parked at the front of the lot just off the sidewalk, with the Taurus next to it. A technical problem: the motion-sensitive light meant whatever happened would be lit up like daytime. Tommy thought about trying to take out the light somehow but it didn't look easy.

The whole thing could go up in smoke if Salerno left at the same time as the owner of the Taurus. Tommy guessed it would belong to the bartender, in there cleaning up after closing, maybe with the boss at the register counting the receipts. If they left together, it was probably off. Tommy decided to wait and see what happened. Where he was standing he didn't think anybody could see him.

The cold was a bitch. It made Tommy question the whole thing a couple of times, but he had learned patience in the army, and he figured he could always warm up later.

But it was starting to look like it was never going to happen. He wondered what the hell Salerno was doing in there. It was almost two-thirty. Tommy left his cover and walked along the edge of the lot to the back of the bar. There was a door there next to a Dumpster, and there was a window above the door, with burglar bars over it. Tommy looked around a bit and found an empty milk crate beyond the Dumpster. He set it in front of the door and stood on it, which put him up just high enough to see through the window over the door.

He could see down a short hallway past what looked like restroom doors into the main room of the bar, with a line of chrome bar stools against a long wooden bar just visible to the right and booths along the wall to the left. It was dim inside, but there was enough light coming from behind the bar that Tommy could make out what was going on in his narrow angle of vision.

And what he saw was Joe Salerno zipping up his pants. Salerno was just backing into view, looking down. He finished zipping up and put out a hand to feel for a bar stool and hiked his ass up onto it and leaned an elbow on the bar. He seemed to be breathing a little heavily. Tommy watched Salerno's eyes come up, following something that was rising, just out of sight around the corner. Tommy couldn't see what he had been looking at until she came into the hallway, wiping her mouth with a thumb, lips pursed tight. Salerno was watching her with a faint smile, but the look on her face told Tommy she hadn't enjoyed what had just happened. She was a woman who had been young not that many years ago, with a lot of black hair and a lot of makeup, in very tight jeans, and she wobbled a little on her heels as she made for the first door in the hall, which said "Ladies" on it. She went inside. Tommy stood there and watched while Salerno closed his eyes for a few seconds, still panting a little. He watched while Salerno opened his eyes, shook his head, and slid off the stool. Salerno went out of sight momentarily and then came into view again behind the bar and pulled down a bottle of whiskey and poured himself a drink. He watched Salerno take a couple of sips and then he watched the woman come out of the bathroom and walk with great dignity down the bar toward the front, where she took a coat from a rack and put it on. Tommy watched her turn for the door and then halt as Salerno said something to her, and he saw the look she shot him and the curl of her lip as she answered. He watched her step to the door, turn a key in a lock, and pull the door open and walk out. Tommy watched Salerno leaning on the bar, looking down at his drink, and he thought about how much he was going to enjoy beating that fat face to a pulp. He was ready.

Salerno took another sip and set the glass down and came walking down the bar again, out of sight and then in view again as he turned the end of the bar and headed back up toward the front. Tommy came to his senses and realized a window of opportunity was about to close. Salerno was walking up there to relock the door. Tommy kicked the door, hard.

Salerno wheeled and looked, but froze like he wasn't sure he'd heard anything, so Tommy kicked the door another couple of times. Salerno started walking slowly back toward him, peering up at the window.

Tommy jumped down off the case and ran for the corner of the building away from the parking lot. There was a narrow gangway there, and Tommy went up it in a hurry. He got to the sidewalk in front just in time to see the Taurus peel out of the lot into the street and squeal away to the right. Tommy made for the front door of the bar.

He pushed inside as Joe Salerno was about halfway up the room, coming back toward him. Salerno stopped dead and stared. Tommy shoved the door shut and turned the key in the lock.

"Who the fuck are you?" said Salerno.

"I told you you wouldn't see me coming." Tommy started walking down the room toward Salerno. There wasn't going to be anything subtle about this. "I'm here to teach you some manners."

Salerno stood with his hands on his hips and watched Tommy come. "You," he said, his eyes narrowing. "Get out of my fucking bar."

"Not yet. I want to know what kind of a miserable asshole treats the help like I just saw you treat that lady." Tommy already had the adrenaline buzz going. He was remembering the barmaid in Texas telling him about the boss hitting on her, a bitter look on her face.

The look on Salerno's face said he couldn't believe what he was hearing. "You're a fucking nut case."

Tommy pulled up about three feet from him. "And you're an emergency room admission. About a half hour from now."

Salerno swung but Tommy was ready for it. He had read the whole sequence, from the eyes to the weight shift to the untrained punch powered by panic, and he got his left up to block it so it glanced off the side of his head, giving his ear a hell of a pop. It stung but Tommy was beyond feeling it. "That's it, huh? That's the one supposed to put me on the floor?"

Salerno thought for a second about trying again, and then he turned and ran. He wheeled around the end of the bar, and Tommy knew what that meant. He tore a couple of barstools out of his way and put both hands on the bar and vaulted over it, landing a step or two from the cash register. Salerno stopped in his tracks, about the same distance from the register on the other side of it. His eyes told Tommy where the prize was. Tommy stooped and looked and sure enough there it was, at the back of the shelf just under the cash register. It was an automatic, maybe a SIG-Sauer.

"Well, shit. You gonna shoot me?" Tommy took a step backward. "Be my guest." Tommy didn't know where the hell that came from. Adrenaline could do strange things to a man. "You got a choice," he said, perfectly calm, the diverging paths in the next few seconds laid out in front of him. "You want to go for the gun, who's gonna blame you? Only thing is, you go for the gun, I'm gonna kill you. I'll have to. Now, you want to take your beating like a man, you just turn around and walk back around the end of the bar."

Tommy could see Salerno thinking about it: a big mean bastard not used to having tough choices. Tommy could see him wondering, looking for Tommy's piece, looking in Tommy's eyes to see what was there. Tommy really didn't know at that moment what he wanted to happen. He had come there with the intention of beating the living shit out of Joe Salerno, but if things went a different way, he was ready. What he realized as he watched Salerno making his choice was that he had never racked the slide on the little automatic in his pocket. That was going to make things interesting.

He and Salerno locked eyes, and Tommy saw the change in Salerno's expression as he decided Tommy was bluffing. Tommy knew he had to get a head start, so he put his hand in his pocket. That got things moving.

As Salerno lunged for the SIG, Tommy got the automatic out and racked the slide, things seeming to move slowly the way they did at times of crisis, and he knew as he raised the gun, thumbing off the safety, that he had won: there was no substitute for experience. Salerno had to look to find the safety, and that was what cost him his life. He brought up the SIG and squeezed off a wild shot that went past Tommy's head, but it was too late: Tommy had already fired. He had aimed for the center of Salerno's forehead eight feet away, but small automatics being what they are, the shot exploded one lens of Salerno's glasses and popped his right eye. Salerno's head jerked back as if someone had smacked him, and he collapsed on his back, legs bent, his remaining eye open and the shattered glasses hanging off one ear.

Tommy stepped closer and bent over him. He had seen enough head shots to know Salerno was history. Tommy stepped back and took stock.

He had read somewhere about a police detective complaining that with all the protection of suspects' rights in the United States, all you had to do to get away with murder was make sure nobody actually saw you do it and then keep your mouth shut. He also remembered something he'd read about professional hit men: they never got caught with the murder weapon on them. He took a quick look around and grabbed a damp towel from under the bar. He gave the little gun a quick wipe-down, even though he had also heard it was a lot harder than the TV made it out to be to get good prints off a gun. He dropped the gun on Joe Salerno's body and then wiped the bar where he had put his hands on it vaulting over.

He stepped around Salerno's body, avoiding the blood that was pooling on the floor. He thought for a second about the door up front. He remembered opening it with his shoulder more than his hands. He had shoved it shut with a hand on the glass, though. Tommy ran up to the door and wiped down the area he had touched. He took a look out at the empty street but decided he didn't want to go out that way. Somebody might have heard the shots, and the clock was ticking.

Tommy ran for the back, tossing the towel behind the bar as he went. The back door had a couple of bolts to undo but it didn't take him long. He stepped out into the alley, pulled the door shut behind him and started walking, fast.

At the end of the alley he made himself slow down. He went north for a block, then turned east toward Harlem. A couple of cars went by him. Tommy crossed Harlem against the light and kept walking. When he heard the first sirens somewhere west of him, he went for his car.

Driving back east, Tommy thought about how it had happened. He wondered if in taking the little automatic along with him he had maybe secretly wanted something like this to happen. He didn't waste time thinking about it. He decided things had worked out for the best.

11

Tommy tried not to think too much about Joe Salerno until the following evening. He was cutting up onions to make chili, Brian sitting at the kitchen table bitching about his job, when his cell phone went off. Tommy answered it and heard Lisa's voice in his ear. "Were you watching the news on TV just now by any chance? Channel seven?"

"I gave up on the TV news a long time ago," Tommy said. "How come?"

"He's dead."

Careful, Tommy told himself. "Who?"

There was a pause at Lisa's end, about as long as the one Tommy had made. "Joe Salerno."

Tommy went rapidly through a few different things he could say and settled on, "What happened to him?"

"Somebody shot him."

"No shit?" Tommy tried to sound surprised.

"No shit. It wasn't you, was it?"

Tommy laughed out loud. It felt natural but it was a good way to mask his nervous release of tension. "If I did, do you think I'd tell you?" He broke off to answer Brian's questioning look. "Somebody shot that prick that was bothering Lisa." He watched astonishment bloom on Brian's face as he lifted the phone again. "You sure it was the same guy?"

"Absolutely. They showed his picture and everything. Mary and I were watching and I started like screaming, 'That's the guy! That's the guy!' We're kind of in shock over here, but it's a good shock."

"I bet. They know who did it?"

"No. You want to know the strange part?"

That set off all kinds of alarm bells for Tommy. He didn't like the sound of that, not at all. He didn't want to deal with any strange parts in this business. "What?" he said.

"It turns out he was a gangster. A Mafia guy."

Everything stopped for a second. Tommy said, "You're shitting me."

"No. They're saying it's the first mob killing in Chicago in years. Apparently Salerno's father is some kind of big mob honcho and this could be part of a dispute over who gets to control all the illegal gambling or something. Anyway, I think my problem is solved."

"Well, that's good," Tommy said. "You can rest easy now."

"I can't believe it. One day I'm afraid to go home and the next it's all over. I thought I'd lost everything. And now I'm like . . ." She stopped, and Tommy could hear, very faintly, what sounded like a gasp and then a murmur of voices. A few seconds went by and Lisa was back. "I'm sorry. I'm like losing it here. I just wanted you to know. And to say thank you. You and Brian both. For helping me. I'm going to throw a party. As soon as I'm back in my house. This weekend. And this time nobody's going to interrupt it."

Tommy had missed all the reports on the early evening news, but he and Brian caught it at ten. The title floating on the screen as the anchor lady talked said *Mob Killing?* Tommy didn't like that question mark. He would have been happier if everyone had been sure about it. The picture changed and Tommy's heart skipped a beat or two: yellow crime scene tape across the entrance to a little neighborhood bar in Maywood Park. Tommy sat as still as a rock. "Police tonight are questioning the bartender, who was apparently the last person to see Salerno alive," said the reporter in the foreground, his hair whipped by the wind. "They are being very tight-lipped about what information this individual has to offer."

That worried Tommy a little: the woman he'd seen leaving the bar after being practically raped by Joe Salerno would be a good first guess for a homicide detective. He was going to have to give some thought to what he would do if somebody got charged for shooting Salerno.

"Well, that's Lisa for you," said Brian. "She wouldn't attract just any old jerk. Had to be a real professional major-league jerk."

Tommy didn't say anything. He was listening to the cop who was talking into a microphone on the screen. "At this time we don't have a motive. Because of who the victim was there's a lot of speculation, but we don't know for sure that it's related to any organized crime activity."

"Well, hello," said Brian. "The guy's a mobster. What else is it gonna be?" He looked at Tommy and said, "It wasn't you, was it?"

Tommy grinned. "I'll tell you what I told Lisa. If it was me, do you think I'd say so?"

"I sure as hell hope not." Brian shook his head. "Anyway, I'm just glad Lisa's off the hook. Jesus. What a thing to go through.'"

"Tell me about it," said Tommy, getting up to go to work.

The next morning it was all over the papers. Tommy bought the *Sun-Times* and read it in the coffee shop on Wilson after he finished up at the apartment house. *Outfit boss Salerno's son slain,* said the headline. There was a picture of Joe Salerno, a few years younger, with more hair and different glasses but unmistakably the guy Tommy had killed, and another picture of his father, one of those shots snapped outside a courthouse with the subject glaring at all the people crowding around him. Salerno senior was heavy-set and white-haired and he looked like the kind of ill-tempered man who would take a swing at you if you took his parking spot. There was another mention of the bartender and the grilling the cops had given her, but no indication that they were about to arrest her or anybody else. Tommy figured she was in the clear: since she hadn't done it, there couldn't be any evidence against her.

In addition to the lead article there were a couple of background pieces: the Outfit in the 21st century and Rocco Salerno, the reluctant boss. Tommy had never heard of the Outfit but it looked like that was what the Mafia was called in Chicago. As for Salerno, the reason he was reluctant to be called the boss was that lately all the bosses seemed to die in jail. The article said nobody could even say for sure who was in charge of the Outfit these days, but maybe that was part of the reason Joe Salerno got shot.

The more Tommy read the more he realized how lucky he had been. He had managed to shoot somebody who came with a whole set of reasons for getting killed, none of which had anything to do with Tommy. Tommy had been prepared to ride out a police investigation and even take to his heels if necessary, but it was starting to look like he wouldn't have to sweat it. Everybody was assuming this had something to do with the mob.

It could signal the opening of a new phase in the evolution of the Outfit, some expert was quoted in the paper. *Things have been quiet for years and everyone has assumed that all the spoils were divided. But crime is always evolving, and any time there is change there can be disputes.*

We don't know what it means, another expert was saying. *The word was, Rocco Salerno had kept his son out of the rackets. But our intelligence is always imperfect.*

Way down at the bottom of the lead article, the police chief of Maywood Park was quoted as saying, *We're not assuming it was a hit in the classic sense. It could have been some kind of personal dispute or even a robbery. We're looking at it from all angles.*

Tommy shoved the paper away. He hoped they didn't look too hard.

Walking over to Lisa's on Saturday night, Tommy asked Brian, "What's happening with you and Lisa, anyway?"

"Not a thing, man. We went out a couple of times, and nothing. There was just no spark. And then the last time we were out, what's-his-name the gangster guy shows up, and that about did it. Maybe if I'd put up a better fight it would have been different, but I got my ass kicked."

"That don't mean nothing."

"Yes, it does. Having a woman hold a napkin to your bloody nose doesn't exactly make you look heroic."

"You stood up for her, at least."

"Yeah. But all that happened was, she felt sorry for me. It just ain't happening with us. The way's clear for you, man."

"Me? What the hell you talking about?"

"You're the one she likes."

"Horseshit."

"She called your cell phone when she heard about Salerno. Not mine."

"That's just because I'd talked with her about helping her out."

"Well, I'm telling you. She's yours if you want her. I can tell."

"I'm not interested."

"Why not, man? She's a nice lady."

"Too nice. Too neat, too high-class or something, I don't know."

"That's just the kind that goes head over heels for you rugged individualist types."

"Bullshit. She's not my type."

Brian laughed. "What is your type? You ever had a real girlfriend?"

"I could tell you some stories."

"Okay, I'm not talking about just getting laid. I mean somebody you would consider spending some serious time with. You ever think about getting married?"

"Not much. Mostly for the last couple of years I been thinking about staying alive."

Brian gave it up then and soon they were at Lisa's. It was pretty much the same crowd as had been at the dinner when Salerno showed up, with a few other people he recognized from the party at Mary's. Tommy had been expecting to get the question a few more times, remembering what he had said at the dinner, and sure enough one or two people asked him if he had shot Joe Salerno. Tommy just put a finger to his lips and said, "Shhh. Don't tell anybody." Everyone laughed and Tommy hoped they were all sure it was a joke.

Lisa was dressed in tight jeans and a dark green sweater with a slightly daring neckline, with a touch of makeup, and her dark brown hair swept behind her ears. Tommy looked at her with a little more attention this time, thinking about what Brian had said, but she still wasn't his type. She was pretty and petite, and Tommy had always had a vision in his head of somebody a little on the wild side. But looking at the way Lisa laughed, like a weight had been lifted from her, he was truly glad he had done what he had done.

Tommy had had no regrets, not one, since he had shot Joe Salerno. What he had was a feeling of accomplishment. He had shot up the landscape for a year and a half in Iraq and not accomplished much of anything, so he was overdue.

Tommy was getting himself a beer from the refrigerator when Lisa came into the kitchen. She smiled at him and glanced over her shoulder and took a step toward him. "I wanted to thank you," she said quietly.

For a second, looking into her dark eyes, Tommy was sure she knew. He managed to say, "For what? I didn't do anything."

"Just for being willing to help. It meant a lot to me."

"It was nothing. I'm just glad somebody took care of the problem."

Lisa paused with her lips parted for a second and said, "You know, when I asked you the other night, I didn't really think you shot him."

Tommy realized all of a sudden that a part of him would love Lisa to know what he had done for her, and that was dangerous as hell. He stood there with his mouth open for a moment and then said, "I wanted to."

"So did I," she said, looking grave now. "And I never thought I would say that about anyone."

"That's what being afraid will do to you," Tommy said. "I know. I been there."

12

It was time to get a real job and get his own place. Brian hadn't said a word about it, but Tommy could feel it coming. Something had changed when Brian gave up on Lisa. It was almost as if they were rivals now, even though Tommy still had no intention of getting involved with Lisa or anybody else Brian knew. Tommy just felt he was close to wearing out his welcome. He tried to give Brian a little money toward the rent, but Brian wouldn't take it. "Hell, I ought to pay you, for doing the cooking," he said. But Tommy thought the joke sounded a little forced.

He went back to looking at the want ads. He was starting

to realize that Brian was right: some college would be a big help. All the schools and courses he'd done in the army had made him into a very good combat patrol leader, but he was still basically an infantryman: he wasn't sure how well the skill set transferred. The obvious thing was law enforcement, but now you needed a degree for that. He was starting to think in terms of saving up for more schooling, which probably meant working like a dog for a year or two while living cheap.

Meanwhile there were jobs out there, most of them lousy. Lots of people needed sales clerks, pizza delivery drivers, people to hand out pamphlets. Those jobs were always available because nobody could stand them for long. Somebody was always advertising for a bartender, but Tommy wasn't sure he wanted to get into that racket. A lot of friendly bartenders had greased the skids for his old man on the way down. Anyway, he had no experience on the business side of the bar.

A bakery needed a delivery driver six mornings a week in Wicker Park and Ukrainian Village, another part-time gig but okay money. Tommy figured if he could handle a Humvee he could handle a delivery van. He went in to talk to the guy and after a couple of days got a phone call saying the job was his. It was an early-morning job that he could fit in between the restaurant and the apartment house. With his three shit jobs he was almost making a living and becoming even more of a night owl.

He started to look at apartments again, realizing that all he could afford for a while was a dump. It would be cheaper to have a roommate, but he knew he would be lucky to find anybody as easy to live with as Brian. He was going to wind up in a ratty studio apartment in Uptown, he figured, along with all the other derelicts. But it was a place to start. He wanted to put down roots somewhere, and he knew anywhere he went it would take time. He told Brian he would have his own place by the end of the month and Brian said that was cool.

The cops showed up for the first time a week after he killed Joe Salerno. It had dropped out of the papers, and Tommy had just started to think he'd gotten away with it clean when the doorbell rang, waking him up from his afternoon nap on Brian's couch.

It was only one cop, to be exact, and as he came up the stairs Tommy saw he already knew him. It was Hays, the man he and Lisa had talked to at Area Three. The way he looked past Tommy into the apartment reminded Tommy of the way he himself used to look past people who answered the door in Iraq. "Can I talk to you for a minute?" Hays said.

Tommy didn't move. "What for? What'd I do?"

"You tell me," Hays said with a smile. "I just came to ask you a couple of questions."

"About what?"

"About Joe Salerno."

Tommy just stood there, thinking. Don't tell him any lies, he told himself. Let him do the talking. "Come on in," he said.

Hays looked around the room and said, "Your roommate here?"

"He's at work."

"That would be Brian Dawson?"

"That's right." Tommy sat there frowning at the detective. How did he know about Brian?

Hays just stared back at him for a few seconds. "Well?" he said.

"Well what?"

"Tell me about Joe Salerno."

"I don't know anything about Joe Salerno. Except what I read in the papers."

"You talked to him, didn't you? When he was bothering your friend Lisa?"

Tommy nodded. "You must have talked to her. So you know what happened."

Hays smiled, just a little bit. "I want to hear you tell it."

Tommy shrugged. "I told him to lay off her."

"When was this?"

"After he got into her place and messed with her stuff."

Tommy thought Hays looked a little surprised at that. "He was inside her apartment?"

"Yeah. She said she left a key hidden on the porch and he must have found it. She didn't tell you?"

"No, she didn't tell me. What happened after that?"

"Nothing happened. Next thing I know, Lisa calls me to tell me he got shot."

Hays was a man who liked to take his time, apparently. He just sat there looking at Tommy, elbows on his knees, holding a clipboard in both hands. "Why did she come and tell you about it instead of reporting it to us?"

"You'd have to ask her that. But I think she was afraid you guys weren't gonna do much for her."

"And how were you planning to help her out?"

Tommy met the detective's stare for a few seconds before saying, "Well, I was thinking about taking him down an alley somewhere and beating the shit out of him."

Hays nodded. "Why didn't you?"

"Somebody saved me the trouble."

"I see." Tommy thought it looked like Hays wasn't buying it, but he knew better than to keep talking. "What day was it when she told you he'd been inside her place?" Hays said.

Tommy looked at the floor like he was thinking about it, even though he didn't have to. "The day before he got shot," he said after a moment. "I remember she called me the next evening to tell me about it. She'd seen it on the news."

"So what were you doing the night it happened?"

"I was at work."

"And where's that?"

Tommy gave Hays the address of the restaurant. "After that I went over to the apartment building where I work in the morning. I usually catch a couple of hours of sleep in the basement. That's what I did that night."

"Where's the apartment building?"

Tommy told him. Hays wrote on the clipboard and then looked up and said, "Who can I talk to that can back you up?"

"I don't know. There were some people at the restaurant when I got there. But I was alone after they left. Till I talked to some tenants at the apartment building the next morning."

Hays stared at him for a while. "You own a car, Tom?"

"Yeah."

"You mind giving me the model and plate number?"

"Why would I mind?" Tommy gave him the number of the Chevy. "It's got Texas plates."

"Is that where you're from?"

"I'm from Kentucky. I was in the service down in Texas."

"Really? What branch?"

"Army."

"No kidding. What'd you do in the army?"

"Killed people, mostly." Tommy waited a beat and added, "Over in Iraq."

The look on Hays's face was blank. "When did you get back?"

"Last summer. I was in the hospital for a while."

"You hurt bad?"

"Bad enough. But I'll live."

Hays nodded. "How long have you known Lisa?"

"A month or so. Just since I got into town."

"You like her?"

"What's that got to do with anything?"

"I'm just trying to get things straight. See, I'm the guy that got assigned to Lisa's complaint. And no sooner do I find out who the stalker is than he gets shot. So it makes me curious."

"Well, it was me who gave you his license number."

"I'm aware of that. So what?"

"Just pointing out that I tried to do things legally." He hoped that was ambiguous enough.

"But you were planning to go beat him up."

Tommy nodded. "Yeah, I was. Maybe that was wrong. But the man wouldn't take no for an answer. You gonna arrest me for thinking about it?"

"I'm not gonna arrest you for anything. Salerno's not my case. I'm just tying up loose ends here."

"I'll tell you one thing," Tommy said. "Whoever shot him deserves a medal."

Hays said, "I don't necessarily disagree with you."

13

Tommy walked around for a couple of days waiting for more detectives to show up. His talk with Hays made him think hard about where he stood. For a while he gave some serious thought to throwing his stuff in the Chevy and taking off, and then phoning in a confession from some truck stop somewhere and trusting to luck as a fugitive for a while. It was a big country and he figured he could set up somewhere new, Alaska maybe.

He wasn't sure what stopped him. Maybe it was the thought that if he rode this out he could put down roots in a place he was starting to get comfortable in. The delivery job was a breeze after the first couple of days, when he was finding his way around. He was doing a lot of driving around but that was okay. It gave him time to think.

He was starting to develop a social life, too. Mostly it depended on Brian, who seemed to have a hell of a lot of friends. Tommy admired that in him: Brian was good at talking to people, something that had always made Tommy freeze up. Brian took him along to the bar on Halsted or the occasional party, introduced him to people. Tommy sometimes felt like Brian's little brother, but he also found himself talking to women quite a bit, which was a change of pace after the last year and a half of his life. Nothing had happened with anybody yet but Tommy could feel certain parts of his personality that had been neglected starting to revive. They were coming up on Thanksgiving and Mary was having people for dinner at her place. Tommy was surprised to find he was looking forward to it.

About a week and a half after Joe Salerno got killed, a headline in the *Sun-Times* caught Tommy's eye: *Abbate hit stirs mob war fears*. The subtitle said *Salerno link suspected,* so Tommy had to buy the paper. A gangster named Bobby Abbate had taken a couple of shotgun blasts to the chest in a parking lot behind an adult bookstore on U.S. 41 north of Chicago. The usual experts were analyzing what it meant. The idea seemed to be that Abbate was a rival of Rocco Salerno's, and this was maybe payback for young Joe. But the cops were keeping their lips zipped. Again there were all kinds of background articles. With two Outfit figures dead in ten days, the Chicago papers were treating it like World War III. Abbate sounded to Tommy pretty much like a plain old pimp and no great loss, but he had to wonder if he'd set something off he didn't mean to.

Thanksgiving came. Brian was driving down to Kentucky to his folks' house like he always did, and he invited Tommy to come along, but Tommy had already told Mary he would be at her place. Mary had billed it as the Orphans' Thanksgiving. Her parents were in Minnesota and she didn't feel like fighting the holiday traffic to get there. She had invited a few other people who for one reason or another weren't going to be with their families. "My first grown-up Thanksgiving," she said. Tommy realized that in a lot of ways Brian and his friends were just coming out of adolescence. They were in their late twenties and had responsible high-paying jobs, but they didn't really have any cares and worries. Tommy felt about a hundred years old around them sometimes.

Brian took off on the day before Thanksgiving, slapping Tommy on the arm and telling him the place was his until Sunday and just try not to leave any used rubbers lying around. "If I get that lucky, you ain't getting back in this place," Tommy said.

He worked that night and the next morning, and then had a couple of hours to relax before he headed over to Mary's. The weather was cold, the sky was gray, and Tommy was in one of his moods where the world was a big empty house with the wind whistling through. The only place he felt like he really belonged was back in Iraq with the people he cared about, and that was a hell of a comment. He wound up driving to Montrose Harbor and looking out across the endless water.

At least he had Mary's go to. He had bought some beer to bring along and he was prepared to put up with a fair amount of brainless chatter just for the company. He drove around looking for parking and finally dumped the Chevy on Halsted, blocks away from Mary's.

There were six people there besides Mary, and Tommy knew all but one of them, some kind of foreigner Mary had picked up somewhere. Tommy eventually figured out he was Polish. Jason and Diane were there, and another couple named Paul and Linda he had met once at the bar with Brian. And there at the end of the sofa was Lisa. Tommy was surprised to see her, because Mary had told him Lisa was going to be at her sister's in Schaumburg.

Lisa looked nice in slinky black pants, but then all the women looked nice. Mary was being suspiciously friendly to Tommy. He could do worse, he thought. She looked like she might be fun in bed if she ever stopped talking.

There was a lot of fussing and coming and going from the kitchen. Everyone but Tommy had brought food. The other guys made token efforts to help but eventually wound up with Tommy watching the football game on TV, the Bears getting the shit kicked out of them down in Dallas. Then it was time to eat and there was a lot of milling around the table before they all got settled.

Mary raised her glass to toast. "Here's to us orphans," she said. "Just temporarily, we hope." They all drank, and then she started asking people where their families were that they hadn't been able to get together with them for the holiday. People were all over the map. The Polish guy said his parents were working in Ireland, which Tommy couldn't quite figure out. Jason's parents were in one place and Diane's in another. Paul said his parents were divorced and he hadn't been at Thanksgiving with either of them since they broke up. Linda's parents were in Forest Park but she had had it up to here with family get-togethers because of the fights. And Lisa's sister had decided to spend the day with her husband's family, so Lisa had been left out in the cold. "What about you, Tom?" Mary said, like a game-show emcee.

Tommy wiped his mouth and said, "My folks are six feet under, I'm afraid. I'm a real honest-to-God orphan."

Mary put on a concerned look. "Oh, I'm so sorry," she said.

Tommy shrugged. "They've been gone a long time. I'm used to it by now."

She wasn't going to quit, he could see. "What about brothers and sisters? You have any?"

Tommy hesitated a little, and he even thought about lying, but he figured she had asked, so she had it coming. "I had a sister, but she got killed."

Mary's hand went to her mouth. "Oh, my God. I am *so* sorry, Tom. I had no idea."

The Polish guy was staring at him through his thick glasses. "It was some kind of accident?" He pronounced it "exident."

Tommy shook his head. "No. She was raped and strangled in our living room. By a guy that had been following her around for weeks. We thought he was just a nuisance."

Man, did that ever kill the mood, Tommy thought. He made a quick survey of the appalled looks around the table and said, "You know what? It's okay. It was a long time ago and you get over it eventually. I'm sorry to bring it up."

"Oh God, Tom. I am so sorry," Mary said. She looked like she wanted to crawl away somewhere, and Tommy took pity on her.

"Don't worry about it," he said, smiling. "It's good to talk about it sometimes. I couldn't, for a long time."

A few awkward seconds went by and then from the end of the table Lisa said softly, "What was her name?"

Tommy turned and looked at her and saw something gleaming at the corners of her big dark eyes. "Her name was Beth," he said. "And she was my best friend. But she's in a better place now, so it's okay."

It took a while for the conversation to recover, but it did eventually, and after a few beers and a whole lot of food Tommy was feeling pretty good. He was glad to be there. After they ate they all did some preliminary cleaning up and then sat around the living room for a while shooting the shit until the yawns started. The couples left first and it was just Tommy and Lisa and the Polish guy. Mary was being awfully friendly to the guy now, but Tommy suspected he had his sights set on Lisa. Tommy didn't care how it worked out. He was about ready to take off. He didn't have to work that night and he figured it was a good night to hang out by himself at Brian's place, watch a movie or something. He got up to leave.

"Will you walk me home?" said Lisa.

He thought about offering her a ride, but it was farther to his car than it was to her house. He said sure. He thought the Polish guy looked disappointed. When they were all set to go, Mary gave them both hugs. Tommy wasn't much of a hugger but it felt good. He shook hands with the Polish guy and they left.

There weren't a lot of people out and Tommy and Lisa walked in silence for a while. "That detective came and asked me about you," she said after a while.

"I know. He came and talked to me."

"I hope I didn't get you in any trouble. I didn't tell him about what you said that night."

"What, about shooting the guy?"

"Yeah. I know you didn't mean it."

Careful, Tommy thought. Be careful. He decided anything he said would be wrong, so he kept quiet and they kept on walking.

On Lisa's front steps she turned to face him. She was shorter than Tommy but she was on a higher step and her face was nearly level with his. She gave him a long look with her big dark eyes and said, "Whatever you did, thank you."

Tommy looked back at her and thought, she knows. He let a couple of seconds go by and said, "Don't mention it."

And then Lisa leaned forward and kissed him, just a touch on the lips, but she lingered for a second. "Good night," she said, and went inside.

It was a long cold walk back to his car, but Tommy didn't feel it. He was still feeling that kiss, and seeing new vistas outside that big empty house.

14

The Greek was waiting to talk to him when he showed up at the restaurant the next night. "I had the police here asking about you," the Greek said. "You want to tell me what it was about?" He sounded a little steamed, and Tommy couldn't blame him. Having cops come asking about the help couldn't do much for a business owner's peace of mind.

"Sure," Tommy said. "If they were asking was I here on a certain night, it's because they think I killed a guy that night."

The Greek put out a hand to steady himself, shook his head and muttered something Tommy couldn't make out. Then he gave Tommy a pained look and said, "Did you?"

Tommy had to laugh. "I'm gonna tell you what I been telling everybody. You think I'd admit it if I did?" He let the Greek work on that for a second and then said, "The guy was harassing a friend of mine. I got his license number and gave it to the cops. The cops are going around asking about me because they don't have anything else."

The Greek nodded a couple of times, looking like he wasn't sure whether to buy it, and then said, "You promise me you didn't kill anyone?"

Tommy stood up straighter, looked the Greek in the eye and said, "If you don't trust me, just say so."

The Greek left him alone after that. Tommy got to work and by one o'clock he was the only one left in the restaurant. Shoving the mop around, he kept thinking about Lisa. He had felt like a fourteen-year-old kid all day, circling around the phone, trying to decide if he should call her. He had finally decided not to. In the morning light that kiss on the lips had seemed a little ambiguous. Tommy wasn't sure if he had read it right. Besides, he wasn't much of a hand at the dating game. He liked things to happen naturally, like they had in Killeen, a look across the bar at closing time sending clear signals. Tommy figured if anything was going to happen, he would know when the time came.

Did he want to get involved with Lisa? He was still on the fence. She was still a little delicate for his tastes, but the kiss had felt good.

A sharp rapping noise came from the front of the restaurant. Tommy saw two men standing outside the door, one of them tapping on the glass with a set of keys. He put the mop in the bucket and went up front. When he got close enough,

94

he yelled, "We're closed." But he had a feeling that wasn't going to do it, and sure enough one of the men held a police badge up to the glass. Tommy went and unlocked the door.

"Are you McLain?" the first cop said, putting the badge away. He was short and stocky, with black hair starting to crawl back from his forehead.

"That's me." Tommy closed and relocked the door behind them. "What can I do for you?"

"How about a cup of coffee?" said the second cop. He was tall and blond, with a mustache.

"You're out of luck. You want a glass of water, help yourself."

"You here by yourself?" said the short one.

"Not anymore."

"Cute. I'm Detective Bellini and this is Detective Frazier, Maywood Park police," the bald one said.

Tommy stood with his hands on his hips. This was bad news. If Maywood Park was on his trail it was serious. "Where the hell is Maywood Park?"

"West of here. Where the hell are you from, with that accent?"

"South of here."

"That's what I thought. You got a minute to talk?"

"Do I have a choice?"

"Sure you do. It's a free country. You don't have to talk to us. Of course, a good citizen with a clean conscience is always happy to talk to the police."

Tommy shrugged. "Have a seat." He slid into a booth. Bellini sat opposite him and Frazier leaned against the booth across the aisle, hand in his pockets.

"So you work in here by yourself, huh?"

"It's a one-man job."

"You here every night?"

"Except Tuesday."

"What do you do, just the floors?"

"Floors, bathrooms, miscellaneous. Whatever the kitchen and wait staff miss. They're sloppy sometimes. I always like a restaurant to be clean if I'm gonna eat there, so I make sure I leave the place like I'd want it."

"Man, that's a great attitude. How long does it take you?"

"Couple of hours. I'm usually out of here by two, two-thirty."

"You punch a time clock?"

"Nope. The owner pays me a hundred a week, flat rate."

"I see. Cash?"

"You from the police or the IRS?"

Bellini shrugged. "Just curious. You got any way at all of proving you were here on any given night?"

"You could ask Mr. Karas if the work got done."

"I already did. I'm not sure what that proves."

Frazier spoke up. "You own a weapon, Mr. McLain?"

"No, sir."

"No firearms?"

"Not since the army. I'm done with firearms. I hope." Tommy looked from him to Bellini.

Bellini just blinked at him for a while. "You know why we're asking you all these questions?" he said finally.

"Probably because you don't have any idea who killed Joe Salerno."

Bellini smiled. "Tell me what you know about Joe Salerno."

"He was stalking a lady I know. She talked to the police about it but they couldn't do anything. She came to me and I

96

told her I'd have a talk with the guy. Next thing I knew, he was dead."

Bellini waited a couple of seconds and said, "You left something out, didn't you?"

That gave Tommy a little chill. He kept his face blank. "I don't think so."

"How about the part where you said you'd shoot Salerno like a dog?"

Tommy wondered who the hell they had talked to. Had Lisa given them that? "Yeah, I said that. We were all talking shit that night. The other guys said they were gonna go beat him up. I don't think they did."

"Maybe not, but if Salerno woulda got beat up that night, you can be damn sure we'd be talking to them."

"Okay, you got any reason to think I shot him, arrest me." Tommy hoped he sounded jaded instead of cocky. He knew he was walking a fine line.

Bellini and Frazier exchanged a look. Tommy tried to read it but he couldn't. They asked him a few more questions after that, just probing. Where did he live, what was his schedule like, things like that. Tommy could tell they didn't have shit besides the threat he had made. He was starting to relax. He had figured out that it had to be the Chicago detective who had tipped these guys about him, and all he had was a hunch.

The only thing that worried him was the gun: if they traced it to the punk who had tried to stick him up and the punk told them what happened, that could be trouble. He didn't think that was likely, though.

Finally Bellini stood up. "One last question, Mr. McLain."

"Yeah?"

"Who appointed you Lisa DiPietro's bodyguard?"

Tommy just sat there for a moment. "I guess you could say I volunteered."

"You didn't think the police were capable of protecting her?"

"I know they weren't. That's not what they're there for. You're a cop. What would you say?"

Bellini gave him a long cold stare. "I'd say you were probably hoping to get something out of the deal. Did it work?"

Don't let them piss you off, Tommy told himself. "Why don't you ask her about it?" he said finally.

"I plan to," said Bellini, and then they left.

15

"**D**id some detectives from Maywood Park come and talk to you?" Lisa's voice in Tommy's ear brought him upright on the couch.

"Yeah. Last night."

"I'm sorry. I have a feeling I got you in a lot of trouble."

"What do you mean?"

"They showed up at my place and asked me a whole bunch of questions. Mary was there with me. And she told them about how you said you'd shoot Salerno like a dog."

That figures, Tommy thought. "It's okay. All they did was ask questions."

"Mary was kind of upset afterwards. She knew she shouldn't have said anything about it but they were, like, insistent. And you know Mary can't keep her mouth shut about anything."

"It's no big deal. Tell her not to sweat it."

There was a pause. Tommy sat there with the cell phone to his ear, wondering if she wanted him to say something.

"Do you have to work tonight?" Lisa said finally.

"Not till late."

"Want to have dinner or something?"

"Sure," said Tommy. Then he hesitated: did he? "Tell you what, I owe you one. Want to come over here, to Brian's place? I got a couple of steaks in the fridge and Brian's not due back till tomorrow. I'd hate for 'em to go bad."

"Sounds perfect."

Tommy took a shower and cleaned the place up a little, throwing things into closets and giving the bathroom a quick once-over. Brian was fairly tidy, so it wasn't much work. Tommy had the steaks marinating and was cutting up potatoes when the doorbell rang.

Lisa looked like she always did: pretty and dolled up. Tommy had shaved, put on a flannel shirt and combed his hair. That was about as dressed up as he ever got. "Here," Lisa said, handing him a bottle in a brown paper bag. "I got some wine."

"Okay." Tommy took it out of the bag. "I don't know anything about wine."

"This is Chianti. It's Italian. It goes well with red meat."

"Sounds like it'll work. Come on in the kitchen. I gotta get the potatoes on."

"A man who can cook. I'm impressed."

Tommy shrugged, picking up the knife. "I been cooking since I was in grade school."

"Got a corkscrew?"

"Try that drawer."

"Here we go." She attacked the bottle. "How did that happen?"

"What, me cooking? My mother died when I was six. My sister did all the cooking at first, and then she taught me. We kind of traded off after that."

"What about your father?"

"He was always out working. We had to have dinner ready when he got home."

"What did your father do?"

"He was a sheriff's deputy. Till he lost his job because of his drinking, right at the last."

"Here." Lisa handed him a glass of wine. "Cheers." They touched glasses and drank. She watched him over the rim of her glass, then stood with her head cocked to one side. "You haven't had the easiest life, have you?"

Tommy swallowed the wine, not sure he liked it. "It's had some adversity in it. But like my sister always said, you gotta count the good luck with the bad. I had my mom for six years, my sister for fourteen, and my old man for twenty-two, not counting the last couple of years when he wasn't worth much, so it could have been worse."

"You've got that half-full instead of half-empty attitude, huh?"

"Well, the more you sit around feeling sorry for yourself, the sorrier you get. My father used to say that."

Lisa watched him put the potatoes on the stove and pick up his glass again. "I don't think I've ever met anyone quite like you," she said.

Tommy took another sip. He wasn't sure he could learn to like wine, but he was fairly certain he was starting to like Lisa. "I don't know that I ever ran into anyone like you, either."

Their eyes met and Tommy was a little bit surprised at how comfortable it was to stand there looking into those big dark eyes. Lisa set her glass on the counter. "Will those potatoes keep?"

"If I turn off the heat."

"Can you kiss me without spilling wine on me?"

Tommy took a deep breath. Until this moment he hadn't really been sure what was going to happen. "I can try." He put the glass down next to hers, and she practically jumped into his arms. This time her tongue was right there from the start, and it sent a shock through Tommy's system like a live wire. She was quite a bit shorter than he was and light as a feather, and somehow she wound up with her legs clamped around his hips. Tommy swayed a little holding her like that for a few seconds and then she pulled her mouth away from his and whispered, "Is there a bed in this place?"

"We ain't using Brian's. I couldn't do that."

"Then it'll just have to be that rug out there, won't it?"

"Looks like it," said Tommy, starting to move.

Afterward they lay on the couch with Tommy's sleeping bag over them, skin to skin, all the lights out and dinner forgotten. Tommy was amazed. He didn't know where this little tiger had come from. He couldn't believe he had been granted the taste and smell and touch of her. In twenty-four hours his world had changed.

After a while they talked. Tommy told her about Kentucky, the army, good times and bad. He told her things he hadn't told anyone. He stopped and said, "You want me to shut up, just say so. I ain't talked this much in my whole life."

"I can tell." Lisa ran a finger across his lips. "Keep going. I love to hear you talk."

Eventually they got up and dressed, at least partially, and had their dinner, late. Tommy had talked himself out, and when he wasn't cooking he just stood there and held her. Lisa reached inside the flannel shirt and traced the scars on his torso and kissed his bare chest. Tommy kissed the top of her head. He had messed up her hair and smudged her makeup a little but she looked good.

"I gotta go to work," he said, around eleven-thirty.

"You can't blow it off for once?"

"Not really."

"No," Lisa said, looking up at him with her big dark eyes wide open. "You can't, can you? Not you."

16

This time he saw it in the *Tribune* first. *Third killing signals mob power struggle.* Tommy grabbed the paper and went into a café. Somebody named Vincent Spina had been shot six times just inside the entrance to a fast food joint on the Southwest Side. Two men had been seen climbing into a pickup truck and driving away. Spina was a reputed associate of Rocco Salerno.

Tommy sat pondering with his coffee for a while. He wondered how much of this would be happening if he hadn't shot Joe Salerno and how bad he should feel about it. He didn't come up with an answer right away. Vincent Spina had been a loan shark collector and had done time for attempted murder, so once again Tommy couldn't see how he was any great loss to the world.

He had to admit the whole thing was starting to bother him a little, though. He didn't really want to think about it, not with this thing going on with Lisa. He had been walking around in a daze ever since it happened. Going to work that night had been surreal: leaning on the mop with his eyes closed, hardly believing it had really happened. It had been hard to stay motivated.

It was also hard to be without her: he itched to see her again, ached for it. She had called him the next day and said she would be busy all day. Tommy had been afraid she was having second thoughts, about to brush him off. But she had said, "That was nice last night. Let's do it again," and he had said sure and then got tongue-tied. Tommy wasn't good at tender words, and he was glad she seemed to be okay with that. They had agreed to get together at her place on his off night.

Who could have imagined what good things there were in that small package? Tommy was amazed.

Brian had come back from Kentucky and Tommy hadn't been able to bring himself to tell him about it. He felt uncomfortable even after Brian had said basically she was all his. It was getting to be time to get his own place. He looked at a studio on Magnolia just off Lawrence that he could more or less afford and put down a deposit. He could have it on the first of December.

He was working pretty much all night and into the morning now with his three jobs, but he had his afternoons and evenings free, which he liked. Tommy could have gone on like that for a while. He was making enough to eat and pay for his own place, barely, and he was starting to feel like he might have a life after all. He knew that sooner or later he had to give some thought to the future, but for the moment he was cruising.

He didn't know what was going to happen with him and Lisa, but it was truly a joy just to think about her jumping into his arms. That made up for a lot of things.

He was in the bar on Halsted with Brian when the story came on TV. The title on the screen caught his eye first: *Confession in mob hit.* He couldn't hear the TV too well over the the jukebox, and at first he thought the anchorman frowning into the camera was talking about Vincent Spina or maybe Bobby Abbate. But then the picture changed and Tommy was startled to see a place he knew: the inside of Joe Salerno's bar. The video clip showed the stools Tommy had toppled lying on the floor, then shifted to a shot of the space behind the bar, complete with bloodstains.

Tommy walked down the bar to be closer to the TV set. "Maywood Park police say the man surrendered to detectives this morning," he heard. The picture changed again and Tommy was looking at the man who had rapped on the glass at the restaurant a week before, Detective Bellini. Bellini was talking into a mike somebody was holding up to his face.

"This individual has made a full confession," Bellini said. "The motive appears to be personal. It is not related in any way to organized crime activity."

Tommy couldn't believe his ears. He wondered if he had misunderstood something: was this the same Salerno? He was confused. How in the hell could somebody else confess to doing what he had done?

Brian had come down the bar to join him. "What's up?"

Tommy opened his mouth and almost threw his whole life

away right there. He stopped himself just in time from telling Brian that some son of a bitch had confessed to the crime he himself had committed. "The guy that shot Salerno just confessed," he managed to say.

"Shot who?"

"Lisa's stalker."

"No shit? Who was it? Some mob thing, right?"

"That ain't what they're saying." Tommy was trying to listen but with the music and the laughter he couldn't follow it. He shrugged and pushed away from the bar. "Who the hell knows?" he said.

Both papers the next day put it on the front page. *Suspect surrenders in Salerno hit* said one. The other one had *Did it for sis, says Salerno killer.* Tommy grabbed the papers when he got done with his delivery job and took them into a diner on North Avenue. Wondering about it all night long had practically driven him crazy. He ordered breakfast and read everything both papers had.

According to the reports, Michael LaRussa had turned himself in to the Maywood Park detectives and told them he had shot Joe Salerno because Salerno was sexually harassing his sister, Victoria LaRussa, the night bartender at Salerno's bar. The harassment had been going on for months and Victoria LaRussa had not dared to complain because she needed the job: she was a divorcée with two children to feed and her ex-husband was a deadbeat who had skipped town.

Tommy knew damn well Salerno had been harassing his night bartender, but he also knew damn well Michael LaRussa hadn't shot him. He thought for a second and then he could see what must have happened, why LaRussa would turn himself in for something he hadn't done: he was protecting his sister. He had to be convinced she had done it. She had been the last person to see Salerno alive. The cops would have raked her over the coals, and she must have looked like a pretty good suspect. If they had turned up something about the harassment on top of her being at the scene at the right time, that would have been hard to argue against. Michael LaRussa must have bought it just like the cops did and been afraid they were going to charge Victoria.

Tommy had to admire the guy. Now that was a brother. The paper said Michael LaRussa had had his own troubles with the law, having done time for cocaine dealing in his twenties. So he knew he could do prison and maybe figured with mitigating circumstances he could get a reduced sentence. Still, that was a hell of a lot of devotion to a sister.

Tommy couldn't let him do it, of course. For a bad moment he thought he was going to have to stand up himself, face the music. Could he do prison? He didn't know. Then Tommy asked himself why he had to think along those lines. He still figured he had done a good thing by killing Joe Salerno, and he decided he was damned if he was going to go to jail for it. All he needed was a way to get this Michael LaRussa off the hook.

The anonymous phone call was a classic, but Tommy didn't know what kind of technology the police had nowadays, whether they recorded all the calls that came in to them. He had heard they could identify your voice like a fingerprint now. He knew they could identify handwriting, too, not to mention fingerprints on a letter. Typewriters were no better: he'd read about the Secret Service finding people who had threatened the president by tracking down the typewriter that had been used. He didn't know about computer printers, but he knew he had to be careful.

Finally he decided that a fax machine could be a useful way of putting a layer between him and the police. If he wrote in capitals or cut out the letters or something, nobody was going to identify his handwriting, and nobody was going to be able to analyze the paper it was written on because it was going to be destroyed before they were done reading the fax. All he needed was a fax operator who could be counted on not to pay attention to the contents. Tommy had sent a few faxes in his life and he had never yet seen an operator read what he was sending.

Anyway, was anybody going to run after him out of the currency exchange because he had asked them to send a message saying he shot somebody? Or remember his face if the cops came calling? Tommy thought it was a safe bet.

He did his apartment job and went home to Brian's. He gave the whole thing a little more thought and then looked up a fax number for the Maywood Park police on the computer and jumped in his car. He drove to a Kinko's on Clark Street and typed his letter on one of their computers, in small type:

Michael LaRussa did not shoot Joe Salerno. Ask him which eye he hit Salerno in and how many shots Salerno got off. Then let him go.

Tommy figured that ought to do it. He could have faxed it right there at Kinko's, but he figured he had already left enough tracks in the place. He got back in the car and drove some more, finally winding up at a currency exchange on Halsted where he handed in the fax to be sent. He filled out a cover sheet with the fax number on it and sure enough the lady who put it through never looked at the fax. Tommy tore up the letter and the cover sheet and threw them in a Dumpster down an alley. Then he got back in the car and went home.

Lisa called him on Monday afternoon to confirm their date. "Did you hear about the guy who confessed to shooting Salerno?" she said after a pause.

"Yeah."

"You think he really did it?"

Tommy figured he knew exactly what she was saying: I thought you did it. He was conflicted: he wanted her to know the truth, but he couldn't say it, not even to her. It bothered him to let someone else take the credit, but he would be a fool to claim it for himself. Anyway, she would go back to wondering soon enough when the cops cut LaRussa loose. "Why would he confess if he didn't do it?" he said.

A few seconds went by. "I guess he wouldn't," she said.

"Unless he thought he was covering up for his sister." Tommy couldn't stop himself from saying it.

"God, you think she did it?"

It was getting harder for Tommy to stick to his resolution not to tell anybody any lies. "I think it's gonna be interesting to see who else gets arrested."

The silence was a little longer this time. "What do you want to do tomorrow?" Lisa said. "Dinner and a movie?"

"Sure. Whatever you want to do."

"Why don't you come over to my place and we'll play it by ear?" she had said, and Tommy felt his stomach turn over.

Tommy had a hard time making it through the day. He rang Lisa's doorbell at seven o'clock. Walking up the stairs after she buzzed him in, Tommy had a moment of panic: did she expect him to have flowers, a bottle of wine? Would she want him to grab her and lay one on her, sweep her off her feet? Or play it cool? All of a sudden he wasn't sure how you acted with a girl like Lisa after you had slept with her once.

He felt better when he saw her standing in the doorway waiting for him, smiling. She looked happy to see him. He couldn't help himself: he grinned back at her.

"Hey, there," Lisa said. "You are a sight for sore eyes."

Tommy just reached for her. He wasn't any good with words. She turned her face up to his, standing on tiptoes, and put her hands on either side of his face. The kiss was perfect, easy and natural.

"You forgot to shave." Her breath tickled his lips.

"I'm sorry."

"No, I like it." She ran a hand over his cheek. Looking into her big dark eyes, Tommy couldn't believe this was the same woman he had thought was too delicate for him a week or two ago. "You hungry?" she said.

"Not especially."

"Me neither. Want to go to bed?"

All Tommy could do was nod. Somehow the door got closed. After that it was easy.

It was nice in her bed: lots of room, covers to throw over them when they were done. Tommy dozed off with Lisa in his arms and woke up in the dark to hear water running in the bathroom. He lay there thinking that he was in one of those moments he would remember all his life. He felt peaceful and contented, and that didn't happen to him a lot. He felt lucky. He felt like his life was turning around. In a minute she was back, slipping in beside him again. "Ooh, my God, you're warm. Hold me."

Tommy held her. After a while she reached out and turned on the bedside lamp. She propped her head up on an elbow and ran a finger over his lips. "You know what I thought when you walked into Mary's place with Brian, that first night?"

"What?"

"I thought, 'This guy's dangerous.' "

Tommy laughed. "Dangerous?"

"Yeah. You had a kind of look, like you were sizing everybody up and not liking what you saw. And it was pretty obvious you could take anybody in the room."

"I didn't mean to scare anybody."

"No, I could tell that, once you opened your mouth. You didn't sound like the type of person who likes to throw his weight around."

"You didn't think I sounded like a dumb cracker?"

"No, I thought you sounded like a really smart cracker."

"Watch it."

"Seriously. I try not to make assumptions about people on the basis of things like that. Maybe because people make assumptions about me."

"Like what?"

"Well, what did you think when you saw me?"

Tommy smiled. "I thought you looked like a really nice girl. About the last girl who would want to get involved with a cracker like me."

"See? Did I surprise you?"

"Big time," said Tommy.

17

B rian took the news pretty well when it finally came out. Tommy answered a call from Lisa on his cell phone at Brian's one evening and then had to explain. "You sly dog," said Brian, staring wide-eyed at Tommy. "I told you she wanted you. What'd she have to do, come over here naked and roll you off the couch?"

"Practically." Tommy was embarrassed by the whole thing. The last thing he wanted to do was brag about it.

"You didn't do it in my bed, did you?"

"Dammit, Brian, would I do that?"

"Chill, will you? I'm shitting you."

Brian seemed to find it funny but Tommy knew there had to be at least a little hurt pride somewhere. He was anxious to move out now. In a couple of days he would be in the studio up in Uptown. He had mixed feelings about it. It would be nice to be in his own place but he realized he would miss the companionship. He owed Brian a lot for putting up with him.

He had momentarily forgotten about Michael LaRussa when the headline caught his eye: *Salerno confession unravels.* Tommy had been expecting it. This time he read the story in the diner on Wilson after his morning job. *Cops say suspect tried to shield sister,* the subhead said. This article was shorter than the ones that had told about LaRussa's arrest. All it said was that Maywood Park detectives had determined that Michael LaRussa had made a false confession. He had been unable to corroborate certain crime scene details, according to the chief of police. "We are considering obstruction-of-justice charges," the chief was quoted as saying. But Michael LaRussa had been cut loose.

Tommy was relieved. He was sorry about the obstruction charges, but at least he had gotten LaRussa off the hook for murder. What really concerned him was that attention would shift back to his sister now. She was the one with no alibi. Tommy hoped the cops were smart enough to ask Victoria LaRussa the same questions he had suggested they ask Michael. At the end of the article was a sentence or two about the formation of a task force, bringing the Chicago police in on the case. Tommy figured that meant two things: they were clueless, and they were worried. They didn't want any more mobsters going down. They wanted things to be quiet again. Tommy was with them on that one.

In the meantime, there was Lisa. She was driving him nuts.

So far she was keeping her distance a little. She would call and set a date a few nights ahead, and then he would hear nothing from her. It wasn't that Tommy wanted to spend hours on the phone with her or make eyes at her over dinner every night. Tommy knew they were just having a fling, the kind of thing that would run its course in a month or so. The rational part of his mind told him that was fine, about what he could expect for two people so different. He wasn't going to get ideas above his station.

It was just that another part of him was so hungry for her that it was hard for him to make it through the day. He ached for her; her absence was almost a physical pain. It wasn't just the sex: it was the newness, the adventure, the glimpse of a different kind of life. Tommy had never been involved with anyone like her before. The nice girls, the college girls, had always been off-limits. The idea that he could have a place in Lisa's life, even if it was just for a moment, made him think there could be more to his own life than he had thought. It was broadening his horizons.

Until he got hurt, Tommy had always figured he was going to be an army lifer. Now he was starting to get a glimpse of the million different things he could do. He started looking into schools again. Truman College was right there at Wilson and Broadway, and it might be a good place to start. It was cheap, you could study part time, and from what he could tell it was considerably easier to get into than Harvard. Tommy didn't know what kind of student he was going to make. He'd done pretty well in high school in spite of everything, well enough to get into the army, anyway, but it had been a while since he'd had to do any homework. He figured he could handle it, though. He made a tentative decision to work his ass off until next fall and then enroll.

Tommy felt like he was waking up from a long, troubled dream.

He moved into the studio apartment on Magnolia on the kind of day that drove people south to warmer climes: a hard gray sky clamped down low over the city with a wind off the lake that jumped you at the corners and sucked the life out of you. He threw all his stuff in the Chevy and moved while Brian was at work, then stood at the window in his new place looking out at rooftops and a cemetery across the way. He felt lonesome as hell. The place smelled of insecticide and it was just big enough for him to stretch out and do push-ups if he moved the chair. He was already homesick for Brian's couch.

Tommy wanted to take Brian out for dinner as a reward for putting up with him all those weeks. He told Brian to choose the place, money no object. "I owe you big time, man. I can spring for a nice dinner."

"Well shit, in that case. I think you can probably feed a couple of people at Ambria for under five hundred." Tommy just looked at him. "Okay, how about Café Ba-Ba Reeba? It's Spanish."

It didn't sound Spanish to Tommy, but he said it was fine.

Brian had a mischievous look in his eye. "I don't know how many people you want to pay for, but it would be more fun if it wasn't just us two. You want to bring Lisa?"

Tommy shrugged. He was still a little uncomfortable on that score. "Sure."

"I'll call Mary, see if she wants to come. Don't worry, I'll pick up the tab for her if you want."

"Naw, forget it. I'm buying. You all been good to me."

Tommy felt for a second like he'd been hustled, but then he told himself not to be a cheap bastard. They set up the date for Friday night and Tommy spent the rest of the week looking forward to it. His routine was a little easier now that he was living closer to his Uptown jobs. He still had to drive down to Wicker Park in the middle of the night for the delivery job, but now it was a short haul home after the apartment gig and he could be asleep in his own bed by ten o'clock. He got up around five and had a free evening ahead of him.

Friday came and the roof fell in. Tommy heard it on the radio this time, driving up Ashland after his delivery job. *"A man released by police earlier this week after being questioned in the murder of mob figure Joe Salerno was shot to death last night on the West Side. Michael LaRussa was slain in the parking lot of a doughnut store at North and Naragansett by two gunmen who accosted him as he left the store."*

Tommy swore out loud. He listened to the rest of the report and cussed again. Speculation was that the killing was retaliation for Joe Salerno. How in the hell could that be? LaRussa hadn't done it. Tommy pulled over to the curb and just sat there for a while, leaning on the steering wheel. How could they kill Michael LaRussa if the cops had said he didn't do it? Tommy knew the answer to that one—the cops got things wrong all the time. Somebody hadn't believed them. The radio kept going but Tommy wasn't listening anymore. After a while he turned it off. "God damn it," he said. He put the car in gear and pulled out.

Now he had gotten somebody else killed. Or had he? What were the ethics here? He hadn't asked Michael LaRussa to go in and lie about killing Joe Salerno. But the fact remained that

117

Michael LaRussa would probably still be alive if Tommy hadn't shot Salerno. Of course, Salerno would still be alive, too, and still sticking it to Victoria LaRussa and harassing Lisa to boot. In spite of everything, Tommy figured he had done a good thing. It was like Iraq—say what you will, but if Tommy and his friends hadn't gone over to put their lives on the line, Saddam and his asshole sons would still be sticking it to the whole Iraqi people. Could he write off Michael LaRussa as collateral damage?

Tommy had had a lot of trouble with the collateral damage he had seen, and sometimes caused, over in Iraq. It bothered the hell out of him. And this was going to bother him, too.

He didn't know what to think. It bothered him all through his janitor job and it kept him awake for a couple of hours back at his place. He didn't know what to do.

Evening came. He picked Brian up first and then they went and got the girls at Lisa's place. It was a short drive down Halsted to the restaurant. Tommy would have driven around till he found a place to park, but Brian told him to leave it with the valet parking guys. Tommy didn't like the idea of giving his car key to some guy who barely spoke English, but Brian laughed at him. "What, you're afraid he's gonna run off with this luxury vehicle of yours?" Tommy handed over the key.

Inside it was loud and crowded. The food was nothing like Mexican, a point Tommy had been uncertain about. Some of it was pretty good. Lisa looked like a million bucks, like she always did. Mary was talking a blue streak as usual. Tommy tried to forget his worries and have a good time. When the drinks came he raised his beer. "I want to thank you all for laying out the welcome mat. You made this here soldier feel at home, and that's a feat."

They clinked their glasses against his. "I'm just glad you got out of Iraq okay," said Brian.

"Hear, hear," said Mary.

After a moment Lisa said, "I think I'm the one who should thank you." She was giving him a serious look. There was a silence that got a little awkward. "For getting that guy off my back, I mean."

Tommy shrugged. "I didn't do anything." He wondered why the hell she was bringing it up. If she thought she knew what he had done, she should keep it quiet.

Lisa said, "You got the police onto him. They would have done something eventually even if he hadn't gotten killed."

Tommy stared back at her for a moment. He wondered if maybe she didn't suspect after all. Maybe he was imagining things. "All's well that ends well, I guess."

Afterward Tommy drove them all back to Mary's place. They sat around for a while drinking and shooting the breeze and then Brian said he was taking off. He shook Tommy's hand and wished him luck. After he left, Lisa asked Tommy if he would walk her home.

"You okay?" Lisa asked him as they walked, holding hands, shoulders hunched in the chill.

"Yeah, why?" Tommy had been thinking about Michael LaRussa.

"You seem kind of bummed this evening."

Tommy realized he wanted to tell her. He wanted to talk to somebody about it. A secret like that was hard to keep. For a dangerous moment he considered telling her. "I'm just thinking about all the money I spent." He laughed a little to show her he wasn't serious.

"It was nice of you." They went a few steps and Lisa said, "You have to work tonight?"

"Yup."

"But not till midnight?"

"Right."

"Then we've got nearly an hour." She squeezed his hand.

Tommy squeezed back. All of a sudden he couldn't believe his luck, walking along hand in hand with this pretty girl, heading for her place.

"You got a way of cheering a guy up," Tommy said.

18

Tommy bought the papers and read what they had on Michael LaRussa's death. It was as bad as he'd thought. The cops were saying it was a mistaken hit, based on the idea that LaRussa's confession had been for real. They were repeating that he had clearly not been at the crime scene, and they had hauled Rocco Salerno back in for questioning. Nobody had been able to prove anything, but everybody figured he was giving out the orders for retaliation.

The thing that bothered Tommy the most was reading that Victoria LaRussa had gone into hiding. Tommy had heard that mobsters didn't hit women, but anybody that would hit

Michael LaRussa even though the cops said he hadn't done it was on a serious rampage.

Tommy went back to his place and tried to sleep, but he couldn't. On top of the LaRussa business, he couldn't stop thinking about Lisa. It had been hard to tear himself away last night when their hour was up. His work ethic was being undermined. Something was going to have to change.

He dozed off finally, and when he got up in the afternoon his mind was clearer. He knew what he had to do. Tommy jumped in the Chevy and drove out to the West Side. He figured he knew where to start to find old man Salerno. He found Joe Salerno's bar and drove a couple of blocks past it before he parked and walked back, still not wanting anybody to notice those Texas plates. The neon signs in the window were turned on and it looked open. Tommy went inside.

It hadn't changed since the last time he'd been in here. They'd picked up the barstools and that was about it. If an extensive police investigation had disturbed the place, they'd done a pretty good job of cleaning up. There was an old man behind the bar now, and a couple more on stools in front of it, making a little huddle near the register. All three of them stared hard at Tommy as he walked up to the bar.

"Help you, son?" the bartender said. He had a worn-down, disappointed look on his face.

"Where can I find Mr. Rocco Salerno?" Tommy said.

A couple of seconds went by. "Who?"

Tommy wasn't going to waste time. "Cut the shit, will you? You don't know where to find him, say so. Don't tell me you don't know who he is."

"Who the hell are you?" said the customer closest to

Tommy. He had white hair but he looked as if he would go down hard in a fight. Tommy gave him a three-second look and turned back to the barkeeper. "I got some important information for Mr. Salerno. About his son's death."

That got their attention. For a moment nobody said anything. "You ain't a cop," the bartender said.

"No, I ain't. Now how can I find Mr. Salerno?"

"You can tell me the information."

"Are you Rocco Salerno?"

"No."

"Then don't waste my time."

The bartender gave it some thought and said, "Have a seat. I'll see if I can get in touch with him."

Tommy took his cell phone out of his pocket and laid it on the bar. "You got a number for him, just dial it on that and give it back to me."

The old man laughed. "Salerno don't talk on the phone. You kidding me? He has people to do that for him."

"So call one of them."

"It ain't that simple. I'll have to do some calling around. Just have a seat, have a beer, I'll see if I can contact him. He'll probably send somebody over to pick you up."

"I said how can I find him, not how can he find me."

"Look, hotshot, I don't know what you got, but if you think you can get somebody to tell you where Rocco Salerno is when they don't know who the hell you are, you're fuckin' dreaming. Especially now."

Tommy stood there and thought for a second. He could see he hadn't considered things from Salerno's point of view. "Okay," he said. "I'll wait."

"You want a beer?"

"Make it coffee if you would."

Tommy stood at the door of the bar looking out into the street while the bartender went into the office at the far end of the place and made his calls. Tommy could hear him talking but couldn't hear anything he said. He sipped coffee and thought about what he would and wouldn't agree to. The old man came out of the office and said, "Sit tight. Somebody will be here in a few minutes."

Tommy went to a table and sat watching the door. After fifteen minutes, two men came through it. One of them was short and stocky and somewhere past fifty, with gray hair that looked as if it didn't get combed much, and an expression on his face that said whoever he was looking at was in the way. The other one was in his early thirties, well-dressed in a black leather jacket and well-groomed, black hair slicked back from a high forehead. He had a narrow face with dark intelligent eyes that were sizing Tommy up even as he walked toward the bar. The old man just nodded in Tommy's direction.

The two men came over to Tommy's table. "Who the hell are you?" the young guy said.

Tommy watched them come to a halt, six feet away. "I'm a concerned citizen. Who the hell are you?"

The young guy said, "My name's Steve. What is it you're concerned about?"

"I need to talk to Rocco Salerno."

"Does he know you?"

"No. But he'll want to hear what I have to say."

"You think so, huh?"

"I know who killed his son."

The guy called Steve gave Tommy a long look. "So do I," he said.

"If you think it was Michael LaRussa, you're wrong."

After a moment Steve said, "You sound pretty sure."

"I'm sure."

"So who was it?"

"I'll tell that to Mr. Salerno, if anybody ever gets around to telling me how I can do that."

The two men traded a look and Steve said, "Talking to Mr. Salerno is a little complicated right now."

"If you think I'm gonna try and shoot him or something, you can search me."

"Don't worry, we will. If we get that far."

"Well, if we're not gonna get that far, I'd appreciate it if you'd tell me now, so I don't waste the rest of the day. I got things to do."

Steve smiled in a way that said he wasn't especially concerned about Tommy's time. "Don't get impatient," he said. He walked away toward the door, pulling a cell phone out of his jacket. He went outside and stood where Tommy could see him through the door, talking on the cell phone. After a minute or two he came back in.

"Stand up," he said.

Tommy thought about it for a second and stood up. Steve said, "Vince here is gonna make sure you're not carrying anything that might worry Mr. Salerno. Just raise your arms and hold still." Tommy did as he was told. He had searched plenty of people himself, and he could tell Vince knew what he was doing. He gave Tommy a careful going-over, back, legs, crotch and all, and looked bored while he did it. Finally he turned Tommy around and pulled his wallet out of his hip pocket.

Tommy wheeled and grabbed Vince's wrist. "I ain't gonna shoot Mr. Salerno with a wallet. And my name's my business for now. I'll tell Mr. Salerno who I am if he wants to know."

Vince didn't bother to try to break Tommy's grip. All he did was look at Steve, and Tommy knew he was looking for permission to take it to the next level. Tommy said, "You want to make an issue of it, the whole thing's off and Mr. Salerno can spend the rest of the day wondering what it was I had to tell him."

Steve had that little smile on his face again. "Okay, have it your way. Give the man his wallet."

Tommy put it away and said, "We ready to go?"

"Whenever you are."

A black Buick Century was parked in the lot outside. Vince got in the driver's seat. Steve opened the passenger side door for Tommy. "You get shotgun," he said. "I'll ride in back."

"You guys are nervous, aren't you?" said Tommy.

"Careful," said Steve. "We're always careful."

They pulled out and went east and south. Tommy was starting to get a little bit familiar with the West Side suburbs, and when Vince pulled into the parking lot of a pancake house on the north side of North Avenue east of Harlem, Tommy knew they were in Chicago: across the street was Oak Park. "Now we wait," said Steve from the backseat. Tommy shrugged. He was looking at cars on either side. One car parked outside a restaurant with guys sitting in it wouldn't have turned his head. Three was a whole lot.

"Where you from, anyway?" said Steve from the back seat. "I mean, if you don't mind my asking. Texas, I'm guessing."

"Close," said Tommy. He wasn't going to play games.

"Louisiana? Oklahoma? What the hell's close to Texas?"

"Mexico," said Tommy. He was looking at escape routes now. He was going to need a way out.

Steve said, "Mexico? I don't think so."

"Suit yourself."

"Okay, tell me this. How come you're so anxious to tell Mr. Salerno who killed his son? What's in it for you?"

"That's my business, too."

"You think he's gonna pay you? You looking for a favor? What's the deal?"

"The deal is, the wrong guy got blamed for it," said Tommy.

"So how do you know who killed him? You do it yourself?"

Tommy managed not to flinch at that, looking out the windshield. "I'll give Mr. Salerno a full report," he said.

"You were in on it, maybe? You helped stick the place up?"

Vince was looking at Tommy with disgust. "That's it. He's scared. He's gonna give up his partner so he don't get killed."

"That so?" said Steve. "Is that what's going on?"

Tommy figured it wasn't going to hurt anything to let them think that. "I'll tell Mr. Salerno what happened, and if he wants to tell y'all, I'm sure he will."

Steve said, "Well, get ready to talk, because here he is." A dark blue Impala had pulled into the lot and was easing into a slot beyond one of the other occupied cars. "Okay," said Steve. "Here's how it works. You go and get in and talk to him. You do anything that looks hostile or even a little bit sudden, and you're likely to get shot. You got it?"

"I think I got it." Tommy had the door open already. He got out and walked over to the Impala and got in on the passenger side. "You Mr. Salerno?" he said to the driver.

There had been another picture of him in the paper that

morning, and the old man hadn't changed much since it was taken. Some men mellowed out with age and some men just went sour, and Rocco Salerno was one of those. He had white hair, yellow skin and black eyebrows, and he looked like he hadn't smiled in about thirty years. He was wearing a corduroy jacket with a fleece collar, and the hand resting on the steering wheel looked like a chicken claw.

"No, I'm Little Black Sambo. Who the hell are you?" Salerno had a smoker's voice, a truck-rolling-on-gravel voice.

"I was with your son the night he got shot," Tommy said. "I know who shot him."

"Keep talking." The look on Salerno's face almost made Tommy think twice about the whole thing. He hadn't anticipated all the manpower, and he knew he should have. He had been hasty, and that made the risks a lot higher.

"I can tell you who shot him, but there's a condition."

The old man's nostrils flared and his eyes widened a little. "And why do I take your word for it?" he growled.

"Because I was there when it happened."

"Where the fuck you been?" Salerno said. "You could have saved a hell of a lot of trouble."

"I been minding my own business. But I'm giving up the man who shot your son. The thing is, in return you have to leave Victoria LaRussa alone, because she didn't do it. Her brother didn't have anything to do with it either. He was just trying to protect her. So if you had anything to do with killing him, you made a bad mistake."

"You better watch your mouth."

Tommy could tell he was about out of time. "I'm telling you the truth, Mr. Salerno, no bullshit. I got nothing to gain from all of this. Now, you give your word Victoria LaRussa doesn't get hurt?"

"I don't give a shit about her. Talk."

Tommy let a second or two go by. "I shot him," he said. "He was a no-good low-life bastard and he had it coming. You want to take it out on me, you're welcome to try. But it's between you and me, nobody else."

Salerno's mouth had come open. He looked as if somebody had smacked him in the face. Tommy pushed open the door and got out, trying not to hurry. He walked toward the street, looking at the traffic. He heard a car door come open behind him. When Salerno started leaning on his horn, he broke into a run.

Tommy dodged three cars and a bus as he cut across North Avenue, drawing some angry honks as he went. On the Oak Park side he went down an alley, ran for fifty feet and ducked left between two houses. He cut through to the street beyond, crossed it, ducked up another gangway and kept walking. Whatever happened behind him he never knew, because nobody ever caught him.

19

After a certain amount of tramping around Tommy grabbed a cab on Harlem and took it back to Maywood Park to retrieve his car. He figured it was a big town. Rocco Salerno would have to be lucky to find him. All they had was his face, and Tommy didn't plan to hang around the West Side anymore. He hoped he had done what he wanted to do, take the heat off people who had suffered from his actions. He was through playing Lone Ranger. All he wanted now was to go to work, save up money, and see what was going to happen with Lisa.

She was still keeping her distance. Tommy walked around

waiting for his cell phone to ring, but every time it did it was some stupid problem he had to deal with at the apartment building. Tommy could have stood to spend a lot more time with Lisa, but he wasn't going to crowd her, and he wasn't going to beg. He didn't have a lot of experience with stable relationships, but he figured she was probably a little ambivalent about the whole thing. Tommy didn't have any illusions: he wasn't the sort of man that a girl like Lisa would set her sights on with anything long-term in mind. He was a novelty, a thrill ride. He figured it was a matter of weeks before the thing ran its course.

The hard part was, he woke up in the twilight in his shabby little room wanting her. He wanted that tenderness she showed him, lying together after they were done. He was starting to realize he hadn't had enough of that in his life.

Meanwhile, he kept working. Three days after he talked to Rocco Salerno, he was finishing up at the restaurant about two in the morning, knotting the last trash bag he had to take out to the Dumpster. He took the two-by-four that barred the back door out of its brackets and set it down, pulled open the door, and hauled the bag out into the alley.

Tommy knew he was in trouble when he smelled the cigarette smoke. But it was too late by then. When it happened he thought for an instant he'd been shot again: all of a sudden, all he knew was bright lights and pain. He didn't quite go out but nothing made sense for a little while: hands tugging at his shirt, falling over in slow motion, a hell of a jolt, bad news all over. By the time he figured out that he had been walloped on the head his impressions were starting to stabilize and he was being dragged back inside the restaurant. The door slammed shut and

Tommy managed to focus on the man who had shut it, looking down at him.

"Surprise," said Steve in his black leather jacket, still looking as if he was just out of the barber's chair. "Remember me?"

Tommy waited for the pain to subside enough that he could talk. "Sure," he said. "What the fuck hit me?"

Vince the fireplug moved into Tommy's field of vision. In his hand was a long narrow flat-faced leather pouch with a handle on it. "He sapped you," said Steve. "That's a good old-fashioned sap. Cops used to use them before they were outlawed. Filled with lead shot. Don't see 'em much anymore." He could have been discussing antique cars or old baseball cards.

"Can I get up?" said Tommy.

"Sure. Why do you think we're here, Tom?"

Tommy got to his feet slowly, steadying himself on the stove. His head was clear enough to wonder how they had found him, how they knew his name, but he had more serious things to worry about. He could see the two-by-four out of the corner of his eye, leaning against the wall by the door, a long lunge away. He could see the knives stored over the counter on a magnetic rack, way out of range. He hadn't seen any guns yet but he figured they had to be there.

Tommy had had to clean up after a few street shootings in Iraq, and he knew that a lot of victims were too paralyzed by fear to put up any kind of fight. Tommy wasn't going to go easy. It was a lot harder to shoot an active target, even at close range. He looked Steve in the eye. "Probably because Mr. Salerno told you what I told him the other day."

"Yeah. Well, Mr. Salerno wants to talk to you again."

The word "talk" gave Tommy a little hope, but it wasn't a

lot to hang on to. "That's okay by me," he said. "But I gotta close this place up first."

"Don't worry. We're not going anywhere. Mr. Salerno's on his way."

Tommy shrugged. "Can I finish cleaning up?"

"Why don't you just sit tight for a while? You can finish after we're gone."

Right, thought Tommy. That was the oldest one in the book. Tommy didn't doubt for a second that they intended to leave him lying on the floor with a couple of holes in his head. "Can I sit down?" he said. "I don't feel so good."

Steve gave him a look that said he didn't give a shit. "Shoot him in the leg if he does anything you don't like," he said to Vince. Tommy saw that the sap had disappeared and been replaced by a big old M1911 automatic, the classic .45 hole-blower. Vince was aiming it more or less in his direction. He didn't look like he would be particularly good with it, but this close he wouldn't have to be. Steve pointed at a chair that sat in the corner of the kitchen for the cooks to collapse on at slack times. "You can sit there," Steve said. Tommy almost bolted toward the front of the restaurant but knew he would never get the door unlocked in time. The chair would put him a little closer to the knife rack, and he figured he had to wait for his chance. He sat down.

Steve was wandering around the kitchen, poking at things. "How the hell did you get mixed up with Joe Salerno?" he said.

Tommy just looked at him. He didn't intend to make any admissions. "You know the guy?"

"To know him was to love him." Steve looked at Vince, who gave a grunt of laughter. Steve said, "You ask me, they should give you a medal. But then, he wasn't my son."

That surprised Tommy a little, but he wasn't going to let anybody fool him into letting down his guard. He knew he was in a bad situation.

The back door of the restaurant opened and two men came in. One was a bulldog, short and thick and bald, a bad-looking piece of work. And the other one was Rocco Salerno. He had a trench coat draped over his shoulders and he moved slowly, as if his back hurt. He had the same sour expression on his face, and it only got more intense as he came slowly across the kitchen looking at Tommy.

Get tough, Tommy told himself. The fun's about to start.

Salerno just stared at Tommy for a while. Tommy stared right back. His heart was beating a little faster and he was feeling for all the psychic supports that had gotten him through bad situations in Iraq. "You killed my son," said Salerno. He said it with a note of angry surprise, the same way he might snap at someone who had spilled beer on him or stepped on his foot.

"Yes, I did," said Tommy. "And like I said, he had it coming."

Salerno kept on staring with that sour expression. "I'm sure he did," he said finally. "He could be a real prick sometimes."

That was about the last thing Tommy had expected to hear, but he kept his expression blank. "Just for your information," he said, "he had a piece, too. And he got off a shot at me. So it wasn't like I shot him in the back or anything."

"A fair fight, huh?" Salerno's face said he didn't believe it.

Tommy knew there could be an argument on that score, but he said, "He had his chance."

"You did it for the girl, huh?"

"You could say that. I just have a thing about the kind of

man that makes a woman suck his dick to keep her job. That bothers me."

"I ain't talking about the barmaid. I'm talking about your girlfriend."

That surprised the hell out of Tommy: how could he know about Lisa? He blinked a few times and said, "Maybe I did it for both of them."

"You're some kind of Boy Scout, huh?"

"Trustworthy, loyal, helpful." Tommy didn't give a shit what he said anymore: he was thinking hard.

Salerno made a sound deep in his throat. "Well, good for you." He sighed, his eyes roaming the kitchen. When they came back to Tommy he said, "My son and I didn't get along too good. His mother spoiled the hell out of him. But he was still my son."

Tommy had a feeling his time was running out. He was trying not to look at Vince, starting to judge distances and reaction times. "Well, then I guess you got a bone to pick with me."

Salerno's eyes narrowed. "Why do you think you're still alive?" he said after a moment.

"I was kind of wondering."

Salerno made the sound in his throat again. Tommy realized that was what passed for a laugh. "You're still alive because I haven't told anyone to kill you yet."

"That's nice of you."

Salerno peered at him for a moment. "You don't show it, do you?"

"Show what?"

"How scared you are."

"I been scared before."

Salerno nodded. "I can tell. And that's the main reason you're still alive. I think you got something I can use."

"What's that?"

"Balls."

All of a sudden, just for an instant, Tommy got a glimpse of something called a future. He couldn't quite see where this was going, so he kept his mouth shut.

Salerno said, "You owe me. You killed my son, you owe me. Agreed?"

"Sure."

"When somebody owes me, they have two choices." Salerno stopped like he was waiting for Tommy to say something, but Tommy wasn't going to help him. "One, they pay up. In your case, that would mean your life. That would mean I kill you like I would kill a fucking cockroach. You understand that?"

"Sure."

"Two, I own 'em. And I mean I fucking own 'em. Body and soul. Till the debt's worked off. That seem fair to you?"

Tommy wasn't going to go into the ethics of the thing. "Sure."

"Okay, here's how you can work off the debt. I got a job for you."

Tommy tried to keep the lid on his feeling of relief. He'd heard a lot other offers in his life that turned out to be too good to be true. "What's the job?"

"You know who Pete Catania is?"

Tommy knew that from reading the papers. "Yeah. He's in your line of work, I believe."

"Yeah. And right now we ain't getting along too good. He killed one of my guys the other day."

Now Tommy thought he saw where things were headed. He asked anyway. "So what's the job?"

"You kill Pete Catania for me. Then we're even."

Tommy blinked at him. He said, "Free and clear, huh?"

"Free and clear. And I think that's pretty goddamn generous."

No shit, Tommy thought. If that truly was the deal, Rocco Salerno was the greatest philanthropist since Andrew Carnegie. Even if there was more to it than that, it looked as if it meant living till sunup at least. Tommy said, "I kill the guy, we're done? I don't have to go around looking over my shoulder?"

Salerno's eyebrows rose. "Well, shit. You're never gonna be on my Christmas card list. But if somebody shoots your dumb cracker ass after that, it won't be one of my guys."

Tommy nodded, thinking about all the fine print he'd failed to read in his life. "Can I ask a couple of dumb cracker questions?"

"Go ahead."

"Why don't you just use the same guys that shot Michael LaRussa and the other guy, what's-his-name?"

Salerno's eyes were dead, his face completely blank. "Who the fuck says I had anything to do with any of that?"

Tommy shrugged. "Okay, forget it." Tommy thought he knew the answer anyway. There had to be a lot of law enforcement heat on Salerno and all his men right now, and it would be hard for them to make any kind of move without setting off alarms. Salerno needed somebody who was off the radar, both the cops' and Catania's, and he was it. "How do I find the guy?" he said.

"We'll help you. Steve will tell you everything you need to know."

Steve answered Tommy's look with a nod. Tommy turned back to Salerno and said, "You supply a weapon? I'm fresh out."

"Steve'll make sure you have what you need."

"A job like this can take some time to set up. How much time do I have?"

"Three days."

"Three days? That sounds a little tight to me. How about a week?"

Tommy saw he'd gone too far: Salerno's mouth tightened. He looked at Steve and said, "Can you believe this shit?"

Steve said to Tommy, "Look, Tom. This is a take-it-or-leave-it offer."

Tommy nodded. He was calm now, knowing he was going to live. "Okay. I'll be working on my own, I assume?"

Steve answered. "We won't be going to the bathroom with you. But we won't be too far away."

Tommy thought hard for a second, looking at Salerno, and then said, "All right, here's a real dumb question. What's to stop me from jumping in my car and hauling ass out of here the second you cut me loose?"

Salerno smiled a little and shook his head, like a man who can't believe how stupid some people can be. "Well, now let's see. What happens when you skip out on a bond? Besides they come looking for you, I mean."

Tommy shrugged. "You forfeit the money. You want me to put up a bond?"

"You already did."

Tommy didn't like the sound of that. "What do you mean?"

"What's a bond, anyway? It's just something you value. Except in your case it ain't money."

Tommy nodded. "I got it."

"Do you? I want to make sure." He shot a look at Vince. Tommy watched Vince put the gun away inside his jacket and move toward the stove. He said, "You don't have to do that. I get the point." He didn't expect it to stop Vince, and it didn't. Vince took a hot pad from a hook above the stove and reached for the big ten-gallon soup pot that the cooks had left to simmer overnight. "I said I get the point," said Tommy. He watched as Vince heaved and tomorrow's soup stock went all over the floor with a crash and a splash. Tommy watched the flood tide come across the freshly mopped floor and reach his toes. "You son of a bitch," he said.

Salerno and Steve had moved toward the door to avoid the mess. Salerno said, "Don't worry. No harm done. You'll get it cleaned up. It's not like a busted window, or a fire or something."

"Got it," said Tommy, looking at hours of extra work and a tough explanation to the Greek. "Loud and clear."

"Yeah, a fire would really fuck things up." Salerno turned to Vince and said, "What's it look like over there on Burling?"

Vince said, "The fire trucks was just getting there when we went by. Everybody was out on the sidewalk in their pajamas and shit. It ain't every day you see a nice red Mustang go up in flames."

Tommy sat there looking at them, feeling the freeze work its way up through his torso. Tommy knew he was watching professionals at work.

Salerno said, "You might want to go by and check on your pal. He may need a shoulder to cry on."

Tommy said, "He gets hurt, I'll kill you. "

Salerno smiled. "I like your attitude. You might even be good enough to do it, if you can kill about a dozen other guys first. But what good would it do you? By then it'll be way too late for your friend. You fuck up the job, you try and run, we'll hit his house next. Every day you don't come back we'll hit something else. Till there's nothing left to hit but him. You understand?"

"I understand," Tommy said.

Steve said, "You got a lot of exposure in this town. Remember that." His look said he knew Brian wasn't the only friend Tommy had in Chicago. It was a message.

"Okay," said Tommy. "You got a deal."

20

Tommy stood at the end of the block looking at the smoking hulk of Brian's car. The Mustang was destroyed, and the cars at either end of it had taken their licks, too. There was one fire truck still on the scene but the crowd was starting to thin. There were no ambulances, so people were going back to bed. Tommy spotted Brian next to a fireman, looking beat down and dazed.

One part of Tommy wanted to go over and fess up to Brian, but he knew he couldn't face him. He also knew he couldn't get bogged down in explanations, not now. He wheeled and went back to his car. He spent an hour cleaning up the mess in the restaurant and left a note for the Greek explaining how he had upset the soup pot. That was the best he could do. Then he drove home and stood at the window of his room looking out at the cemetery. He was in deep shit and he knew it.

The cops, Tommy thought. Go to the cops and start talking. He should have done that first instead of trying to take things into his own hands.

Except there were problems in that direction, too. There was only one way Salerno could have known about the restaurant, and about Lisa and Brian, and it made Tommy sick to think about it. He had to have gotten it from the cops.

Tommy knew there were cops who were cozy with the bad guys. It was a fact of life. He had heard his father complain about deputies who had taken a few dollars to make sure a pot farm didn't get raided. But this was different. Tommy didn't understand how a sworn police officer could pass information that might get somebody killed. It had to have been the Maywood Park cops. They'd had all Tommy's information, and they could have gotten Brian's car registration. Maybe it hadn't been the detectives: all it took was a crooked clerk with access to the files, but somebody had talked to Rocco Salerno's people.

So he had to be careful about cops, the suburban variety anyway. Would talking to the Chicago department be any better? Tommy was in over his head.

His cell phone rang. It was five in the morning: who the hell was this? He answered.

"Tom? Where the hell are you?"

It took Tommy a second to recognize the voice, and then he said, "Shit." He had forgotten all about his morning job, just flat-out spaced on it. That was what a whack on the head and an offer you couldn't refuse could do to you. This was his boss. "Jerry, I'm sorry. I been dealing with a big-time personal problem here. I should have called you, I know. Can you get somebody to cover for me this morning?"

"Just like that, huh? You got a personal problem, so to hell with me, huh?"

"I ain't making no excuses. You want to fire me, fire me. You want to wait, I can be there in maybe an hour."

"In an hour I start losing accounts. Tell you what, you're not here in twenty minutes, you're history."

Some decisions were easy. "I'm history anyway. I'm real sorry about leaving you hanging like this, but I ain't coming back. Keep what you owe me and call it quits."

"What the hell's the matter with you?"

"More than I can explain right now." Tommy switched off the phone. There it was: he was burning bridges. He had a feeling the next three days weren't going to leave him a lot of time for sweeping floors, either. He was going to have to call the Greek, hand in his resignation.

Before leaving, Steve had given Tommy a cell phone number to call for instructions, later in the day. He had a few hours to figure out what to do.

There was only one thing to do, and that was go to the cops. If the Maywood Park cops were dirty, he didn't see any reason to think Hays was, and Hays was the one in charge of protecting Lisa, which was Tommy's priority. Tommy left the apartment and went and got in his car.

It was a nasty cold morning just starting to lighten to a dirty gray. Tommy was getting tired of Chicago weather. He drove down to Belmont and swung west. Hays would be off duty, but there would be somebody at Belmont and Western who could tell him what to do. Traffic was sparse, not too many people unlucky enough to have to go somewhere in the cold when most people were still under the blankets hanging on to that last restless dream. Tommy looked at people shivering at bus stops, hunched over steering wheels at stoplights, and thought about how lucky they were. He would have given a lot to have nothing more to worry about than getting his bread route done today.

Can you do jail time? Tommy was starting to think seriously about consequences. Talking to the cops meant coming clean, and that was going to hurt. Tommy was going to have to tell them everything. There was no way he could salvage anything by telling half of the story, or trying to lie about this or that. Cops were very good at making your lies work for them and against you. It was going to be come clean or keep your mouth shut.

And Tommy knew that coming clean meant there was no way he could get out of a felony charge. He had gone looking for Joe Salerno with a gun, and he had shot him. He wasn't sure he could make it out to be self-defense, not with the way he had challenged Salerno.

Tommy pulled over to the curb just shy of Western Avenue. He parked and sat there with the engine running, thinking about what a good lawyer might be able to do for him and where the hell he was going to find a good lawyer, much less the money to pay him.

Tommy was pretty sure he was tough enough to do jail for a few years, but the thought that it might wind up being more than a few was starting to bother him. He'd rather get shot to pieces in a Baghdad alley, with his friends around him, than spend his life in jail surrounded by assholes.

And there were other things to consider, too. All of a sudden it seemed as if Tommy had a lot to lose. He tried to picture Lisa on the other side of a pane of glass, talking to him on a telephone. She would be good for two or three visits before she stopped coming, if he was lucky.

The idea of going to jail was looking worse and worse with every tick of the clock. Tommy wasn't sure he could do it after all.

There was another choice, and it was simple. Pete Catania didn't mean a goddamn thing to Tommy. He was just another thug. And if Rocco Salerno was willing to call it quits with Tommy afterward, then that was okay by Tommy. He had killed people before.

Tommy looked at his two choices side by side and wondered how he could have even thought about going to the cops. He put it in gear. He would have time to do his morning job and catch some sleep before he had to drive out to the West Side.

There were two choices, and the only sensible one was clear: do the job.

"Damn, Brian. I mean, shit." Tommy stood looking at the wreck of the Mustang, shaking his head. It looked like Hummers he'd seen taken out in Iraq, except, mercifully, there were no smoking bodies, no moaning survivors in this one. "Holy shit."

"That's what I said." Brian had taken the day off work to deal with the mess: he was waiting for the insurance adjuster. He stood slump-shouldered next to Tommy with his hands in his pockets, unshaven, his hair sticking up every which way. "The noise woke me up and I kind of wondered, but I didn't get out of bed till I heard the sirens. I practically shit my pants when I saw whose car it was. What really sucks is, this is like the one time I had a parking place within sight of my house."

"What did the cops say?" Tommy couldn't look at Brian: he had a guilty conscience but he couldn't afford to give anything away.

"Not much. The arson squad's supposed to come by this morning. The fire department guys said somebody had to have fucked with it. Cars don't just blow up, especially when they're sitting there parked. The cops asked me who might have a grudge against me."

He fell silent and Tommy finally had to look at him. The look on Brian's face wasn't suspicious or angry or anything besides worn out. "What are you thinking?"

Brian shrugged and said, "I'm thinking it was some lunatic, or a mistake. There's this prick at the bank I don't get along with, but I don't think this is exactly his style." He looked Tommy in the eye and said, "Only thing I can think of, the only confrontation I been in lately, was the mobster dude. But he's dead. And I don't think anybody's gonna come after me because I took a couple of swipes at him and got my ass kicked, right? Unless they got me mixed up with you or something. You're the one that got in his face. But then, how would they know it was my car?"

Tommy could see the question in Brian's eyes. He said, "Brian, I don't know who did this. If I find out who it was, and it had anything to do with me, I'll take care of it, I promise." It was not quite a lie, but not quite the truth. He meant the promise, but he didn't know how he was going to keep it.

Brian laughed. "I'm just talking out my ass." He shook his head. "Damn, that was a pretty car."

21

In Iraq Tommy had spent a certain amount of time trying not to get informants killed, which meant he was familiar with the kind of cloak-and-dagger bullshit you needed to make sure you could have a private conversation without the wrong people finding out about it. The instructions Steve gave him on the phone didn't surprise him.

There was a Starbucks in a strip mall on Harlem Avenue north of Fullerton. Tommy pulled in and parked just before two and went in and stood in line to order a cup of coffee. He spotted Steve sitting at a table with the *Sun-Times* but ignored him. When he got his coffee he went to a chair by the window and sat down and looked out at the street. For a few minutes nothing at all happened, and then Steve's cell phone rang. He answered, listened, said something Tommy couldn't hear, and then stood up, folded his paper and left. Tommy gave him a minute and followed.

Steve was waiting in a black Chevy Trailblazer, parked at the end of the lot and idling, exhaust rising in the cold air. Tommy tossed the rest of his coffee into the gutter, stuffed the cup in a trash can and got in. "How's your head?" Steve said. He put it in gear and backed out.

"Head's fine. Where we going?"

"What do you care? I'll bring you back here when we're done."

"We're just going for a ride, huh?"

"You're being taken for a ride, that's what's happening."

Tommy looked to see if he was smiling, but he wasn't. He turned south on Harlem and they went for a few blocks in silence. "So how do you get into this line of work you're in?" Tommy said.

"What line of work would that be?"

"This taking people for rides."

"I filled out an application. There's a waiting list."

Tommy could see he wasn't going to get a straight answer. He was curious, though: he'd never run into a real gangster before, except for the Iraqi variety. Besides, he figured a little small talk couldn't hurt with a guy he would prefer to be on good terms with. His impression of Steve was of somebody he might get along with if circumstances allowed it. He didn't seem like a thug. "Are all you guys Italian, like in the movies?"

Now Steve was smiling faintly. "You bet. Everything's just like in the movies. I got a tommy gun in a violin case back there." Steve drove for a while and said, "Forget the movies. It's a business. It's the business of running things the government doesn't like but everyone else does. Somebody's got to keep things quiet and profitable. And we were doing a pretty good job till you showed up."

Tommy could see the justice in that. He said, "I never intended to stir things up. I just wanted that prick to leave my friend alone."

"Well, you stirred things up pretty good. And that's why I'm taking you for a ride."

Tommy could tell the small talk was over. "Well, let me know when we get there," he said. He pulled the bill of his cap down over his eyes and slumped down in the seat with his arms folded. He figured wherever they were going he would live till they got there, and he could use the rest.

He dozed off after a while, and when he sat up and looked, woken up by the slowing of the car, they were pulling into a parking lot next to a big barnlike building. Tommy took a quick look around: he could see trees and a gas station with a few semis parked next to it and a traffic light at an intersection a few hundred yards away, and that was about it. At some point they had left the city, but they weren't exactly out in the country. They were in that kind of no-man's-land of truck stops and expressway ramps and busted farms waiting to be housing developments that half the country seemed to have become. As Steve rolled toward the building Tommy took a look at where the ride had brought him.

It was a big prefabricated metal building with no windows

and a billboard on the roof. The billboard showed a ten-foot-high blonde in a bikini cocking her hips and shooting a pouting look at any man who happened to be driving by, a look designed to make him jam on the brakes and wheel into the lot. There was a door in the side with an awning over it and above it a sign that said *Gentleman's Club*. There were half a dozen cars parked near the entrance. Steve pulled up in the shadow of the building and put it in park. "You awake?"

"More or less."

"You will be once we get inside, I guarantee you."

"What kind of business we got in a strip joint?"

"You got moral objections, is that it?"

"I just don't know if I'm enough of a gentleman to get in."

Steve smiled a little, opening the door. "You got money, you're a gentleman, as far as they're concerned. But don't worry, we're comped today."

They got out and Tommy followed him into the place. As soon as the door opened, the sound hit Tommy: music at top volume, a thump-thump beat with a female singer whining high above it. Inside there was a kind of lobby with some places to sit and a cashier's booth at one end staffed by a woman with peroxided hair, and right by the door a defensive-tackle-sized bouncer on a stool that looked a little frail for his weight. The bouncer had been looking at a magazine, but he rolled it up and slid off the stool when they came in, giving them the eye. He and Steve shook hands and then put their heads close enough together to shout at each other for a few seconds, and the bouncer looked at Tommy the way he might look at a stray dog that had slipped in when nobody was looking. The bouncer nodded and lost interest, and Steve beckoned to Tommy to follow him.

They went down a short hall and through a wide doorway to where the noise was coming from. It was a big room with a long bar all along the far wall with a bartender behind it chewing on a fingernail and staring at a cocktail waitress in a miniskirt who was leaning on the bar. There were booths in the back and tables in the middle and a brightly lit stage up front with a brass pole in the middle of it. The room was mostly empty, but there were a couple of occupied tables up at the front by the stage, two or three guys at each of them, watching a girl dance. The girl was naked except for a garter on her right thigh and she was doing things on the brass pole that the firemen had never thought of. The men were watching her with completely blank looks.

Tommy stood there watching for a moment. Naked women had the same effect on him as they had on most guys, but it was embarrassing to stand there with a dozen other men watching it. He looked at the men, saw them trying to look nonchalant about having this girl six feet away pushing her snatch at them, and he wondered what kind of guy could afford to spend the afternoon in a place like this instead of holding down a job. He wondered about the girl, too, but that was a mystery he wasn't going to solve.

He saw Steve looking at him with a faintly superior smile. Tommy shrugged and Steve jerked his head toward a door in the back. Tommy followed him. When they got there he saw it was the restroom. Normally he would have run the other way if a guy invited him into the can, but the coffee had circulated through and he had been thinking about it anyway. They went in and stood at the urinals. There were speakers in the ceiling and the music was almost as loud in here as it was out in the room. It occurred to Tommy that was why they were here: nobody was going to hear much on any kind of recording device.

Steve finished first. Tommy was in full spate when he heard the door open behind him. He finished his business and zipped up, listening. It sounded like half the clientele was coming in, but nobody was talking. By the time he turned around Tommy had figured out he wasn't going to have a chance to wash his hands.

Three guys had come in and were standing there looking at him. Tommy had seen one of them before: Vince. The other two he thought had been at one of the tables up front. They were more in his age range but bigger. Tommy figured they were there mainly for deterrence. He met their stares and said, "She done already? Don't tell me you came in here to look at me. That would worry me."

"Keep your fuckin' mouth shut." Vince took a couple of steps toward him. Tommy just glared. From the way everyone was behaving, it looked like he was about to take a beating, but that didn't make sense.

Steve finished washing his hands and peeled off a paper towel. He said, "Take your clothes off."

"Fuck you." Tommy didn't know what was going on, but he wasn't having any of that.

Vince drove a very hard fist into Tommy's stomach. Tommy's reactions were good enough to deflect it a little, but not enough to keep it from jolting his tender insides hard enough to send him to his knees, with his head on the cool tiles. He had figured he was all healed inside from the surgery but he was finding out different. All of a sudden he felt like he had when he had been shot, with that same sense of deep-seated damage. "Fuck you, too," he managed to wheeze.

"Just do it, pal," he heard Steve say. "Look, what do you think I would be worried about, in a situation like this?"

Tommy didn't answer until he was able to push up to a kneeling position. When he could breathe a little easier he said, "I ain't wearing a wire, you dumb son of a bitch."

"I may be dumb, but I'm not dumb enough to take your word for it. Now strip. You asked why we came to a strip joint, this is why. Take your clothes off."

Tommy did it slowly, throwing the items at the older man as he did. "Underpants, too," Steve said when he got that far. Tommy did it and then stood there buck naked with his hands on his hips. "What the fuck happened to you?" Steve said, looking at his scars.

"A guy tried to kill me," Tommy said. "But I killed him instead." It was horseshit, but it was the kind of horseshit guys like these appreciated. Steve's expression didn't change: he just shook his head.

Tommy watched as the three men went through pockets and felt linings and poked at his cell phone and his watch. His stomach hurt like hell but he wasn't going to show it. Vince pulled a latex glove out of his pocket and wriggled it onto his right hand. "Forget that shit," said Tommy.

Steve said, "The G's been known to tape a microphone under a guy's dick. Just hold still and there's no need for anybody to get upset."

"How the hell you think I feel about this?" said Vince, moving closer.

Tommy had to laugh at the look on his face. "Shit. You're the ones set this up."

Steve said, "Yeah, and you've had half a day to think about

it and pick up the phone. The G can move pretty fast when they want to."

Tommy didn't move while Vince checked his private parts, gingerly and with his lips clamped tight. "Don't get excited now," Tommy said.

Vince straighted up, stripping off the glove. His face a foot from Tommy's, he said, "Listen, cocksucker. You're a walking corpse right now. Every breath you take is a gift from Rocco Salerno. And he changes his mind a lot. Try to remember that."

Tommy didn't blink. "You done?"

"I'm done." He stuffed the glove in Tommy's mouth.

Tommy spat it out. "Then gimme my clothes."

They threw his clothes at him and he got dressed. Steve said, "Let's go have a drink and talk business."

They went out, and the tough guys went back up front to their table and Tommy and Steve sat in the middle of the room. The girl on the stage was on her hands and knees, her ass toward the audience, writhing. Tommy wanted to get the hell out of there: the whole thing made him sick. His insides ached and he was close to having to puke. The waitress came over and Tommy turned down a drink. He shifted his chair so his back was to the stage. Steve put his head close enough to Tommy's to be heard. "You understand we had to be sure, right?"

Tommy said, "Just tell me what I have to do."

Steve reached inside his jacket and pulled out a road map. Tommy read *Chicago & Vicinity*. "You know where Chicago Heights is?"

"Not really. South, right?"

"That's right." Steve partially unfolded the map and laid it on the table in front of Tommy. "There." He stabbed at it with a finger. "Catania's got a place down there. Down near Balmoral Park racetrack, actually, right . . . there." He tapped on the map with a finger. "He's got himself a few acres, out in the woods. We got information says he's been hiding down there since the shit hit the fan."

"Okay."

"It's not hard to find. Look at this." Steve pulled out another another paper and unfolded it. This one was a hand-drawn map with lines marked *394, Exchange Road, creek, country club* and a few other features, with an X marking the spot. "The entrance is by a mailbox sitting on a brick base. There's no sign or anything. The driveway takes you about a hundred yards back through some trees. The house is near the creek here." Steve folded the map and handed it to Tommy. "You'll need to drive down there and scout the place out."

"Sure."

"If I was you I wouldn't go in the front way. He'll have a bunch of guys with him."

"Terrific. What's a bunch?"

"I don't know. Three to five, probably."

"Jesus. And I'm supposed to walk in there and shoot the guy?"

"They get careless. They get drunk. And they sleep. Nobody said it would be easy, but it's doable. They won't be looking for you."

"How do I know which one's Catania?"

Steve's hand went inside the jacket again. "Here." He handed Tommy a sheaf of newspaper clippings and articles printed out from the Internet. "He's a little older than he looks in this one. Last time I saw him he looked pretty much like this. Don't worry, he's hard to miss."

"No shit." The pictures all showed a bald man in his sixties with thick lips and a world-class scowl.

Steve's look was totally blank as he leaned close to Tommy's ear. "There's not a lot of guys around Catania who have a real serious reputation. If you're careful, you got a pretty good chance of getting away without having to shoot anybody besides Catania."

"Well, that sure makes me feel better. What do I get to shoot with?"

"We'll get you an automatic. As soon as you give me the word you're ready to move, I'll tell you where to pick it up."

"I'd rather have a shotgun."

Steve's eyebrows went up. "That's a lot harder to conceal."

"More firepower, no ballistics. Get me a shotgun. Auto or pump action, I don't care. Find a way to get it to me."

Steve smiled a little and then nodded. "Okay, I'll see what we can do."

Tommy just stared at him. "It's a suicide mission, isn't it?" he said.

Steve shrugged. "You pull it off, you're off the hook with Salerno. I know him, he keeps his word. If you get killed, that's fine with him, too. He'll just try something else. The only other thing is, you chicken out, get caught and squeal, whatever, your friend pays the price. You understand the deal?"

Tommy had looked at a lot of bad deals in his life, and he knew when he could negotiate and when he just had to take it. "I got it," he said.

22

It took Tommy an hour to claw his way down through the South Side, through the industrial wastelands and drawn-out suburbs and out into the flat open country. Night was falling by the time he had oriented himself on Steve's hand-drawn map. He was out in the middle of nowhere, but it was a nowhere somebody had plans for: there were traffic lights and gas station mini-marts where the county roads intersected with the highway, and signs saying *For Sale—Prime Development Site* stood in the fields.

Tommy had decided there was no sense in putting things off. He figured the best time would be just before dawn, just like for an infantry operation. This was reconnaissance, finding the place and looking at approaches.

Tommy turned off the highway, made a couple of turns and found the brick column supporting the unmarked mailbox, just where it was supposed to be, along a wooded stretch of blacktop road. Beyond the mailbox was a gate in a wire fence, closed. He drove on past without slowing down. The area was a lot more developed than it had looked at first glance. This was farm country having an identity crisis, everyone wanting to live on an estate but not too far from the Wal-Mart and the liquor store. It was basically fields broken up by scattered woodland, but the woods were full of houses, and in two minutes Tommy found himself driving into a town. He drove around just enough to see what was there, which wasn't much. Tommy didn't linger. He wound up going back the way he'd come.

He went back past Catania's place, thinking. He was going to need a place to ditch the car for a while. A big crowded shopping mall parking lot would be good, but he didn't know if there was one in hiking distance of Catania's place. Pulling off the road into the woods was tempting but it was a risk: if anybody stumbled over the car they'd be sure to remember it. It was a problem.

The road had gone over a stream just shy of Catania's place. Tommy turned off onto a road that ran to the left, trying to keep oriented. The road ran through woods on both sides now, houses set back in the trees here and there. On his left the woods ran downhill, toward where the stream would be.

He went for about half a mile, went around a bend, and came to what he needed. A big lighted sign announced the entrance to a country club. Tommy slowed to turn in through a gate into a fair-sized lot with a dozen or so cars grouped at the far end, next to a long, low brick building. He rolled slowly across the lot and parked between an SUV and a Caddy. He got out and went slowly toward the clubhouse. He scanned as he went, looking for anyone looking at him, but he didn't see anybody. He could hear music. Whatever was going on at the country club tonight, it was happening indoors.

Tommy walked on past the entrance to the clubhouse and around a corner, as if he knew exactly where he was going. He kept walking past tennis courts and garages, toward the woods. Away from the clubhouse it was dark. Tommy slipped into the woods and made his way downhill. He was pretty sure he was alone, anybody who had any sense sticking indoors on a cold evening.

He went downhill until he heard the trickle of water and turned upstream. A look at the stars showed him he was heading roughly south, toward where Catania's place should be. The trees had thinned out on either side but in the depression of the stream bed nobody was going to see him unless they were right on top of him. The stream was a trickle over rocks and a slick of mud at the edges. Tommy stayed clear of the mud, thinking about tracks.

He took his time, stopping every once in a while to listen. He counted his steps as he went, knowing he had about half a mile to cover. Without a map he was guessing, but he had an infantryman's instincts.

The headlights took him by surprise: in the dark he'd almost reached the road without seeing the culvert that carried the stream under it. He watched a car sweep by and knew he'd guessed right. Catania's place had to be somewhere up the slope to his left. Tommy started climbing.

When he got to the trees he ran smack into a fence with two strands of barbed wire along the top. Tommy sat down to watch and listen for a while. The only thing that really worried him was dogs. If Catania had a dog or two it was going to be tough. The wind was out of the east, so it wasn't going to give him away, but Tommy didn't want to get within a few feet of the house and set some dog to barking. He could see lights through the trees, and every once in a while a car went by on the road, but mostly there was just the whisper of the wind, the countryside shutting down as the winter night settled in. Tommy shivered a little and dug his chin down into the neck of his sweatshirt.

After a while he decided the only way to find out about dogs was to go over the fence. He got over it with some minor damage to his jeans, and then sat and listened some more. After a while he got up and started walking. First he went toward the road: he had to make sure he had the right place. On his left he could make out lighted windows, a hundred yards away. When he reached the road he went along it until he saw the mailbox on its brick base, then turned back toward the house and went slowly, following the driveway.

The dog showed up when he'd gone maybe fifty feet. Tommy heard it come bounding through the dark, barking. He couldn't be sure, but it looked like a good-sized dog, maybe a Shepherd. There was only one thing to do, and Tommy did it; he went down on the ground into a fetal position and stayed there. Everything depended on whether this was a trained attack dog or just a plain old farm dog; if it was the former, Tommy had a problem.

The dog hauled up just shy of Tommy and barked at him

a few more times. Tommy didn't move. He knew most dogs wouldn't attack if you didn't give them a reason to. He also knew all bets were off where animal behavior was concerned. Tommy wasn't too worried about getting hurt, but if the dog didn't shut up soon it was going to deep-six his whole approach. Tommy waited it out, arms over his face, the dog barking its head off, three feet away.

The dog finally shut up, and then Tommy heard something that was worse than the barking: he heard a door open. Tommy heard footsteps on concrete and started thinking about escape routes. The bad part was, running almost always set a dog off.

He waited. A couple of hundred feet away, somebody spoke, not too loudly. Somebody else answered, just audible, and that got Tommy seriously worried. Two men and a dog were going to make it interesting. The dog barked again, but Tommy didn't move. There was a long moment of silence and then the dog took off toward the voices in the dark. Tommy heard it bark once or twice more and thought that if he was going to take off, this was his chance. He almost broke and ran, but the voices stopped him, muttering in the dark not quite close enough for him to make out words.

Time went by. "Probably just turned up a rabbit or something," somebody said quietly but distinctly, maybe a hundred feet away.

Tommy could just barely hear the response: "Shut up." Everyone listened some more. The dog came running back toward Tommy and circled him, but didn't bark. Then it ran away again.

After a minute Tommy heard footsteps moving back toward the house, grass and leaves rustling, muttered conversation moving away. A door opened and shut. Tommy waited a minute and then slowly uncurled, stretching out his limbs. The dog came back and Tommy lay still. The dog sniffed and barked once, then sat down. Tommy said, very quietly, "Easy, boy."

All it took was patience, and most people didn't have it. Tommy lay there in the dark with the dog and let it get used to him. When he was sure this was just a big friendly farm dog, he started petting it, taking every step slowly. Tommy knew he had gotten lucky: the dog had been an easy conquest because Catania had a lot of extra people around the place and the dog had gotten used to strangers. After fifteen minutes Tommy stood up, patted the dog a couple of times, and started moving carefully through the dark, the dog trotting with him.

The trees were sparse near the house and Tommy circled, scoping it out. It was a long, low ranch house in the shape of an L, the driveway leading to a patch of asphalt nestled in the crook of the L in front of a two-car garage. There were a couple of cars parked on the asphalt, a Cherokee and a Grand Am. Looking in windows as he moved around the house, a hundred feet out, Tommy was able to get an idea of the layout. The garage wing of the house also contained the kitchen, then there was a living room with big picture windows where the two wings met, and finally bedrooms in the other wing of the house. Tommy glimpsed at least two men through the kitchen windows; all the other windows had curtains pulled over them. Behind the house were a couple of sheds, padlocked.

Tommy retraced his steps and found a comfortable spot at the base of a pine, on soft needles and sheltered by the lower branches, where he could see the front of the house. The dog stuck with him for a couple of minutes and then went off to do whatever dogs do. Tommy was getting cold, but he knew he had to put in the time and do the homework if he wanted to get away with this. He needed to get into the house, find Catania, deal with any opposition, do the job and get the hell out. Then he would have to get back to his car and get away, all without leaving any traces. That was the hard part: in a real infantry operation nobody gave a shit about leaving a mess behind.

Tommy lay there in the dark thinking and watching and wondering how in the hell he had gotten into shit this deep and how the hell he was going to get out of it. A man came out of the house, got in the Cherokee and drove away. A Dodge Dakota rolled up and two men got out and went into the house. The man in the Cherokee came back with a bag of groceries. A man came out and got in the Grand Am and drove away. The garage door went up and a Buick Riviera backed out, nearly clipped the Dakota, and went off down the driveway. Tommy had seen enough. He moved carefully out of his hiding place and back toward the stream. In fifteen minutes he was back at his car at the country club.

He had a phone number to call when he was ready to pick up the weapon. Tommy had turned off his cell phone because he knew it could betray a man's movements if somebody got access to the records, so he had to look for a pay phone. He finally found one at a Shell station at a crossroads and dialed the number Steve had given him.

He had to wait while the phone rang a few times, but finally a voice said, "Yeah."

Steve had given him a code to use, more bullshit but probably a good idea. "This is Stanley," he said. "I need to talk to Mr. Roberts."

"He ain't here," said the voice. "Try the Round the Clock, at Sauk Trail and 394. Look for him at the counter."

"Okay, I'll do that." The phone went dead.

The Round the Clock was a country pancake house with a big lighted sign and a moderately crowded parking lot. Tommy parked at the end of a row and went in. He'd been hanging out in places like this all his life: fluorescent light, plate glass windows, booths along the wall filled with kids on dates and farmers on a big night out, and a long counter with the loners piling eggs into their mouths or staring into their coffee. He joined the loners.

He didn't see anybody he recognized but he figured somebody would show up. He ordered dinner. He was halfway through the pork roast when a man sat down two stools away from him. Tommy glanced at him: he had a shaved head, a goatee and a leather jacket. He didn't look like a farmer.

"Pass the sugar there, will you?" the man said when he had ordered coffee. Tommy slid it over.

"What you need is in the Dumpster out back," the man said quietly, leaning over to return the sugar. "The one on the left." Tommy nodded.

The man finished his coffee in about a minute and left. Tommy cut off a piece of pork and wrapped it in a napkin and put it in his jacket pocket. Then he waved off dessert, settled his tab at the register, and went to the pay phone by the door.

Last chance, he thought. Last chance to cut and run. Jump in the car and jam down the accelerator, don't stop till you clear the Mississippi. He didn't know how far Rocco Salerno would go in taking it out on Brian, but he knew he couldn't leave his friend hanging like that. There was another choice: drive to the nearest police station and start talking himself into a twenty-year jail term, hoping the cops could salvage something.

Neither one sounded like a good option. Tommy pushed quarters into the phone and dialed the number of the restaurant in Uptown. He wasn't going to make it in to work tonight. The Greek wasn't there, but Tommy left a message. "Tell him I'm sorry, but it's an emergency. I'll be in touch." He hung up and went out into the cold.

He got in his car and drove around the corner of the building to the Dumpsters lined up by the back door. He parked and got out, leaving it idling. He raised the lid of the Dumpster on the left and saw his package right away: a burlap-wrapped bundle tied with twine, about two and a half feet long, nestled in the near left corner of the bin. Tommy pulled out the bundle and put it in the trunk of the Chevy. It weighed about what he thought it should.

Tommy drove back to the highway and turned south. He had been thinking about the car again; he didn't want to push his luck with the country club. He also didn't want to get caught toting that bundle around the countryside.

He drove back past Catania's place one more time, pushing his luck, and stopped where the road went over the stream. There were no headlights in his mirror or ahead of him. Tommy cut his lights and quickly got out and opened the trunk. He took out the bundle and tossed it down onto the bank of the stream in the darkness below.

He found the place he needed fifteen minutes later, in a run-down area a mile or so north. There were some slummy-looking houses widely spaced and a couple of sheds and a long-busted gas station overrun with weeds, and next to it, just where the town petered out, a gravel lot with a few cars parked on it, with For Sale signs in the window. Tommy turned in and parked and shut it off.

If he stopped to think about it, he would lose his nerve. The lot was dark and nobody was going to see him. Tommy took a screwdriver out of the glove compartment and got out and had his Texas plates off in a couple of minutes. He locked them in the trunk and took off walking. If anyone did notice the car, it was just another junker.

He estimated that he would only have to hike along the road for a quarter mile or so before he could duck off the road onto the country club golf course. The recon was paying off. Two cars passed him while he was hiking, but with the hood of his sweatshirt up nobody was going to make out his face, even if they did remember him later. When he saw the golf course opening out on his right, he only had to make it over an eight-foot chain-link fence, and he'd been hopping fences since he was ten years old. He checked for cars and went.

Straight south took him across a few fairways toward the lights of the clubhouse, and then he hit the stream, on the opposite side from where he'd been. He went upstream again, hit the culvert, climbed up to the road and crossed, then dropped down again and found the bundle right where he'd tossed it.

Tommy crept up into the shadows under the trees before he unwrapped the package. He didn't need much light to handle firearms. He stripped off the burlap and found himself holding a pump-action sawed-off, a Remington 12-gauge maybe, from the feel of it. It had once been a nice gun for bird hunting, and it was pity to spoil it by hacking off the stock and the barrel to turn it into something that had only one purpose: to blow big messy holes in people. Tommy pulled out the magazine to see what he had. Somebody had thoughtfully provided him with five shells, which he hoped to God was enough. He fed the magazine back in and worked the action to chamber a round.

Tommy listened for a moment and then stood up and carefully leaned over the fence to set the gun on the other side. Then he stepped a few feet away, went over, retrieved the gun, and started walking toward the house. When he heard the dog coming he sat down, pulled the chunk of pork out of his pocket and waited for the dog to get there. The dog barked a couple of times but shut up when Tommy offered him the pork. Tommy sat with the dog until he was pretty sure he could move without setting off another round of barking, and then he picked up the gun, stood up, and started walking toward the house.

23

With all those cars at the house, Tommy figured there would be a certain amount of coming and going as the evening wore on. He hoped it would involve that garage door going up at least once more, because otherwise he didn't know how the hell he was going to get into the house. He truly did not want to have to shoot his way in.

All he needed was patience. He had warmed up nicely at the restaurant, but now he was getting cold again. It wasn't going to be fun. Tommy moved carefully through the trees, the dog trotting this way and that nearby, waiting for more meat.

Tommy waited for a long time behind a tree fifty feet from the garage, just making sure there was nobody else out looking at the stars or peeking out from behind a curtain on this side of the house. He could see the place where he needed to be, and he wanted to be sure he could get there without being spotted.

The way the driveway curved meant that Tommy would be able to see any lights coming along it from the back corner of the house, near the kitchen door. He didn't know if the Riviera was still out and about, but if it was, he meant to be ready when it came back. He waited a while longer and then walked across the open space to the corner of the house and sank down with his back to the wall, cradling the shotgun. If he turned his head to his left and looked around the corner he would be able to see the traffic on the driveway. There wasn't much light back here, and as long as nobody actually stepped out the kitchen door he figured he was pretty safe. The dog lingered for a little while and then lost interest.

Tommy knew how to wait: military life involved a lot of it. He was also used to discomfort, but sitting there in the cold was hard. After a while he started to shiver. Time passed. Occasionally Tommy heard noises from inside the house, very faintly: music, voices, a laugh or two. If he was in the middle of a gang war, it didn't sound like people were taking it too seriously. He heard the sound of a car engine and got down low to peek around the corner of the house.

Lights were coming along the drive, maybe the Riviera. The lights wouldn't catch him until the car was lined up to pull into the garage, if that was what it was going to do. Tommy pulled back around the corner and listened for the sound of the garage door going up. The grass and trees to his left were lit up as the car turned, and sure enough, he heard the door start to go up. The dog had come out of nowhere and started barking, somewhere on the other side of the garage. Tommy had forgotten to take the dog into account but it was time to take a risk: he watched the pattern of the headlights on the grass.

The car stopped short of the garage, idling, and nothing happened for what seemed like a long time. Then the arc of grass that was lit up by the headlights started to shrink, and Tommy knew the car was heading into the garage. It was time.

Tommy got to his feet and went around the corner of the garage, fast. He came up the side in a hurry, knowing he had maybe three seconds to get to where he needed to be. The dog had stopped barking but now it started again, which was okay with Tommy as long as it didn't get in the way.

The door had started to come down again, the car all the way into the garage, when Tommy took a quick look around the corner just to make sure nobody was standing there and then rolled, the shotgun tucked close to him, too low, he hoped, to be seen in the driver's side mirror. He rolled to a point directly behind the Riviera and started crawling on his belly as fast as he could go, because he had to beat that door coming down.

The door almost caught his feet, but most of Tommy was out of sight under the car when the door hit the floor with a thump and the motor cut out. Tommy froze. The dog stopped barking, outside. There was a brief silence, and then car doors opened on either side of Tommy and he watched feet hit the floor. The ones to his right were female, judging from the high heels, while the ones to his left wore loafers.

"Fucking mutt," a man's voice said. "One of these days he's gonna get run over."

Tommy was watching the feet: if they came toward the rear of the car he was screwed. The woman headed away to the right, where Tommy could see the bottom of a door leading into the house. After a second the man's feet moved, toward the front of the car. Tommy held his breath as the door opened and he watched both pairs of feet go through it. The door slammed and Tommy breathed again: he was in.

Now all he had to do was wait. The light in the garage timed out and left him in darkness. He could hear voices through the door, very faintly. Gradually they died away. It wasn't much warmer in the garage than outside and the cold concrete was sucking heat out of him. It was going to be a long night. He could just make out the throb of music through the door, and an occasional swell of faint voices. Somebody was having fun while he was out here freezing, and from the sound of things it was going to go on for a while.

He was going to cramp, too, if he had to lie here in the same position all night, but as his eyes readjusted to the dark he thought maybe he wouldn't have to. There was another set of wheels in the garage, and this one belonged to what looked like a big pickup. Tommy waited a while longer and then crawled out from under the Riviera.

It was a Ford pickup, and the bed had nice high sides and was empty. It looked like a more comfortable place to spend the night than the floor, and if the Riviera went out again he would still be hidden. Tommy reached over the tailgate to lay the gun down gently in the back of the pickup and then climbed in after it. He lay down on his back with the gun on his chest and settled in to wait. If somebody took a notion to go out in the pickup it would get interesting, but he didn't think that was likely.

Tommy lay there in the dark and thought about Iraq and all the people he had killed. He hadn't ever taken any pleasure in it: it was what you had to do so they didn't kill you. It was always good to nail somebody with a skillful shot or finally bag some asshole who had been making your life miserable or had killed one of your friends, but it wasn't a warm glow type of good feeling. It was just a job well done, that's all. This was a job Tommy wasn't looking forward to, at all. He just didn't see a way out of it.

What he wanted most of all lying there was Lisa. He wished he had made time, found a way to talk to her tonight. He wanted to hear her voice in his ear again. He wanted to hold her again, take her to bed one more time. He knew it was over for them and he was sorry: he hadn't had nearly enough. He hadn't had enough of those pretty eyes, that small tight body, that secret heat. He was going to have to cut and run, and while he was fairly sure it wasn't going to hurt Lisa, it was sure as hell going to hurt him. He wondered how he had screwed things up so badly. He knew the answer to that, but then he just couldn't find it in his heart to be too sorry about shooting Joe Salerno. He had done it for Lisa.

Time went by and Tommy heard voices outside, a car drive away, a door shut. He hoped the party was starting to break up but then for a while he heard voices closer at hand, in the kitchen maybe. Tommy finally let himself sleep a little. He had time to wait and some catching up to do. From what he had gathered about the gangster lifestyle, things inside wouldn't quiet down for a few hours yet. He knew that as long as he was awake before sunrise he would be fine.

He still panicked a little when he woke up, just for a second, just like all the times in Iraq when he came awake and didn't know for a moment if what had woken him up was about to kill him. He lay there waiting for his heart to slow down and after a while he checked his watch. It was just past four in the morning.

Tommy gave it another half hour. He didn't hear anything from inside the house. At four-thirty he climbed out of the bed of the pickup truck, reached back in for the gun, and made his way softly through the dark to the door that led into the house.

He stood there with his ear to the door for a long time. He could hear something a long way off, voices and then music and then voices again. After a while he decided it was a television program. That worried him, until he remembered how many times he had fallen asleep in front of a TV set.

Sooner or later he was going to have to do something. He figured now was as good a time as any. Tommy reached for the doorknob and tried it, gently. He knew it was asking too much for the people inside to be that careless, and sure enough the door was locked. Tommy thought about it for a second and then took off his jacket and laid it on the floor and tucked it into the crack at the bottom of the door. If somebody was awake, he didn't want them seeing a light in the garage. He found a light switch by feel and flicked on the light. The door was the typical composition piece of junk with a knob lock, nothing hard to get through except for the need to do it quietly. The door stop was just a flimsy piece of molding that Tommy's pocket knife had pried away from the frame in under a minute. Then it was time for the credit card, Tommy getting more use out of it in the last couple of weeks than he had in a year and a half. He switched off the light, put on his jacket and went to work, using the edge of the card to force back the latch. In a few seconds it gave and the door swung open.

Tommy stuffed the credit card in his pocket and went for the shotgun as he looked down the hallway that was revealed to him by the light in the kitchen beyond it. It was about fifteen feet long, with two doors opening off it on the right and one on the left. In the kitchen Tommy could see a long marble countertop with cabinets above it and an island with more counter space and a grill and a hood over it. At the far end was an archway that led into the living room: Tommy could see curtains over a picture window. Now he could hear the TV more clearly. He listened for a moment and realized he was hearing an infomercial. That reassured him a little: nobody who was actually awake ever sat and watched infomercials.

It was time. Tommy raised the shotgun, flicked the safety off and started down the hall. The first door on his right stood open, revealing a laundry room. The second was ajar just enough to show him a bathroom. The kitchen was deserted and somebody was going to have a big cleanup job in the morning. There were empty bottles and glasses, a couple of pizza cartons, and a lot of dishes in the sink. Tommy listened to the TV for a moment and then moved toward the living room.

He went in with the gun up and ready to shoot, but his guess was correct. The living room was lit by two shaded lamps, and it held a lot of massive furniture and one sleeping man, sprawled on a couch opposite the fireplace that dominated one wall. The man was fat, but he had too much hair to be Pete

Catania. He was snoring gently, but Tommy hadn't heard it over the noise of the TV. A bottle of vodka and an empty glass stood on the coffee table in front of him.

Another hallway led off to the right: that was where the bedrooms would be. Tommy moved, thankful for the thick carpeting and the covering noise of the TV.

The master of the house would be in the master bedroom, Tommy figured. That would be the one at the end. From outside it had looked as if the room at the end occupied the entire width of the wing, and the door Tommy could see at the end of the hall had to lead there. He went fast now, figuring a night of drinking had pretty much knocked everyone out.

Tommy stopped at the end of the hall to listen again. He didn't hear any snoring behind the door. He didn't hear anything except the voice in his head telling him it wasn't too late to bail out. Tommy put his hand on the doorknob and turned.

He went in fast and shut the door behind him. There was a little light in the room, coming from a lighted bathroom beyond a door that stood slightly ajar. Tommy stood still by the door and waited for the stirring on the bed, the raised head, the sleepy question. Nothing happened.

Tommy could see two people in the bed. One of them was Pete Catania, unmistakable with the shiny dome and the heavy jowls. The other was a woman, the one he'd seen from under the Riviera, judging by the red high-heeled shoes that lay on the floor in a jumble of woman's clothing. Both of them were dead to the world, Catania on his back, chest heaving gently, and the woman on her side facing Tommy. She looked to be in her forties and was blond and tousled and not quite as nice-looking as she must have been before her makeup had gotten smudged.

Tommy shook his head. The woman was going to complicate things a little.

Tommy lowered the shotgun and put the safety on. He stepped carefully across the carpeted floor to an armchair that sat in the corner of the room facing the foot of the bed. He lowered himself into the chair, leaned the gun against the wall within easy reach, and settled in to wait for Pete Catania to wake up.

24

Tommy had known for several hours that he couldn't kill Pete Catania in cold blood. He had known it ever since he had seen how easy it was going to be. What he hadn't known was what the hell he was going to do instead. He still didn't quite know, sitting there in the armchair with light starting to show around the edges of the curtains, but he had an idea or two.

It was the woman who woke up first. She stirred and muttered something, then rubbed her eyes and thrashed her way out from under the covers and staggered toward the bathroom, still half asleep. She was buck naked and pretty well preserved for her age, but Tommy had too much on his mind to get excited about it. He sat there and listened while she used the toilet, wishing like hell he were somewhere else. When the woman reappeared she was a little more awake, but she still didn't see Tommy right away. She stood at the side of the bed giving Catania an amazed and disgusted look, as if she couldn't believe she had spent the night with him. Then she got back in bed as gingerly as possible, trying to avoid waking him up. Finally, propped up on an elbow and tugging at a pillow, she caught sight of Tommy and froze.

Tommy put his finger to his lips. She drew a quick breath, but before she could scream, Tommy said quietly, "Wake him up if you want, but don't wake up anybody else."

It stopped her from screaming, but she started hyperventilating, and Tommy had to say, "Look, I ain't gonna hurt nobody. Just wake up the boss there. And keep it quiet."

When she grasped that, she reached over and shook Catania by the shoulder. It took a few tries: he rolled over, grumbled in his sleep and, when she kept doing it, swore at her. Finally he rolled back toward her, opened his eyes and said, "What the fuck is wrong with you?"

She just pointed at Tommy. He watched Catania clear away the cobwebs enough to sit up and look where she was pointing. Tommy couldn't believe she'd slept with him either: he was a mountain of blubber. Catania focused on him, blinked a few times, and said, "Who the fuck are you?"

Tommy smiled. "I'm your new security consultant," he said.

Catania was getting wider awake with every second. His eyes went to the shotgun propped against the wall and then back to Tommy. "What the fuck?"

"You heard me. I'm the man who's gonna tell you how to stay alive in this here gang war you got going."

Catania's eyes narrowed. "How'd you get in here?"

"Boy, that's a good question, ain't it? The truth is I just walked in. I'd take a long hard look at my security arrangements if I was you."

Catania looked as if he were going to have a heart attack. Maybe he was. He kicked at the sheets and said, "I'm gonna fucking kill somebody."

"If you live long enough," said Tommy. "Right now I'd be worried about whether somebody's gonna kill you." Tommy picked up the shotgun, which stopped Catania with one fat hairy leg over the side of the bed. Tommy held the gun in one hand, pointing at the ceiling. "That's what I was sent here to do," he said. "You're lucky I thought better of it. Now just get back in bed and listen to me for a while."

Catania pulled his leg back under the covers. "Okay," he said. The woman was trying to hide, sliding down under the covers and cowering behind Catania.

"I'm gonna tell you what you need around here," said Tommy. "Pay attention."

"Okay." Catania nodded.

Tommy lowered the shotgun. "You need a less friendly dog, to start with. You need better fences and better locks, too. Most of all you need better people. If I wasn't such a nice guy, your brains would be all over the sheets by now and I'd be ten miles away. You never would have woke up, but she would have, and she'd be having nightmares about it for the rest of her life. I'd probably have had to kill that joker out there in the living room, too. It would have been messy. You know how come it didn't happen?"

"How come?"

"Because you need me and I need you."

The new day was evidently presenting Pete Catania with more than he was prepared to handle right away. He sat there with his mouth open, just staring at Tommy, and finally said, "You mind if I put some clothes on?"

"Tell you what," said Tommy. "I'll go out there in the kitchen and get some coffee started. When y'all are ready, we can talk." Tommy stood up. "Remember, I could have killed you and I didn't. That's what they call a good-faith gesture. I'm gonna assume you're smart enough to accept my offer. Just in case you're not, I've still got the gun. Does Sleeping Beauty out there have a weapon on him?"

"He's supposed to."

"I'll take it off him. But if nobody tries anything, and that includes telephone calls, jumping out the window, whatever, then nobody's gonna get hurt. As of right now we're on the same side. That okay by you?"

Catania blinked at him and said, "Sure, whatever you say."

Tommy left them. He went down the hall into the living room, gun up and ready to shoot somebody if he had to. The man on the couch was still asleep. Tommy reached down and pulled up the tail of his sweater and tugged an automatic out of his waistband. He put it in his jacket pocket. The man started a little but didn't wake up. Tommy went over and turned off the TV: it was starting to bug him.

In the kitchen Tommy poked around in cabinets until he found coffee and got the coffeemaker going. Before it was done brewing Catania came into the living room, fully dressed. He looked awake now, but he didn't look happy. He went over to the couch and stood for a second looking down at the sleeping man. Then he grabbed him by the hair and pulled him off the couch. That finally woke him up. "What the fuck?" he said, on all fours on the rug, looking bewildered and more than a little hung over.

Catania kicked him in the face. "Don't worry," he said. "This is just a dream."

"Jesus, Pete." The man put a hand to his nose and then stared at the blood on it. "What are you doing?"

"Waking you up, asshole." Catania kicked him again.

"Fuck! Cut it out, will you?" The man rolled to a sitting position, the alarm on his face fading to wonder as he stared up at Catania. "Jesus. I must have dozed off."

"No shit? You mean you missed the parade?"

"What are you talking about?"

"Where's your fucking gun?"

"Right here . . . shit."

Catania was stalking toward the kitchen. "You're history, Bobby. I don't wanna see your face again."

"Pete, Jesus Christ." Bobby had made it to his feet, dripping blood onto the carpet. He followed Catania into the kitchen and then froze, looking at Tommy.

"Morning," Tommy said.

Bobby looked at Catania and back at Tommy with the shotgun in his hand. "What's going on?"

"You been replaced," said Catania. "Get the fuck out of my house."

"Hang on a second," said Tommy. "Before anybody leaves, I want to make sure we're all on the same page. Why don't you just sit down and have some coffee?"

"I think my fucking nose is broken," said Bobby. Behind him the woman came trotting into the kitchen on her high heels, dressed but not quite ready to face the world, her hair flying and her makeup still a mess. "Can somebody give me a ride?" she said.

"You're not going nowhere," said Catania. "Not yet."

Beyond the woman a voice said, "What the hell's going on out here?" A man had come out of the bedroom wing, wearing nothing but boxers and black socks. He had a gun in his hand.

"You're fired, too," said Catania. "Put that fucking gun away before you hurt somebody, you useless son of a bitch."

The man halted in the archway, the gun dangling at his side. He was tall and gray and lean except for the paunch hanging over the waistband of the boxers. He looked at Tommy and started to raise the gun.

"I wouldn't," said Tommy. He had the big ugly sawed-off bracketed on the man's chest. The woman shrieked and ducked behind Catania again.

"Put the goddamn thing down," said Catania.

"On the counter there." Tommy pointed with the gun. "And then step away."

The man obeyed. "So who's this?" he said, cocking a thumb at Tommy.

"He's the guy that just took your job," said Catania.

"You fuckin' kiddin' me?"

"You're lucky I don't let him shoot you. The both of you. Now shut up and listen."

"Coffee's almost ready," said Tommy.

"Talk," said Catania. "What do you mean, I got something you need?"

Tommy stirred sugar into his coffee. Catania had packed the gunmen and the woman off to the living room, where Tommy could hear them muttering. He and Catania faced each other across the island, sitting on high stools. Tommy had both pistols in his jacket and the shotgun close at hand. "What I most need is to be somewhere else with nobody looking for me," he said. "You can help me do that."

"How?"

Tommy drank coffee. "Rocco Salerno sent me here to kill you. But I don't think he really expected me to succeed. I think he figured your guys would kill me. So he won't be too surprised when he hears that's what happened."

Catania peered at Tommy, a professionally suspicious man. "How's he gonna hear that?"

"You're gonna tell him. Call him on the phone, send a guy, however you usually do it. And you're gonna show him this." Tommy took out his wallet and pulled out his military ID card. He had saved it for old times' sake, but he was going to need his driver's license, so the army ID had to go. He reached for a paring knife that was sitting on the countertop and put it to the heel of his left hand. He made a quick slit in the flesh, wincing a little. He dripped blood onto the card and then smeared it. When it was splotched and gruesome-looking he shoved it across to Catania. "You show him that and you tell him he's got to send somebody better if he wants to get Pete Catania. Or you negotiate a truce with him, call it even, whatever you want to do."

Catania shook his head. "You're a fuckin' nut case."

Tommy went to the sink and rinsed his bloody hand, then pressed a paper towel to the cut. "Very possibly," he said. He took a Band-Aid out of his wallet and got it onto the wound.

183

"But I can still make your security a lot better. Even if those dumbasses out there are all you've got to work with. They just need a little training. Give me a morning to work with them. All I want in return is for you to convince Salerno I'm dead."

Catania hadn't reached his relatively advanced age in a field like his by taking things at face value. He sat and looked at this one for a long time, taking the occasional sip of coffee, before he spoke. "That's all you want, huh?"

Tommy gave him a blank look. "If I wanted anything else I'd have taken it, after I'd killed everybody in the house."

Catania stared a while longer and then shook his head. "You sure you don't want to hang around, work for me?"

"I got places to go," said Tommy. "Things to do."

25

Bobby gave Tommy a ride back to his car in the Riviera. Bobby's nose had stopped bleeding and he didn't seem to hold Catania's kick in the face against Tommy, though he hadn't exactly been an eager pupil during Tommy's security lecture after Catania had relented on the firings. He and his partner had pretty much scowled at Tommy through the whole thing, Tommy telling them in a calm tone all about their carelessness and their weak spots and the useful things he'd learned in Iraq about keeping people alive in a hostile environment.

The last thing he'd done was to get the story straight with

Catania. "You probably don't need to tell him much of anything," he'd said. "Just send him the card, let him draw the conclusions. All's I need is for him to think I'm dead so he won't come after me."

Catania had grunted and picked up the blood-smeared ID card by a corner. "What'd you do to that prick Salerno, anyway?"

"I know better than to answer that question," Tommy had said, and Catania had smiled.

Tommy put his plates back on the car and took off. He hit the highway and went north, going fast. He pulled off Lake Shore Drive at Montrose and went and parked by the harbor and sat looking out at the lake. He had been heading for Uptown, with the idea of going in and doing his morning job at the apartment, but just in time he realized that he couldn't do that. If he was going to sell the story about his getting killed, he had to just disappear. He couldn't go back to his place, either. Let the landlord keep his security deposit and to hell with the lease. There wasn't anything there he really valued, just a few clothes. He had everything he really needed on him.

His time in Chicago was over. He felt bad about the Greek, he felt bad about Brian, he felt bad about Lisa. He felt bad about a lot of things, but there was a big country out there. He figured this time he might try out west. Tommy had cousins in California: he could take his time getting there, see a little of the country on the way. He could use a vacation.

Could he afford to talk to Brian and Lisa before he left? He didn't want to make them have to lie to anybody who might come looking into his disappearance. It would be safer, for them, to leave them in the dark just like everybody else. But he couldn't bear to go without seeing Lisa one more time. He sat there for a long time fighting it, but he couldn't.

Talking to her meant trusting her, trusting her to keep the secret that he was alive. And explaining all that meant taking her in on another secret. Or did it? There were some tough calls here. Tommy looked at it for a long time and decided he would just go see her, tell her he was leaving, and let her draw her own conclusions.

She would be at work. Tommy still had his cell phone turned off, which he knew was the only reason he wasn't fielding frantic calls from the Greek. The cell phone had to be history, too, because the cops could get access to the logs and Tommy wanted to be dead as of last night. He needed a pay phone.

He found one on Montrose and called Lisa at work. She had her own line, and Tommy didn't think anybody was recording her calls, so he wasn't too worried. "I gotta see you today," Tommy said.

"What's the matter?"

"I just need to see you. Can I pick you up after work?"

"That's awfully mysterious."

"I just want to see you, Lisa." That was the plain truth, the best Tommy could do.

There was a brief silence. "Okay, why wait till after work? I go to lunch in half an hour. Where are you?"

"On my way," said Tommy.

Lisa worked at the Merchandise Mart, a huge hulk of a building on the river downtown. He picked her up at the main entrance. When he spotted her he had to take a deep breath. Suddenly he didn't know how he was going to leave her. Coming across the sidewalk on her high heels, hair flying free in the wind, she was the prettiest thing in sight. He couldn't believe this high-class girl was getting in the car with him.

"Hey there," she said, and leaned across to kiss him. "What's going on?"

Tommy pulled away from the curb. "I gotta leave town," he said.

She didn't say anything while Tommy jockeyed through the traffic, not really knowing where he was going, and got onto LaSalle Street going north. "When?" she said finally.

"Pretty much now. Where we going for lunch?"

"What happened?" She was staring straight ahead.

Now you have to tell her everything, Tommy thought. Or lie to her. "I got myself in a shitload of trouble," he said.

"Because of me?" Now she was looking at him.

"No. Because of me." Tell her, one of his voices was saying. "I pissed some people off."

"Does this have something to do with Joe Salerno?"

Keep your mouth shut, said another voice. "Yeah, it does. Some of his friends think I shot him." Tommy waited for the question, wondering how he was going to answer it.

Sure enough, here it came. "Did you?"

Tommy just drove for a few seconds. "If I did, I'd be a damn fool to admit it, even to you," he said.

"Okay, forget I asked."

Nobody said anything for a block or two. "So where we going for lunch?" They were almost at Grand Avenue.

Out of the corner of his eye Tommy could see Lisa watching him. "I don't want lunch," she said. "Are you really going away, like forever?"

"For a while. Till these guys forget about me. Listen, the

only thing I'm worried about is if they hold it against you. But I think I fixed that. I made it look like I'm dead. And if I'm dead there's nothing in that for them. I'm just gonna have to disappear. So people are gonna come asking about me, okay? And you gotta tell them you never saw me since the last time we were together. Anybody you know see me pick you up?"

"I don't think so. I came down by myself. Tom, what the hell have you been up to?"

"I can't tell you that, Lisa. The less you know, the better."

They were at a stoplight and Tommy looked at her. She was staring at him with her big dark eyes, and the look on her face made Tommy think maybe she was as sorry about his going as he was. He was glad to see it but it made it tough to go. "You don't want lunch?" He felt like a fool as soon as he said it.

Somebody behind him honked and he had to drive. "No," said Lisa. "I want to go somewhere with you and say good-bye."

Tommy's stomach turned over.

Tommy lay on his back with Lisa in his arms, her face nestled against his neck. He wasn't sure if she was awake. Her body was featherlight on top of him, warm, her skin slick with sweat next to his. Tommy lay looking at the stuccoed ceiling and wondering how he was going to give her up.

They had wound up at one of the Lincoln Avenue motels on the Northwest Side, the ones that had been orphaned by the interstates but survived by catering to the kind of guest that didn't need the room for more than an hour or two. Tommy couldn't believe it when Lisa steered him in past the sign saying *Free Adult Videos*. She was full of surprises. She had called in sick to her office on her cell phone and there wasn't any rush. Up in the room she had jumped into Tommy's arms, staggering him.

He couldn't believe her heat, he couldn't believe her tenderness. He didn't want to let go, ever. Tommy knew it was a good-bye fuck, had to be. But it was going to be awfully hard to tear himself away. How long can we stay in this room, he wondered. He was already thinking about spending the night here, ordering in a little food if they got hungry, making love again, as many times as they could before he had to jump in the car and go. Tommy knew it was over, had to be. But it hurt him.

Lisa stirred, kissed his neck, propped herself up on an elbow, caressed his face. "Hi there, hero."

"I ain't no hero."

"Yes, you are. You're my hero." Her hair fell on his shoulder, his chest.

Tommy just stared at her: he wanted to lose himself in those big black eyes. She kissed him on the lips, gently. "Nobody's ever done anything for me like you did for me," she said. "Ever."

"Don't mention it."

"You saved my life."

"I don't know about that."

"I do. You rescued it, gave it back to me." Her breath was warm on his lips. "Did I ever say thank you?"

"I got thanked pretty good."

She smiled a little and let her head sink back on his shoulder. "So where are you going?"

"I don't know. California, maybe."

After a silence she said, "I'll miss you."

Tommy knew what that meant. He knew as far as Lisa was concerned, things had run their course. She had had her adventure, she'd thanked him, it was over. Tommy knew how the game was played. He'd played it. But it had never hurt this much before. Knowing as he opened his mouth that it was stupid, he said, "Maybe you could come see me some time."

A few seconds went by and Lisa said, "Maybe I could."

"'Cause God knows I'm gonna miss you."

Lisa was caressing him again, whispering. "Tommy, Tommy, Tommy."

When he got his voice back he said, "Nah, don't call me that. My sister's the only one ever called me Tommy."

They lay still for a while. Gravely she said, "You don't blame yourself for what happened to her, do you?"

"Every single day."

"But you can't do that. You can't let that rule your life."

"Yeah, that's what everybody tells me."

After a while she said, "Well, you didn't let me down. You have to let that count for something."

No, I didn't let you down, Tommy thought. He wanted to say it but he knew he'd admitted too much already. "I probably oughta get going," he said.

He drove her to her place. Neither of them said much on the way. In front of her apartment building he put the Chevy in park and just looked at her for a while. She was looking back with something he couldn't quite read in those big dark eyes: sadness, maybe, but not enough to make her want him to stay; maybe some relief, too. It hurt him to look at her, he wanted her so much. He felt that tenderness going out of his life again, draining away like water through his fingers.

Shutdown time, thought Tommy. It was time to shut down the emotions again for a while. He'd had a lot of practice.

There were times when you just had to screw the lid down tight if you wanted to go on functioning, and this was one of them. "Bye, Lisa," he said.

She threw her arms around his neck and kissed him once, hard, then whispered bye in his ear and got out of the car in a hurry. Tommy wanted to watch her go up the steps into her place but instead threw the car into gear and left some rubber on the street pulling away.

26

Tommy thought about going by his place and grabbing his stuff but decided not to. Everything he really needed he had on him. He was going to put some distance between him and Rocco Salerno before he worried about trivial things like buying a change of clothes. He drove up to Irving Park and headed west toward the expressway.

When the cops pulled him over Tommy thought for a second he'd blown a red light or something, but he knew right away that was too good to be true. He sat watching the two cops in his rearview mirror as they got out of their squad car, thinking he could have been three hundred miles away if he hadn't had to see Lisa. Tommy rolled down the window. "What'd I do?"

"Get out of the car, please." Tommy could tell it wasn't a traffic stop: most cops didn't have their hand on the butt of their gun when they pulled you over. "Slow," the cop said. "And keep your hands where I can see them."

Tommy got out and put his hands on the hood of the car, following instructions. The lead cop started patting him down while the other one walked around the car, looking inside. "What the hell'd I do, run over an old lady?" Tommy said.

"Just keep your mouth shut." The cop pulled Tommy's knife out of his pocket, took out his wallet, felt him up and down. He looked in the wallet and said, "You Thomas McLain?"

"You're standing there looking at my driver's license. What do you think?"

The cop gave him a look and said, "I asked you a question."

"I'm Thomas McLain. Can I ask you a question?"

"No. Put your hands behind your back."

"You gotta be shittin' me."

"I don't shit nobody, pal. Let's have the hands."

Tommy obeyed and let the cop cuff him. People on the sidewalk and in cars going by were staring at him. It embarrassed him even though he had more important things to worry about than what these idiots thought. He looked at the other cop and said, "You guys gotta help me out here. I'm doing my damnedest to remember all the stop signs I might have gone through, and I'm coming up empty. What the hell am I charged with?"

The other cop was younger and looked as if he didn't give

a damn about much of anything. "You're not charged with anything yet." He reached in through the window and pulled out Tommy's keys.

"Then how in the hell can you arrest me?"

The first cop put his hand on Tommy's arm and led him toward the squad car. "I can arrest you if I don't like your fuckin' haircut. I might have some trouble making the charge stick, but that's my problem. In your case, somebody put out a stop order on you."

"A stop order. What's that?"

The cop opened the back door of the squad car and put his hand on Tommy's head to force it down. "That means somebody wants to talk to you. Probably one of the dicks upstairs."

The cops got in and they pulled out. "What's gonna happen to my car?"

"Don't worry. They'll tow it to the pound and you can pick it up there."

"It's those Texas plates that caught our eye," the other cop said. "They stick out a mile away."

They took him to Belmont and Western. Tommy was starting to get to know the place. Up on the second floor they took him to a windowless interview room and left him. They closed the door and went away and nothing happened for a long time. After an hour or so the door opened and two detectives came in. They were in shirtsleeves, with the ID on the lanyard, the gun on the hip. Tommy hadn't seen these two before. They were both young, one taller and balder and blonder than the other one. "How you doing?" said the tall one, dropping a clipboard on the table.

Tommy was hungry, thirsty and needed to piss, but he wasn't going to start whining. "I'm okay," he said. "But I'm still wondering what the hell I'm doing here."

The shorter dick sat on Tommy's left, with the taller one directly across from him. "You're here to help us out," said the short one. He looked like the bad cop: he reminded Tommy of a lieutenant he'd suffered under at Fort Polk for a while, with the same short hair and hardass look.

"My pleasure," said Tommy. "What can I do for you?"

"You can tell us what you know about how Joe Salerno got killed," said the tall one. "I'm Detective Getz, by the way. This is Detective Hanratty."

"Pleased to meet you both. I don't know how much I can help you, though."

"Just tell us the truth," said Hanratty. "That's all you have to do." He was looking at Tommy with the same contemptuous look the lieutenant had affected until his obvious incompetence had lost him his command.

Tommy had had a lot of time to think about what they could know, what he could say and couldn't say. The main thing he wasn't going to do was start lying. "I been through this before. With the Maywood Park guys. They evidently didn't think there was much of a case against me. Why don't you check with them?"

"We had a nice long talk with Maywood Park. They think there's a great case against you. They just haven't made it yet. Look, why do you think you're sitting here?"

"I just got done asking you that."

"You're here because when you shot Joe Salerno you set off a gang war. People are dying. It's not just a Maywood Park thing anymore. There's a regional task force now to investigate the killings and try to choke off the war. And we believe the best way to do that is find out why Joe Salerno was killed in the first place. And we think you're the only one who can tell us that."

"What the hell makes you think I shot Joe Salerno?"

"You said you were going to do it, that's why. You announced your intention."

Tommy frowned. "I think what I said was, if it was up to me I'd shoot him like a dog. That's a ways from announcing my intention to shoot him."

"Jesus." Hanratty leaned forward, getting into Tommy's face a little. "You confronted him and identified him. We have that on record. Then you threatened to kill him. Then he got shot. Then when questioned you gave vague and evasive answers or no answers at all. You got no alibi for the time he was shot, none. You got a better suspect than yourself for us, I'm listening."

The guy had a good stare, wide-eyed and tense, suggesting he was having a hard time keeping himself from taking a swipe at Tommy, but Tommy returned it without blinking. He knew now he was supposed to fold and start crying, confess to everything. But Tommy had been intimidated by the best, and he wasn't going to let these two rattle him. "You think you can charge me, go ahead," he said. "I ain't going nowhere."

"You're right about that," said Getz. "I want you to think about something. While you're sitting in here, half a dozen dicks are out there working this case. I don't care how careful you were, somehow you left a trace. And we're gonna find it. And when we do, we're gonna charge you with first-degree murder. And then you're fucked. On the other hand, if you talk to us now, tell us the truth, then we can maybe work something out. It looks to me as if you did it to protect the girl, which I can understand. The word is, Joe Salerno was a real son of a bitch. If there were mitigating circumstances, that's something we can take into account when we take it to a State's Attorney. We can plea-bargain it down to where you'll get a lesser charge. Six years or even ten downstate is a lot better than life. But you got to come clean. The more you make us work, the harder we'll make it on you in the end. You understand what I'm saying?"

Tommy understood, and he had to admit it was tempting. It was how they always got people to talk. For a second Tommy wavered. But he had gone over things enough in his mind that he knew they couldn't have any real proof: otherwise they'd have charged him already. "I understand," he said. "You want to charge me, go ahead."

"It's just a matter of time," Hanratty said.

Tommy shrugged. "Let me know."

Getz was giving Tommy a sympathetic look. "Did Salerno go for his gun first?" he said. "That would make it self-defense."

Tommy looked at him. That was the closest he came to breaking, right there. "Charge me or don't charge me," Tommy said. "Wake me up when you make up your mind." He pushed away from the table and tilted his chair back until his head and shoulders were resting against the wall. He put his feet up on the table and clasped his hands on his lap and closed his eyes.

After a few seconds he heard the two detectives stand up and open the door. "Sleep while you can," said Hanratty. "They say it's tough the first few nights in the joint."

Tommy never got to sleep. He was too worried. He didn't

think they could prove anything, but who the hell knew? His dad had told him about cases where people had kept digging until they turned up something that sent someone to jail. He spent a little time second-guessing himself about not coming clean. Maybe a good lawyer could make a self-defense case out of it. But that would be a hell of a chance to take, and what really worried him was publicity. He'd been counting on Rocco Salerno thinking he was dead, and if he got charged it was going to be all over the papers, and then Brian and Lisa were at risk again. Tommy sat there pretending to sleep, but he was thinking hard.

The door opened again. Tommy opened his eyes to see two men in suits coming into the room. Where the hell did they get these guys? There was an endless supply of them. These two were different, though, starting with the nice suits. They had nice haircuts, too. They looked like lawyers, and for a second Tommy wondered if that was what they were, prosecutors getting their first look at him, maybe.

"Mr. McLain? I'm Special Agent Stefanovich, FBI." Tommy's feet hit the floor. The guy flashed an ID at him and put it away. "This is Special Agent Foss. How they been treating you?" The lead guy was forty or so, just starting to go gray, while the other one was ten years or so younger and looked like a jock, a thick neck straining the collar of his shirt.

Tommy just stared: they'd caught him by surprise. "FBI? Now you really got me confused."

"Do we? Sorry about that." Stefanovich smiled as they took their seats. "Maybe we can clear a few things up for you. First, you want a cup of coffee or something? You've been in here a while, I understand."

"You could bring me a cup of water. Then I can piss in the empty cup."

The G-men traded a look. "I think we can arrange for a trip to the john." When Tommy's needs were taken care of they all went back to the interview room and sat at the table like coconspirators, elbows on the table. "Okay," said Stefanovich. "Now tell us what you were doing down at Pete Catania's place last night."

27

Tommy was glad he'd been getting lots of practice keeping his expression blank. This one rocked him a little. "Who says I was?"

Stefanovich sighed. "Show him."

Foss opened a folder and slid a photograph across the table to Tommy. It was a printout of a color digital photo of his old blue Chevy, taken from a distance but magnified, the license plate legible, on what looked like a country road. Just visible beyond the car was the brick column that supported Pete Catania's mailbox. "Damn," said Tommy. "You guys got great equipment." He slid the photo back. He was kicking himself: of course the FBI would be watching Catania's place.

Stefanovich waited for him to say something else. He raised his eyebrows, questioning, then said, "So? Want to tell us what you were doing down there?"

"I went for a drive. Down south, near Chicago Heights."

"And?"

Tommy shrugged. "Did I break any laws?"

"We don't know. What did you talk to Catania about?"

"Who says I did?" Tommy figured it was worth a try, but he wasn't surprised when Foss pulled another photo out of the folder. This one was a view through trees of three men in front of Catania's place. It wasn't exactly a close-up but Tommy recognized Bobby, his useless partner, and himself, gesturing at something. He knew when it had been taken: during his little security lecture that morning. Tommy nodded. "That could be me, for sure." Tommy's blood was running cold: he had almost walked right into a nest of FBI agents, shotgun in hand.

Stefanovich watched Foss put the photo back in the folder. "You want to tell us what you were doing there?"

Tommy gave that one some genuine consideration. "I was talking to Mr. Catania about a possible job," he said finally, which was not too far from the truth.

"I see. What was the job?"

"He wanted me to take charge of his security team. I have some army experience and he asked me to help him tighten things up. I gave him a little free advice, but I turned the job down."

"Who put you in contact with Catania?"

Tommy blinked at him. "I'm not trying to be difficult or anything, but why is that your business? Did I break any laws just talking to the man?"

"I won't know till you tell me what you two talked about."

"I just told you."

"And I just asked you how you got hooked up with Catania." Stefanovich leaned back on his chair, crossed his legs and clasped his hands on one knee, like he was about to deliver a lecture. "See, Tom, I'm an FBI agent, assigned to the Organized Crime squad. I'm real interested in people like Pete Catania, especially now, when we've got mobsters dying like flies all over town. And I'm interested in anybody that gets involved with them. Especially guys who claim to have expertise in what they call 'security,' which probably involves the use of weapons, but aren't connected with any legitimate law enforcement agency. Especially when they're suspects in the murder that set off the whole chain of events. You understand why you're all over our radar screen?"

"I can see that."

"So tell me. How did you get hooked up with Pete Catania?"

Tommy knew he had two choices: Tell them everything or tell them nothing. Either way he had problems. He looked at the whole thing for a while and decided again he was better off keeping his mouth shut. He said, "If you think you got a federal case here, let me know. Otherwise I think the Constitution says I can go back to sleep."

Stefanovich shook his head. Foss let out a little puff of a laugh. Stefanovich looked at Foss, and sure enough Foss opened the folder again. Tommy had to smile. "You got another rabbit in that hat, huh? Well, let's see it." Tommy couldn't think what more they could have.

This rabbit wasn't a picture. It was a sheet of paper covered with typing. Stefanovich took it and said, "Tom, this is the transcript of a conversation we recorded between Rocco Salerno and one of his guys last night. Let me read a little part of it to you."

"Go ahead."

Stefanovich frowned a little, again making it look like a practiced effect. "This is in the context of one of Salerno's guys reporting to him about some matter we're not clear on. But Salerno says here, and I quote, *'Best thing would be if the hillbilly gets Catania and then Catania's guys get him.'* Then the other person says here, *'More likely the hillbilly will get his dumb cracker ass shot up for nothing.'* And then Salerno says, *'Which makes us even, so fuck him.'* " Stefanovich looked up from the paper.

Tommy let a few seconds go by and then said, "And you think they're referring to me."

This time Foss laughed out loud. Stefanovich said, "Just a hunch, Tom, just a hunch."

Tommy put on a frown of his own. "I'm not real sure what you think you have there."

"What I have here is somebody who seems to be indicating that you were sent to kill Pete Catania."

Tommy shrugged. "Did he get killed? He seemed okay when I talked to him."

"No, he apparently didn't get killed. But that's real interesting, too."

Tommy said nothing. He was starting to get a bad feeling about where things were going.

Stefanovich said, "Let me read you the rest of this. I didn't quite finish. Salerno says here, *'I just hope he don't chicken out and try to go to the cops.'* And then the other one says: *'Then he'd have to tell them about doing Joey, and I think even a dumb hillbilly's not that dumb.'* " Stefanovich put the paper down on the table.

Tommy just stared at it. After a little while he said, "I ain't a lawyer, but I don't think anybody's gonna get convicted with that kind of evidence."

"Maybe not. But what do you think your CPD pals out there are gonna think when they see this? They already have a pretty good idea you shot Joe Salerno."

"That there's proof, is it?"

"Maybe not. But this insures that they're gonna be in your face and on your case until they pin it on you. The first thing they'll do is haul in Salerno to ask him about it, you gotta know that."

Tommy did know that, and it worried him, but he wouldn't know how much until he had a chance to think about it. He said, "I'll take my chances."

Stefanovich shoved the paper back to Foss. "Okay, it's your funeral. But think about this. The CPD might not be your biggest worry here. Your biggest worry might be how Rocco Salerno's gonna react when he finds out you double-crossed him."

There it was, out in the open, and Tommy knew they had him. They had him two ways, in fact. They had him good. Tommy knew the answer to his question before he asked it. "How's he gonna find out?"

It was Foss who spoke up, finally. "How's he *not* gonna find out, when we question him about that conversation and show him the photos so he can identify the hillbilly?"

Tommy looked at Foss for a long few seconds, not blinking. "They teach you guys that kind of thing at Quantico, do they?"

"Day one," said Foss, smiling.

Tommy looked from one to the other and back again a few times. He was thinking hard and trying not to show it. He said, "What exactly do you guys want?"

Stefanovich smiled, just a little. "We want your cooperation. We don't give a damn whether or not you killed Joe Salerno. By all accounts he wasn't much of a loss. The CPD may care about that, but they don't have to see that transcript. All you need to do is agree to help us."

"How?"

"Well, for example, you could take that job with Pete Catania."

"It might be a little late. I told you, I turned it down."

"Tell him you changed your mind. He offered you a job. He must think he can trust you."

"Maybe."

"I'm sure you can figure out a way to get close to him. And that's what we need."

"You want to wire me up, huh?"

"We'd wait until you were in pretty good with him."

"You make it sound like applying for a job at the Wal-Mart. I just go back and get him to hire me, huh? That easy?"

"You just told us he offered you a job. You won't be the first person to change his mind about turning down a job."

"He's gonna smell something funny if I go back."

Foss said, "With all due respect, Tom, that's your problem."

Stefanovich said, "Look, we realize it may not be easy. We also realize you've already had some kind of dealings with a guy

206

we're very interested in. You may be our best chance to put someone close to him. All you need to think about is, if you cooperate, we'd forget all about what's on that tape. And somewhere down the road we could put you in the Witness Protection Program, get you set up somewhere else."

"If I don't get killed first."

Stefanovich shrugged. "There's always that possibility, I guess. You picked a dangerous bunch of people to get involved with. You have to look at your choices realistically."

Tommy knew that was true, at any rate. He sat there and thought about it. It was another tempting offer, and that all by itself made him think harder. He wasn't sure he wanted the FBI to own him, and if he agreed, they would own him like a dog on a leash. Of course, it was starting to look as if they owned him either way.

But he wasn't sure it was bad enough yet for him to cave. The more he thought about it, the more he thought the G-men were bluffing about giving the transcript to the cops. Whether they had gotten it from a wiretap or a guy with a wire on, they wouldn't want to blow the source by letting anyone know they had it until they were ready to haul Salerno in. So that had to be a bluff. Which meant Tommy could probably ride out his seventy-two hours in custody uncharged. The serious threat was the FBI showing Rocco Salerno he was not only still alive but talking with the enemy. That would be a hell of a dirty trick, but Tommy wasn't sure the FBI was above things like that. His priority had to be making sure Brian and Lisa were safe from fallout. And once Salerno found out he was in police custody, all bets were off. Tommy had to avoid that if he could. He just had to hope he could stay dead until the feds could put Salerno away. What it boiled down to was, he needed the feds to give him time until he could sort something out. And it looked as if there was only one way to buy it. "I've worked for the federal government before," he said. "I guess I can do it again."

28

Tommy figured the binoculars and the telephoto lens were bracketed on him as he slowed for Catania's driveway, but he still hadn't been able to spot where the G-men were hiding. There were a few houses and parked cars scattered through the woods nearby, and they had to be in one of them, but they weren't making it obvious. Tommy had to hand it to them.

He had been released to the custody of the Federal Bureau of Investigation late the previous night. He didn't know exactly what the Bureau had told the CPD, but he could see the local cops weren't happy about it. They had passed Getz in a hallway and the detective had said, "Lots of luck, chump," with a look on his face that said he wished he could be there at the execution.

Stefanovich and Foss had taken him to a Best Western motel near O'Hare Airport and spent a couple of hours laying out what they expected of him and the dire consequences that would follow if he let them down. They had had forms for him to fill out and papers to sign, the same obsession with paperwork that had amazed Tommy in the army. "You try and run, we'll give CPD that transcript and every law enforcement officer in the country will be on the lookout for you," Foss had said. Tommy knew that was hyperbole but he'd nodded as if he were solemnly impressed. The big deterrent to his running had nothing to do with keen-eyed state troopers.

His new owners had given him contact numbers and strict instructions about how to use them, more cloak-and-dagger bullshit. Tommy had been hearing rules read to him his whole professional life, and he had listened with one ear while buzz-sawing through the pizza they'd ordered in for him. "Remember," Stefanovich had said in parting. "You belong to us now."

"Till when?" Tommy had said. "How long does the contract run?"

"Till we indict Pete Catania," Stefanovich had said. "Simple as that."

In the morning they'd come back to get him and dropped him off at the police auto pound at Grand and Sacramento, where he'd spent three hours jumping through hoops to get his car back. Tommy was not in the best of moods by the time he rolled up Pete Catania's driveway. The dog came out of nowhere as he approached the house, barking and coming close to getting run over, and Tommy could see how Catania might have thought it was a deterrent, at least to people who were afraid of dogs.

Tommy had thought hard all night and morning. If he stayed the course, all he could see in front of him for weeks was the misery of hanging out with these idiots and trying to get to the point where he could put his life at risk by getting them to say something incriminating into a microphone stuck up his ass, hoping all the time word didn't get back to Rocco Salerno that he was still alive. It wasn't much of a future.

There was one car parked in Catania's driveway, a green Dodge Neon Tommy didn't recall seeing before. He parked and went to lean on the doorbell by the front door. Nothing happened and he leaned on it again, shivering in the wind. Finally the door opened and there was Bobby, shirtless in a pair of jeans with the belt undone, gut hanging out, hair standing up, and with a red swollen nose and a big purple shiner where Catania had kicked him. He looked like hell, and at the sight of Tommy on the doorstep he reared back as if somebody had just kicked him again. "What the *fuck* are you doing here?" he said.

"Sorry if I woke you up," Tommy said. It was two in the afternoon: Tommy couldn't believe the lifestyle these dumb sons of bitches led. "I need to talk to Mr. Catania."

Bobby stared for a moment longer and then said, "Well, what the fuck are you doing *here*, then?"

One sentence was about all Bobby was good for, Tommy could see. He waited for more and saw it wasn't coming. Bobby couldn't be especially fond of him, and being woken up to answer the door hadn't helped. Tommy figured he would be lucky if he got any kind of an answer, but he tried anyway. "This is his house, ain't it?"

Bobby took a step forward and Tommy got ready: he was having the kind of day where giving the dumbshit a matched set of shiners would be good therapy. Bobby stopped just short of the point where Tommy would have no choice but to hit him and said, "You stupid cracker bastard. You think after yesterday he's gonna sit around here with his thumb up his ass? You fuckin' scared him out of his fuckin' mind."

"That's good," said Tommy. "That might keep him alive."

"Yeah, well I got stuck with the housekeeping, cocksucker. Thanks a million."

Tommy shook his head, a man looking at a hopeless case. "Where'd Catania go?"

"*That's none of your goddamn business!*" Tommy took some flecks of Bobby's spit in the face. Bobby stepped back and put his hand on the door, ready to slam it. "Now take a fuckin' hike."

Tommy had enjoyed just about all he could take. Before Bobby could make the grand gesture Tommy had bull-rushed him and knocked him clean across the entry hall into the opposite wall, which he hit and slid down until he was sitting on the floor. Tommy closed the door gently behind him. "You're what we call a slow learner, aren't you, Bobby?" he said.

Bobby tried to get up but Tommy stopped him with a foot on his chest. "Number one," he said. "If you're expecting trouble, don't answer the door without looking to see who it is first. Number two. If you're really expecting trouble, don't answer the door. Number three. Learn to tell your friends from your enemies. All you had to do was tell me where Mr. Catania is."

"Fuck you."

"Where is he?"

"I said fuck you."

Tommy shook his head and took his foot off Bobby's chest. "What do you think he's gonna say when he finds out I couldn't get his money to him because you wouldn't tell me where he was?" Tommy figured money was always a good approach with lowlifes: greed was what they understood. He turned his back on Bobby and started walking toward the living room, hearing Bobby scramble to his feet behind him.

Tommy stopped at the door to the living room because all of a sudden everything became clear to him. Strewn around the living room floor were various articles of clothing, men's and women's, prominently including a pair of red high-heeled shoes. The woman was peeking out from behind the end of the couch, just her head showing. "Well, shit," Tommy said. "My apologies, ma'am."

There was a commotion behind Tommy and he turned to see Bobby leveling an automatic at him, holding his jeans up with the other hand. "Get ready to die, asshole."

"You gonna shoot me before or after you finish fucking her? Either way, it's gonna put a crimp in your style." Tommy figured he had to do some fast talking. He'd pushed Bobby pretty far.

"I'm gonna blow your fuckin' head off right now."

Tommy cocked his chin in the woman's direction. "Maybe you should run that by her. Some ladies think it kind of spoils the mood having a dead body laying there where they're trying to make love. Oh, and what's the boss gonna say when you tell him you shot somebody in his living room? You might want to clear it with him first." Tommy gave it a couple of seconds where he truly wasn't sure how it was going to go, Bobby glaring at him over the wavering muzzle of the gun, and then he said, "Look, man. I don't give a shit what goes on in here. I just want you to tell me where Mr. Catania is. And he won't find out from me who you're banging in here on his nice rug. Unless you make me work too hard to find him. You know I will eventually."

It was a close call: Tommy stood there and thought about his chances, watching the gun muzzle waver. "For Christ's sake tell him," said the blonde, shrieking just a little.

Bobby said, "Pissing me off is a bad mistake, you dumbass hillbilly motherfucker. You'll find out." The gun muzzle dipped a little and he said, "He's laying low somewhere. Try the pizza joint. They'll call him for you. Now get the fuck out of here." Bobby waved toward the door with the pistol.

"Which pizza joint we talking about?"

"Jesus. Alfano's. Where the hell you think?"

"You gotta help me out a little here. I'm the new guy. Where's Alfano's?"

"It's in Blue Island. You know where Blue Island is? Illinois? The United States? Ever heard of it?"

"Sounds kind of familiar." Tommy started moving. "Sorry about the intrusion. Case anybody asks, there wasn't nobody here but you when I called."

"It fucking better stay that way," said Bobby. He was still tracking Tommy with the pistol. "You don't want to get on my bad side, I promise you."

"If you got a good side, brother, that's where I want to be," said Tommy, heading for the door.

Tommy found Blue Island on his map. It was a suburb hanging

on to the southwest corner of the city, a few miles north of where he was, another workingman's town cut up by railroad tracks. Tommy had to ask at two different gas stations before somebody was able to tell him where Alfano's was. It turned out to be a shabby storefront in a two-story brick building with a big picture window and the usual sign painted in red and green hanging over the door, a not especially prosperous-looking joint in a not especially prosperous-looking town. Tommy went past it and pulled over half a block away. It wasn't a jumping downtown and there were plenty of parking spots. He sat for a while looking at the place in his mirrors, trying to make a decision.

The last thing in the world Tommy wanted to do was spend the next few weeks of his life pretending to be a gangster. He just couldn't see any way out of it. Even if his stunt with the ID card convinced Salerno he was dead, the FBI could show him the pictures, tell him when they were taken. Salerno would see through it. Sitting there in the car, Tommy thought hard about just taking off. He could drive about a mile east to U.S. 57 and be in Memphis or Kansas City by midnight. It was a hell of a temptation.

He knew he couldn't do it. He didn't know how long he could last as a federal fugitive, and there was no predicting what would happen to Brian, maybe even to Lisa, if he split. Until Catania was dead, he was in Rocco Salerno's shithouse. Until Catania was in jail, the FBI had him on a leash. He couldn't see that he had any option but to try to give the feds what they wanted and hope they could nail Salerno, too, to get him off his back. Tommy was starting to wish he'd let the police handle Joe Salerno. Had going to bed with Lisa a few times made it worthwhile? He was starting to doubt it.

Tommy got out of the car and walked back to the pizzeria. He looked in through the window and saw chairs upturned on tables. He tried the door anyway and it was locked. The business hours posted on the door said they ought to be open, but they weren't. Tommy swore and backed away a couple of steps. He looked up at the second floor windows: somebody had an apartment up there. Tommy thought that looked like a more likely place for Catania to do business than a closed pizzeria. There was a door to the left of the storefront with a doorbell next to it above an empty slot for a name tag. Tommy pressed the button a couple of times but nobody answered.

Fuck this, thought Tommy. He thought about calling his handlers and telling them he was stumped, but he knew he wouldn't get any sympathy from them. Tommy walked back to his car. He didn't know what the hell to do. He started the car and sat there idling, looking for an excuse not to drive away and get drunk somewhere.

There had to be a back door. That would be on the alley that ran behind the place. Tommy drove around the corner and found the alley. He had counted: the pizzeria was the fourth building from the corner. Tommy went up the alley. There was a white van sitting about halfway down the alley, leaving just enough room for Tommy to squeeze by. As he approached it, he saw that it was parked at the back door of the pizzeria. On it was painted *J&J Medical Equipment*.

Tommy thought that was peculiar. He braked and sat there for a moment just looking at it, wondering why a medical supply company was visiting a pizza joint. He'd been intending to rattle the back door, but now he just put the car in gear and drove on. He went down to the end of the alley and swung across the street, then reversed into a parking spot that gave him a view of the mouth of the alley.

Tommy sat there listening to the radio, wondering what the hell he was doing there, what the hell he was doing with his life. He had just about decided to go plot strategy in the nearest bar when the white van came out of the alley and turned toward him. As it went past, heading east, Tommy got a good look at the driver. It was Bobby's partner, the man who had come running out of his bedroom in his boxer shorts. There was another man riding shotgun Tommy didn't recognize.

A couple of Catania gofers driving a medical equipment van: it was peculiar. Tommy gave them a one-block lead and then put the Chevy in gear and pulled out to turn around and follow.

29

Following the white van was a piece of cake. Tommy gave it a big cushion going up the Ryan toward the Loop, though he wasn't especially worried about being spotted. If the driver hadn't spotted him coming out of the alley he wasn't going to pick him out in the rearview mirror. Tommy had yet to see anything that would go against what Steve had told him about the guys Catania employed. They were idiots.

He didn't know exactly why he was following, except it was something to do. He was on the job, tailing mobsters for the FBI. Tommy felt like an idiot himself. He followed the van through the interchange where the Ryan hit the Eisenhower and followed it out west into the suburbs. It finally got off the expressway at First Avenue, and Tommy followed it south.

When the van turned off First Avenue into a big hospital complex with signs saying *Loyola University Medical Center*, Tommy thought he'd just wasted a whole lot of time and gas. Where else would he expect a medical supply van to go? Maybe the idiot had a legitimate job when he wasn't waving guns around for Pete Catania. Somehow Tommy couldn't picture it. He turned in and followed the van past a parking lot to an entrance with a sign that said *Outpatient Center*. The van pulled over at the curb just beyond the entrance and put on its flashers. Tommy went on by and turned into the parking lot. It was a risk passing so close but he didn't think the man in the van had gotten any smarter on the drive. Tommy picked a slot where he could sit facing the entrance and watch. He turned off the ignition.

The man who had been riding shotgun got out of the van and went into the building. He was wearing a white windbreaker with the name of the supply company on the back. Tommy could see him talking to a security guard just inside the door before he disappeared into the building. Then nothing happened for a while. Tommy turned on the radio. People came and went, some in wheelchairs and some on their own two feet. Cars drew up to the curb to pick them up or they managed to make it to the parking lot on their own. The van just sat there. The man who had gone inside came out again, walking fast. He got in the van and Tommy saw the man at the wheel lean forward a little, as if reaching for the ignition. Something about the way the other man had been walking when he came out of the building put Tommy on high alert. The sight of Salerno's gofer Vince coming through the door and digging in a pocket for his car keys made everything fall into place.

By the time Rocco Salerno appeared at the door of the hospital, Tommy had had time to see it all: what was going to happen and what his options were. His first thought was that this was going to solve all his problems. A dead Rocco Salerno was off his back forever. Tommy's second thought was that he was going to have a whole new set of problems if he just sat there and let it happen, because he would still owe the feds and they would want to know what the hell he was doing there with the hit team. By the time he had his third thought he was halfway out of the car.

Tommy's third thought was that he just couldn't sit there and let a man be slaughtered in cold blood, no matter who it was. He'd seen too much of that. Tommy had about a hundred feet to cover. A Cadillac with Vince at the wheel was pulling up to the entrance, and Salerno himself, with a burly young guy Tommy hadn't seen before at his elbow, was starting to come away from the door toward it, looking a little unsteady on his pins. Tommy didn't have a weapon, so the only thing he could think to do was to shout.

"Mr. Salerno!" He had broken into a run. Salerno and the young guy stopped in their tracks. Tommy pointed at the van and shouted again. "In the van!" Vince was bringing the Caddy smoothly to the curb, twenty feet or so behind the van. Everyone had stopped in their tracks: the white-haired lady, the mama with two kids, the elderly hoodlum and his bodyguard. Both back doors of the van swung open.

Tommy saw Rocco Salerno's eyes go wide open. Running at top speed, Tommy hit the near door of the van with his shoulder. The door whipped back and hit something with a clang and there was a tremendous boom and the window of the other door exploded. The door Tommy had hit bounced back open as Tommy sprawled on the pavement. He and the man in the back of the van looked at each other as they both scrambled back to their feet. Tommy was just a hair faster, maybe because he knew his life depended on it: he grabbed the barrel of the shotgun before the man could work the slide again and ripped it out of his hands, pulling the man out onto the pavement. Tommy looked into the back of the van and saw a second man bring up a handgun. He hit the asphalt in a hurry, rolling away from those open doors and coming up with the shotgun pumped. He fired, taking out the remaining window. Three sharp cracks sounded from Tommy's right and he saw Salerno's bodyguard squeezing off shots toward the van, one-handed and wild. Somebody was screaming "Go! Go!" and the van peeled out. The man Tommy had disarmed scrambled after it. He caught up with the van and was pulled on board as it picked up speed. It went careering out of the parking lot and back onto First Avenue, heading south, the back doors still open and feet sticking out.

Tommy ran back to the Cadillac. The young guy was hustling Salerno toward it, still waving his piece. Vince was halfway out of the car, staring at Tommy with his mouth open.

"Who the fuck are you?" screamed the young guy over the roof of the car, pointing his gun at Tommy.

"Hold your fire," Tommy yelled. "I'm on your side."

"Get in, for Christ's sake," yelled Vince, jumping back onto the driver's seat. Two security guards were running out of the building.

Tommy tore open the rear door and got in, still holding the shotgun. The young guy shoved Salerno onto the back seat next to him and jumped in front. Vince peeled out, whipping the Caddy around in a U-turn to take off in the opposite direction from the van. "Where the fuck did you come from?" he shouted.

"Kentucky," said Tommy. He felt like laughing.

"You're supposed to be dead," said Salerno, getting his breath back but not looking like a healthy man.

"So are you," said Tommy.

Vince got them to a garage somewhere in what Tommy thought might be Melrose Park in about five minutes flat. They drew some honks but no cops, which was a relief to Tommy. He had put the shotgun on the floor but knew he was in deep shit if they got stopped. On the way, the young guy had done some yelling into his cell phone. The garage was halfway down an alley that ended at a railway line, and the door was standing open when they got there. Tommy saw machinery, oil drums, shelves loaded with junk.

"Out," Vince growled, the overhead door coming down behind them. Tommy got out and then reached in to retrieve the shotgun. Now he recognized it: it was the same one he'd been given to kill Pete Catania. Somebody on the South Side had a sense of humor.

"Stevie will be here in five minutes," said the man who had lowered the garage door, another guy Tommy had never seen before. "Everybody okay?"

"Fuck no, I ain't okay," said Salerno. "I'm about to have another heart attack."

"What the hell happened?" said the garage man.

Vince said, "Those motherfucking pricks tried to kill him. Catania's people. Assholes."

The young guy pointed at Tommy. "This guy come out of fucking nowhere to break it up. Who are you?"

Tommy cocked a thumb at Salerno. "Ask him."

"This is the guy whose ID they shoved through the mail slot," said Salerno. "The dead guy. You got some fuckin' explaining to do, Mr. Dead Guy."

"It's simple," said Tommy. "I owed you one." He held the shotgun out to the young guy, butt first. "I got your gun back, too," he said. "I'm hoping we can call it quits now."

Everybody just stood there and looked at Tommy for a few seconds. Finally Salerno said, "What the hell do they put in the water down there where you come from?"

They talked over a table in somebody's kitchen, where Steve delivered them in a black Monte Carlo. He had shown up at the garage in a state of agitation and asked the obvious question. "How did they fuckin' know? How did they know you were gonna be there?"

Now, with Steve hovering just down a hallway muttering into a cell phone and a bottle of Jim Beam on the table between them, Salerno asked Tommy the same question. "How did they know I was gonna be there? I only made the appointment yesterday."

Tommy said, "Damned if I know. All I did was follow them."

Salerno seemed to be taking that with a grain of salt. He peered at Tommy for a while and said, "And what was all that shit with the ID card? You trying to put one over on me?"

"Sure I was. I couldn't kill Catania, so I needed a way to get you off my back."

"You got the balls to tell me that?" Salerno looked as if a trip back to the hospital would do him good. He looked as if his head was about to explode. "You know what I do to people that try and fuck with me like that?"

"On the other hand, I just saved your life."

Tommy could see that had gone right over Salerno's head. His eyes were bulging. "If you'd fuckin' killed Catania like I told you, it wouldn't have happened. Why didn't you kill him?"

"He was asleep. I can kill a guy if he's pointing a gun at me, but not if he's just laying there with a lady next to him."

"Jesus H. Christ." Salerno drained his glass and reached for the bottle. "What the hell do you want? Why are you here?"

"I want you to lay off my friends. Forever. You got a problem, it's with me. That's what I'm asking for saving your life."

"The only reason you had to was, you fucked me over with Catania."

"Maybe so. But I could have let them kill you today."

The old man drank again, more than was good for him. "Why didn't you?"

Tommy thought about it. "Because then I'd have had two Salernos on my conscience," he said.

Salerno just sat there scowling at him, clutching his glass to his chest. "I don't give a shit about your friends. As for you, you want a job, I got one for you."

Not this shit again, Tommy thought. He sighed. "Mr.

Salerno, I appreciate the offer, but all I want to do right now is haul ass out of town. I ain't cut out for the lifestyle."

He thought he'd pissed the old man off again, watching his face cloud up, but Salerno just drank more bourbon and set the glass down. He looked whipped, an old man with a bad heart slumped on a chair. "Have it your way. In that case, I see you in this town again, I'll kill you," he said.

"Well, I'd have to say that's fair," said Tommy. He stood up. "If I'm ever dumb enough to come back here, I deserve it."

Steve had appeared in the doorway, standing there watching Tommy with a faint smile on his face. "You want this back?" He pulled Tommy's bloodied ID card out of an inside pocket of his jacket.

Tommy shrugged. "Keep it."

"Where'd you get the blood?" Steve looked at the card for a moment, shook his head, and slipped the card back into the pocket.

"The blood's real," said Tommy, holding up his bandaged hand. "It ain't the first time I've lost blood."

Steve stood there smiling at him. "The way you operate, it's probably not the last, either."

30

This time Tommy was hoping for a clean getaway. If the FBI went back to Salerno now, it wouldn't make any difference. Salerno would laugh at them. Now his only problem was how hard the FBI would look for him. He had torched all the bridges behind him, and Kansas City was starting to sound better and better. The only trouble was, he was down to what he had on his back, the credit card, and the cash in his pocket, which was a couple of hundred bucks.

And the car. Tommy wasn't sure he could risk the car. For all he knew, half a dozen different agencies had it staked out waiting for him to come back, after what had happened at the hospital.

All it took was for one witness to say he'd come out of that blue Chevy over there, and they'd run the plate and connect the dots and he was right where he'd been twenty-four hours before. It was time to ditch the car, along with the rest of his life in Chicago. He needed a bus ticket and a head start.

Steve had dropped Tommy at an El station in Oak Park. He took the train back downtown, feeling the massive city close in around him, miles of hostile streets, and got off at Halsted. He walked down to Harrison and went east to the Greyhound station.

Tommy looked at schedules and fares and figured he could put a ticket on his credit card and be in Los Angeles in three days. He wasn't sure he had the heart for it. He went and sat on a bench and looked at a lot of other lost and aimless people and tried to figure out what the hell he wanted to do.

He wanted to hold Lisa, that's what he wanted to do. Tommy wanted to go and find her and grab her and tell her he loved her and wanted more. He was having trouble shutting down. That last kiss had stayed with him. Tommy was starting to realize he'd been a sad lonely bastard for most of his life. It had never felt that way in the army because of his friends, but the army wasn't going to take him back. Out here he was on his own, and so far he was making a complete Mongolian clusterfuck of civilian life.

He should never have gone after Joe Salerno. That was the rage getting the upper hand again. He should have known better. But some things just set him off. He didn't regret shooting the son of a bitch, but it had sure complicated his life. It meant he had messed up his best chance to fit in with people who had some kind of a normal life going. Tommy would never have thought it was possible, but he was already looking back at things like that Thanksgiving dinner at Mary's place and missing them. They were just a glimpse of a life he could have had, a life that was a little kinder than what he was used to, a life with some wider horizons. But he had fucked it up. He had forgotten that you couldn't approach life here the way you had to approach it in Iraq, locked and loaded all the time. He had brought all the wrong reactions home.

Maybe it wasn't too late: maybe there was a way he could stay, get the feds off his back, keep the cops off him, have a life. He still had the apartment, and he could hide out there and feel the situation out. He could at least pick up some of his things. Maybe if he let a couple of days go by he could even salvage the car.

Tommy knew that was foolish. It was time to go, start over again somewhere else. He was feeling low. There was nothing ahead of him except the lonesome road, and he didn't know where it led. He pulled out his cell phone.

He held it in his hand and wondered if maybe there was a message there from Lisa. He would give a hell of a lot to hear her voice one last time. He turned on the phone and brought up his messages.

Sure enough, there was a pile of them, several from the Greek, going from puzzled to furious, a couple from Brian, wondering what he was up to. Tommy felt bad about Brian. That was going to bother him for a long time. Sneaking out of town like this wasn't right, either: he owed Brian some explanations, a phone call at least. A message came up from a number he didn't recognize.

"Mr. McLain, this is Detective Hays, we spoke before. I was

wondering if you could give me a call. I need to talk to you regarding your friend Lisa DiPietro." The detective's tone was completely flat, bored. He read off a number and the message ended. It had come through earlier that day.

Tommy sat there with the phone in his hand, in shock. There was only one reason he could think of why cops called people about their friends. He had heard his dad make calls like this. Tommy's hand was trembling a little as he punched in the number Hays had left.

Tommy put the phone to his ear and heard the ring at the other end and then Hays's voice telling him he could leave a message or page him. He punched in the page. He got up and went out into the cold and stood on the sidewalk looking up at the buildings looming in the dark and letting the wind suck the warmth out of him, thinking, I did it. I brought it down on her. All he could think was, if something happened to Lisa, a whole lot more than one mobster was going to die this time.

When his phone went off he dragged it out of his pocket, almost fumbling it onto the sidewalk. "Yeah."

"Mr. McLain? Hays here."

"What happened?"

"What do you mean?"

"With Lisa. Is she okay?"

"Far as I know. Why? You worried about something?"

"Jesus." Tommy almost pitched the phone into the street. "What'd you call me for?"

"I need some more information from you."

"About what?"

"Can we do this face-to-face? Whereabouts are you?"

Careful, Tommy thought. "To tell you the truth, I'm getting set to leave town."

"Can I persuade you to put it off for an hour or so?"

"Depends. If Lisa's okay, I'm not sure what we got to talk about. Ain't the case over? Salerno's dead."

"Not quite."

"What do you mean, he's not quite dead?" Tommy almost gave himself away: *He looked pretty dead when I left him.*

Tommy could hear Hays laughing, softly. "I mean the case is not quite over."

"What the hell's left?"

"Why don't we get together so I can explain it to you?"

"Why can't you do it over the phone?"

The phone hummed in Tommy's ear for a couple of seconds. Hays said, "Okay, try this on for size. She lied to me."

Tommy just stood there in the cold wind, cars going by on the street. "What the hell are you talking about? Who lied?"

"Your friend Lisa. I'm wondering if she lied to you, too."

"About what?"

"You want the rest of it, we talk face-to-face."

Tommy let the silence go on until Hays asked if he was still there. Finally Tommy said, "I'm at the Greyhound station, downtown."

"Get yourself a cup of that good coffee out of the vending machine and give me half an hour." The phone went dead.

Hays pulled over to the curb in a dark-colored Impala. Tommy had been watching from inside the station and came out when he saw him. He got in and Hays pulled away from the curb. Rush hour was over and there wasn't a lot of traffic.

"What's going on?" said Tommy. It had been a rough half hour for him. He couldn't think what Lisa might have had to lie about, but he was sure there was an explanation.

"That's what I'm trying to figure out," said Hays. He drove smoothly and not too fast, a man out for a cruise. "Tell me how you met Lisa DiPietro."

"I met her at a party. My friend Brian introduced me."

"Uh-huh. Was this before or after the stalker showed up?"

"After. That first time I met her, we walked her home, Brian and me, 'cause she was already worried about him. And I saw him, too, I think, sitting in his car."

"So Salerno was already after her when you came on the scene."

"Yeah. So what? You mind telling me what's going on?"

Hays didn't seem to be in a hurry. He turned north on Halsted, toward Greek Town. "I'm gonna ask you a personal question, Tom. Don't get offended."

"Whatever."

"You and Lisa an item? Did it get physical?"

Tommy's stomach turned over. Did it ever, he wanted to say. "I don't mind answering, but what the hell's it to you?"

"Did it get physical before or after you went after Salerno for her?"

Tommy had opened his mouth to say "after" when he stopped suddenly, realizing how close he'd come to making an admission. He closed his mouth and started over again. "I'm not sure what you mean by 'went after.'"

Hays laughed, softly. "You're not giving anything away, huh? Look, I'm not trying to nail you for anything you might have done to Salerno. That's somebody else's job. I was assigned to investigate Lisa's complaint. On the basis of your evidence and Lisa's, I made an identification of the alleged stalker and gave her the information so she could get an order of protection. Then all of a sudden the stalker gets shot. Coincidence? You tell me. But it gets my attention. I don't have to figure out who did it, but since I gave her the information, and you were heard to make threats, it bothers me. So I take a harder look at the people involved in the complaint. And what do I find?"

Tommy knew he wasn't going to like what he was about to hear. He was starting to wish he'd told Hays to go to hell and gotten on the bus. "Why don't you get to the point, sir? I'm not a very good guesser."

"I find out Lisa told me a big fat lie. I'm hoping she told you the same thing, because then I don't have to think you're in on it with her."

"Look, I give up, okay? What'd she lie about?"

"She told you she'd never seen Salerno before, right?"

"Yeah."

"Well, that's kind of surprising."

"How come?"

"They used to work together. In the same office."

31

Tommy just sat there watching the city go by as Hays drove, up through Greek Town and beyond, into bleak industrial districts. I could be sitting on a bus, he thought, heading west with a memory of lying there in that motel room with Lisa in my arms.

Tough shit, he thought, that's all gone. "So she knew him, huh?"

"Looks like it."

"So why would she lie about it?"

"Man, that's a really good question, isn't it? I was hoping you could answer that."

"She told me the same thing she told you. She'd never seen him."

Hays made a right and they went over the river, shimmering in the dark. "You see what I'm thinking, Tom?"

"You want me to say she used me. Used me for what?"

"You tell me."

"You think I shot Salerno, arrest me. As for Lisa, that's between me and her. If she used me to try and get Salerno off her back, can you really blame her?"

"That's for you to answer. You're the one she lied to."

"So what am I doing in this car?"

"Telling me the truth, I hope. You strike me as a pretty straight shooter. If there's anything you can tell me that would clarify why Lisa DiPietro would lie about not knowing Joe Salerno, I'd like to hear it. Everyone's got you pinned for shooting him. I don't care about that. It sounds to me like he had it coming, whoever did it. But I don't like being lied to. It pisses me off. I don't think you have, but I know Lisa did. I'm hoping that pisses you off, too, so you might help me figure out what the hell's going on with her. If there's anything she told you that might clear it up, I'd like to hear it. Otherwise, I can take you back to the bus station."

"She told me she didn't know him." Tommy was thinking about all the other things she'd told him, wondering if that had been bullshit, too. "Anyway, we're done. We had a little thing and it's over. I don't really give a damn about anything else. I'm on my way out of town."

Hays turned south down Wells, under the El tracks. "I hope so," he said. "You know what would really piss me off?"

"What?"

"If you messed up my investigation by going back and talking to Lisa about it."

"Why would I go back and talk to her? I told you, it's over."

"Okay, I'll take your word for it. I find out you go after her, I find out you lied to me, too, about anything, I'll smack you with an obstruction charge so fast you won't have time to blink. That clear?"

Tommy didn't answer that. They were crossing the river again, heading into the Loop. Tommy was sick of the city. He wanted to see the sun come up over a clear horizon tomorrow.

"So," said Hays. "You want me to drop you back at the depot?"

Tommy was thinking hard. "Sure," he said. "I think I can still just make the bus."

Tommy watched Hays pull away from the curb and then left the bus station and hiked back to the El. He wasn't sure how to get to Maywood, but he was pretty sure he needed the car again. He also needed a shower, a change of clothes, and some answers.

He caught a cab in Oak Park that took him back to the hospital. He got out at a different part of the complex and made his way carefully back to where he'd left the Chevy. He didn't see anybody that looked like a cop hunkered down on a stakeout, but he still made a pass on foot and then waited a while just inside the door of the pavilion, watching, before he finally went for the car.

He got away without any federal agents jumping out at him and got on the expressway. There wasn't any reason for him to avoid going back to his place anymore, so he drove home to

Uptown and went back to his room and had his shower and packed up all his stuff, ready to hit the road. He lay down but had trouble sleeping. He couldn't stop thinking about Lisa. If she had lied to him, he was sure she had a reason. If she had used him, did that make all those tender words and caresses lies? Tommy was confused.

He finally dozed off and got a couple of hours of fitful sleep. He got up early and went and had breakfast at the diner under the El tracks on Wilson. Then he drove down to Lincoln Park and found a place to park and went and rang Brian's bell.

Brian was putting on his tie, getting ready to go off to work. He said, "Jesus, Tom. I thought you'd left town or something. Where the hell you been?"

"I been kinda busy."

"What the hell you been up to? That cop came around again, looking for you."

"Hays?"

"I guess so. I don't remember his name."

"He found me."

The look on Brian's face told Tommy things had changed: whatever Brian knew or didn't know, suspected or didn't, it wasn't an uncomplicated friendship anymore. Brian said, "You haven't been breaking any laws, have you now, Tom?"

"Not that I'm aware of. I wanted to ask you a question."

"Make it quick. I got to get going."

"Did you tell Lisa about my sister?"

Brian frowned. "Shouldn't I have?"

"You did, huh?"

Brian shrugged. "Yeah, I think so. Sure."

"When? Early on?"

"Shit, I don't know. How come?"

"Did you tell her about Beth before we started going out?"

"Yeah, I think I told her maybe that first night, after we walked her home, you know? She asked about you. I told her all about you. I could tell right then she was more interested in you than me."

Tommy nodded. "Okay. Thanks, that's kind of what I figured."

"Did I do something wrong?"

Tommy slapped Brian on the shoulder. "No, man. You ain't done nothing wrong. I owe you, big-time, for a lot of things."

"What the hell's going on with you and Lisa, anyway?"

"When I find out, you'll be the first to know. Let me ask you another question. Do you know where Lisa used to work?"

"What, before the Merchandise Mart, you mean? No clue. How come?"

"I'm just trying to figure something out. I heard a rumor about her, that's all."

Brian frowned at that for a couple of seconds, but he seemed to buy it. "Mary would know, probably."

"Yeah," said Tommy. "I bet she would."

"I run into her on the El sometimes. You want me to ask her?"

Talking to Mary would be the quickest way for things to get back to Lisa, Tommy knew. "Nah, why don't you hold off on that for a while?"

"Whatever."

Tommy could see Brian was starting to lose patience with all the mystery. "Can I ask you another little favor?"

"Sure."

"Can I use your computer for an hour or two?"

Brian looked relieved. "Sure, man. You know where it is."

Tommy ran the same kind of search on Lisa that he had done for Salerno. He came up with the usual things, a list of places she'd lived including the current one, possible neighbors, possible relatives. She didn't have a criminal record and she didn't own any property. What Tommy really wanted was to see where she'd worked, but he didn't get that. He found another site that would do a Work History Search for him for $39.95, but it would take twenty-four to seventy-two hours to get results. He wasn't sure he wanted to wait that long. He wasn't even sure what he was doing. Why couldn't he just call Lisa and ask her to explain? Did he really give a shit about Hays and his investigation? And why did he need to know? What was he hoping for? Tommy was getting more confused all the time. He was starting to wish he had gotten on the bus. Tommy had a feeling whatever he found out was going to make him hurt.

Still, he had to know who that was who had kissed him and told him he was her hero, told him she would miss him. He had to know what those memories were worth, because they were all he was going to have.

Tommy had a cell phone number for Mary. He called it and got her voice mail. "Hey, this is Tom. I was wondering if I could take you out to lunch. Give me a call." He left his cell number and hung up. Then he collapsed on Brian's couch just like old times and finally fell asleep.

His phone going off woke him up. "Tom?" Mary's voice had a wondering tone. "What's going on? I thought you left town."

"I'm on my way out. I thought I might buy you lunch and say thanks for all you did for me."

There was a silence and Mary said, "Sure, I'd love that."

They made a date: Mary got an hour off from her job in an office on Sheffield near Diversey, starting at noon. Tommy would just have time to meet her if he got going. He jogged to his car.

They wound up at a Subway in a strip mall. Mary talked a mile a minute as usual until they sat down with their sandwiches, and then she fell silent. All of a sudden she looked uncomfortable, chewing and looking out the window. Tommy wasn't really hungry. He picked up his sandwich, put it down, and said, "I wanted to ask you something."

"What?" She looked alarmed, and Tommy wondered if she knew what was coming.

"How long you known Lisa?"

"Oh, about . . . six years, I guess. Since college." Mary wiped her mouth and her look softened a little. "Tom, I really don't want to be put in the middle of this. Whatever happened is between you two. I know Lisa's sorry to see you go, but she's not destroyed or anything."

Tommy saw she didn't have a clue why he was there. "That's not it. What I wanted to ask you was, would you say she's a truthful person? Is she honest?"

Mary looked shocked. She stiffened a little and said, "Sure. Are you kidding? Lisa's probably the nicest person I know."

"I don't mean nice. I know she's nice. I mean . . ." What the hell did he mean? Tommy hadn't really given a lot of thought to this interview. Now all of a sudden he saw he was going to have to be honest himself. He was through being devious. He wasn't cut out for it. "The cops say Lisa knew Joe Salerno from before."

Mary stared for a while before saying, "No way."

"That's what I said, too. But the cop I talked to sounded pretty sure. He said they worked together."

"I don't believe it."

"I don't want to believe it."

"That has to be wrong. Why would she lie about it?"

"You got me. You know where she worked before?"

Mary blinked for a couple of seconds. "Sure. Some real estate company, out in the suburbs. She was office manager or something. That was her first job out of college. She was living in Palatine and hating it. We used to talk on the phone and I'd tell her she needed to move into the city."

"You know the name of the company?"

"I could probably think of it." Mary seemed to have lost her appetite. She slumped back on the bench and said, "Tom, this is creepy."

Tommy nodded. "I'm glad it bothers you. It bothers the hell out of me."

"Of course it bothers me. Star."

"Huh?"

"Star Capital. That was the name of the company. She worked there for a year and then it went bankrupt. She said that was the best thing that could have happened to her. She said it was a bad place to work."

"If Joe Salerno was there, I can believe it."

"But why would she lie about having known him?"

"I don't know. You got an Internet connection back there at your office?"

Mary stared for a second and then started wrapping up her sandwich. "Yeah. And forty-five minutes of lunchtime left."

32

C rain's *Chicago Business* had reported on the Star Capital bankruptcy two years before. According to the article, the company had run into trouble due to too many bad loans and filed for Chapter 11 before being bought out by another company called Premier Enterprises, based in Des Plaines. There weren't many details, and there wasn't any mention of anyone named Salerno. The search had turned up a couple of even more passing references on other sites. It hadn't been much of a story.

"Premier," said Tommy. He straightened up from the desk. "Des Plaines. That's northwest, too, right?"

"A little closer in than Palatine. What are you going to do?"

"I don't know." They just looked at one another for a moment. "Maybe nothing. Maybe I don't want to know anything about it. Do you?"

"She's my friend," said Mary. "Of course I want to know."

"Okay. Then I guess I'll go find somebody who knows something about Star Capital. We're not mentioning this to Lisa, are we?"

Mary had to take a moment to think about that. "I feel bad, sneaking behind her back."

"If she lied to us, what was that?"

Mary shook her head. "I can't believe that."

"So we disprove it. Maybe the cops are full of shit. Anyway, don't say anything to Lisa till I have a chance to talk to a couple of people."

Mary looked dazed. "I hate this."

And you didn't even sleep with her, Tommy wanted to say. "I'll give you a call."

He had made it to the door of her office when she called his name. Tommy looked back to see her beckoning him, wide-eyed. He went back and looked where she was pointing on the screen. She had brought up an article from the *Sun-Times* from two years before. The headline said, *Lombard businessman found slain.* "What the hell's this?" said Tommy.

"Look," Mary whispered, pointing. Tommy read *Sheriff's police say Gagliano was slain execution-style with a shot to the back of the head* and further down, *Gagliano had been the comptroller of now-bankrupt Star Capital in Palatine.*

Tommy found Des Plaines on his map, just north of O'Hare,

and jumped in the car and went. He didn't know what he was doing. He had spent another few minutes at the computer with Mary, but they hadn't found out much more. A guy that had worked for Star Capital had gotten himself killed and the company had gone bankrupt. There hadn't been any mention of Joe Salerno or the mob or anything funny about the company. Tommy had gotten an address for Premier Enterprises on River Road and taken off.

He didn't know what he was going to do when he got there. He didn't know if anybody would want to talk to him. In Iraq he'd found that people could be fairly eager to talk if you busted into their living room in the middle of the night and pointed automatic weapons at them, but that wasn't really an option here.

He didn't even know what he really wanted. He was afraid of what he might find out. His better judgment was telling him to leave it alone. And the rest of him was still remembering the feel of Lisa in his arms, and wondering who that was.

Tommy found River Road in the haphazard sprawl of industrial and commercial development in the orbit of the airport, but he couldn't find Premier Enterprises. Tommy was amazed at how the city had spread like a fungus, eating up the land in every direction. Tommy wondered where the hell they were growing the food these days. He went up and down River Road looking for a sign, unable to spot any numbers on any of the buildings. He finally had to stop at a gas station and ask. The address had to be back the way he had come, he was told.

When he spotted it he was surprised, because there didn't seem to be much to Premier Enterprises. He'd pictured a suite in one of the big faceless office blocks that made the area so bleak-looking. What he saw when he turned off River Road was a low-slung cinder block building stuck at the edge of a big parking lot that seemed to belong to a warehouse beyond it. A small sign over the door said *Premier Enterprises.* Tommy parked and went and tried the door.

It was locked. Tommy rattled the doorknob a little but nothing gave. He stepped back and took a look around. There was a window near the door and he took a peek inside. He saw an office with all the things offices usually had: a counter, some shelves, some files, a calendar or two, a computer on a desk. But he didn't see any people.

Tommy thought that was strange. He figured a going concern ought to be open early in the afternoon on a weekday. He started walking down the length of the building. He rounded a corner and saw a white Pontiac GTO parked in back of the place, hidden from view from the street. There was a back door here. Tommy went and tried the knob but nothing gave. He knocked.

Nothing happened, and he knocked again after a while. That car hadn't driven itself out here. The door opened a foot or so and Tommy found himself looking at Rocco Salerno's gofer Vince.

They just looked at each other in surprise for a few seconds. "Well, shit," Tommy said.

"What the fuck are you doing here?" said Vince. He looked as if somebody had just spit on his shoes.

That was a hell of a good question, and Tommy didn't know how to answer it. "I came out here to talk to you," he said finally.

A look of deep suspicion came over Vince's face. "How did you know I was here?"

"Mr. Salerno told me."

A couple of seconds passed and Vince said, "Bullshit. Rocco said if I ever saw you again it would be shoot on sight."

Tommy nodded. "So what are you waiting for?"

Vince took too long to think about it: he was still recovering from his surprise. Tommy took a chance, figuring one car meant one guy. He put his shoulder into the door and knocked Vince back a couple of staggering steps, going in after him. They were in a hallway going up the side of the building with doors opening off it. Vince got his balance back, swearing. Tommy slammed the door. "We gotta talk," he said.

Vince was used to winning by intimidation. Most of the time when he grabbed a handful of shirt the opponent folded. This time he was surprised: when he shot out his hand Tommy grabbed it and twisted it like a key in a lock, forcing Vince to bend over forward if he didn't want his wrist to snap. Tommy pushed down on Vince's elbow with his free hand, and Vince hit the floor face down. Tommy put a knee on his back. "Vince, you don't calm down and talk to me, you'll never raise that arm above your shoulder again. You understand?"

"Fuck you."

Tommy wrenched Vince's arm behind his back and Vince made a sound like a dog getting hit by a car.

"You lost already," Tommy said. "Now, you ready to have a civil conversation?"

Vince groaned and said, "What the fuck we got to talk about?"

"Star Capital."

"Never heard of it."

Tommy grabbed Vince's hair, keeping the arm locked behind

245

his back. He hauled him to his feet and shoved him down the hall. "March." Tommy took him through the first doorway. The room they went into was another office, but a different kind of office: the customers never got invited back here. There were a couple of desks but no computers, a battered sofa along one wall, a coffee maker and a TV set. Tommy shoved Vince onto the sofa. Vince sprawled, rolled over, sat up massaging his shoulder.

Tommy stood over him, just out of kicking range. "Don't lie to me, Vince."

"Fuck you."

"You gonna make me work, huh?"

"I'm gonna kill you, is what I'm gonna do. Don't turn your back."

"You think you can kill me before I tell Salerno you're wearing a wire?"

Tommy knew it was a hit when Vince went completely still for five seconds. "What the fuck are you talking about?"

"I'm talking about the wire you put on for the FBI."

"You're out of your fuckin' hillbilly mind."

"You think that's what Salerno will say when I tell him about it?"

"There ain't no wire." Vince said it without conviction, for form's sake.

"The hell there ain't," said Tommy. "The FBI's got a transcript of a conversation between you and Salerno. They told me it was from a phone tap, but I don't believe it, because I know Salerno never says anything on the phone. So that means it was from a wire."

"What makes you think it was me?" Vince was still pretending, but Tommy could see it was over.

"My dumbass cracker intuition. Now, tell me about Star Capital."

"Jesus Christ, you dislocated my arm." Vince was starting to list to port a little, grimacing, clutching the shoulder. "What about it?"

"Two things." Tommy had been standing over Vince but now he moved to the nearest desk and started opening drawers. "One, why did the comptroller get killed? What was the guy's name, Gagliano?"

"What the hell do you care?"

Tommy shoved the bottom drawer shut. "Humor me, okay? Why'd he get killed?"

"How should I know?"

Tommy stood up straight. "Vince, my patience is running kind of short right now. I been lied to too much. Now what happened at Star Capital? Why did the guy get killed?"

"Damn. You really fucked up my shoulder." Vince was flopped over on the couch, eyes squeezed shut.

Tommy went to the other desk and pulled the top drawer open. "Okay. Have it your way. But once Salerno finds out about the wire, it'll be too late. You can talk all you want then, and it won't help you." Tommy bent to pull open the second drawer as Vince rolled toward the edge of the couch and reached under it. All of a sudden he was moving fast, hauling the sawed-off shotgun out from underneath the sofa and jerking upright. He had just managed to rack the slide when Tommy brought the pipe wrench he had found in the top drawer down on his shoulder. There was a crack and Vince screamed. The shotgun didn't go off, so Tommy pulled it out of Vince's hands, a little gingerly, making sure to point the barrel away from him.

"Well shit, Vince. Now you got two bad shoulders." Vince moaned, his face buried in the cushions. Tommy checked the gun and saw it was loaded, the safety off. He'd been just fast enough to keep from getting his guts blown out, beyond the abilities of any surgeon to repair this time. It was the same gun that kept turning up. Tommy figured it was maybe time to hang on to it. "Sit up," he said. He grabbed Vince by the hair again and pulled him upright, then backed away a couple of steps and held the shotgun at his hip, leveled at Vince. "Now talk to me, God damn it. I didn't come here to mess with you, and I don't give a shit if you're wired up. Talk to me and Salerno won't find out from me. What happened at Star Capital?"

"Ah, God. My shoulder."

Tommy figured it was time for some more guesses. "Why did Salerno have Gagliano killed? Come on, talk to me."

Vince took a few deep breaths and said, "He was ripping off the company. Son of a bitch skimmed off half a million bucks."

"What did Salerno care? Was Star his company?" Vince nodded, breathing through clenched teeth. Tommy thought for a second and said, "So the buyout, this Premium thing, that was just a way of scamming the creditors and starting over?"

Vince had recovered enough to open his eyes. "Rocco has a lot of companies."

"Okay. Second question. What did Joe Salerno have to do with Star?"

"Rocco put him in there to watch over things. Except he was a fuckup. He let the guy get away with it for years before Rocco finally figured out what was going on."

"And when Star folded, what happened to Joe? His daddy give him another job?"

Vince shook his head. "You shitting me? Rocco was fed up with him. You lose half a million bucks, that's a lot for a father to forgive."

"What, Salerno couldn't get Gagliano to cough it up?"

"Oh, he coughed it up right away. Couldn't wait to tell us where it was. But when we got there, somebody had beat us to it. It was gone. And nobody's ever found it."

Tommy stood there watching Vince hurt. "Man," he said finally, "that's a real heartbreaker."

33

Tommy almost cut and ran. He could have jumped on the tollway right there at O'Hare and been beyond the Mississippi in three hours, with the festering swamp of Chicago far behind him. He almost did it, but he didn't.

He had to know. Tommy was like that: he didn't like liars, and he didn't like people getting away with things. It bothered him. So he drove back into the city with a sawed-off shotgun with three rounds left in it in the trunk, thinking hard the whole way.

He picked Mary up at work as they had agreed. "You find

out anything?" she said, almost breathless as he pulled away from the curb.

"He worked there, all right. Whether they really knew each other, who knows? Maybe he just saw her in the office and fell for her, she never noticed him, whatever. But I don't think it was that big a company. I think Lisa's been fibbing to us."

"But why?"

"Maybe she led him on a little at first, something like that. And then didn't want to admit it. I don't know. I don't know that I really want to confront her with it. He's dead, she's in the clear. It's over."

Mary kept quiet for a while, amazing Tommy, and then she said, "It bothers me."

Tommy saw the whole thing blowing up in his face once Mary started talking. "Do me one favor," he said. "Don't talk to her about it until I have a chance to, okay?"

She agreed and Tommy dropped her off at her place. As he was driving up Broadway his cell phone went off. When he answered, a voice said, "I'm trying to reach Mr. Ahern."

"Wrong number, dumbshit." Tommy hadn't been raised to talk to people that way, but this was the FBI calling: that was one of the codes they'd given him. It meant he was supposed to contact them at the first opportunity. Tommy threw the cell phone down on the seat and kept driving. He drove back to Uptown and parked near his place. He sat for a moment in the car and then picked up the phone and dialed the number they'd given him. "What the hell do you want?" he said when somebody who sounded like Foss answered.

"Watch your mouth when you talk to me," Foss said. "We have a serious problem with you, my friend."

"We friends now, are we?"

"Not if you're threatening to reveal the identity of a federal informant, we aren't. That's an extremely serious matter and we want to see you right now, as in yesterday."

That was fast, thought Tommy. "Relax. I ain't gonna tell Salerno nothing. I just had to get Vince to talk to me."

"I don't give a damn what you think you needed, mister. You've got some explaining to do. Now, where are you?"

"Tell you what, I'll be at your office in about an hour. Wait for me." Tommy cut Foss off in midsnarl and turned off his phone. The last thing he needed was the feds making life harder for him. He was going to have to figure out what to do about them.

He got out of the car and jogged back to his place. He figured he had under half an hour before federal agents came screeching up in front of the building. He went up and grabbed his stuff and hauled it back down to the car and took off.

As of now he was living out of the car, but he had to assume the car was hot again. He had to use it sparingly. Tommy had some time to kill. He killed it driving downtown and looking for a place to park near the Merchandise Mart where he wouldn't get a ticket and wouldn't have to pay a fortune. He finally lucked into a metered spot on Kinzie and hiked back to the Mart. He was through with phones for a while, too. He knew Lisa got off work at five and took the train home. He got himself a cup of coffee at a stand near the exit to the CTA platform and staked it out, scanning the flow of people. He almost missed Lisa in the crowd but spotted her just as she went through the door. He followed her through the turnstiles and out onto the northbound platform. Tommy had been afraid she might be with people, but she was by herself. She went to stand toward the north end of the platform, a nice-looking girl with dark hair in a ponytail, petite and poised, absorbed in her thoughts. It hurt Tommy to look at her.

She turned her head as he approached and started when she saw him. Tommy smiled at her and watched her reaction, looking for signs. After an instant of blank surprise, she smiled back at him. "I thought you were gone," she said. She had a look of wonder on her face now, but Tommy wasn't sure if it was joy or just shock.

"I did, too." Tommy wanted to grab her and kiss her, but her body language wasn't right. "I wanted to see you once more. Just once."

Lisa's mouth opened but nothing came out.

"Don't worry," said Tommy. "I'm not stalking you."

The smile went away. "That's not funny," Lisa said.

"I'm sorry. Tell me one thing and I'm history."

Tommy could see she thought she had a lovesick puppy on her hands. He could see her feeling for the words to tell him it really was over. He could see the dread in her eyes. In that moment, in spite of his own feelings, in spite of all his suspicions, Tommy truly felt sorry for her, and for every woman who had ever had a man after her that she didn't want to see. "What is it?" said Lisa.

"Why did you lie to me about Joe Salerno?"

Her face went completely blank for a few seconds and then she frowned, cocked her head, shook it once. "Who says I did?"

Tommy gave it a count or two, thinking about Hays, and said, "The cops."

Lisa drew a deep breath and let it out. "What did they tell you?"

"They told me about how you worked with him at Star Capital." A northbound train was rumbling into the station and Tommy shot a look at it. "We gonna discuss this on the train? I got my car near here."

Tommy had to give her credit: she recovered fast. "Let's go," she said.

He followed her along the platform and down the exit stairs. On the sidewalk below she marched beside him in silence. Night had fallen and the wind whipped a few random flakes of snow in their faces. They reached his car and got in. Tommy started it up and put on the heater. "You mind if we just sit here for a while? I don't want to drive it around too much. There's still people looking for me to talk about Joe Salerno."

Lisa was staring straight ahead through the windshield. "I'm sorry I lied," she said.

"You want to tell me about it?"

Her head went down, her eyes closed, and she was still for a little while. When she looked up at him her eyes glistened a little in the light from the streetlamps. "I did something really stupid," she said.

"Shit, if I had a nickel for all the stupid things I ever did, I'd never have to work again."

"I almost had an affair with Joe Salerno. When we worked together."

"Well, you might call that stupid. But I understand he was kind of forceful."

"Which is why I bailed out. I came to my senses in time and told him I didn't want to see him anymore. But he wouldn't take no for an answer. That's why I quit that job. I left to get away from him. But he found me. It took him two years, but he found me."

"So why did you lie about not knowing him? You must have known once the cops tracked him down they'd find out you knew him."

"That was *really* stupid, I know. But I was ashamed. See, before I realized what he was like, I had, like . . . I might have led him on for a little while. And I was afraid of what the cops would make of that. I was afraid they wouldn't take the stalking seriously, because I'd encouraged him. I wasn't thinking clearly, what can I say? So I lied. And then of course when they found him they came back and asked me about it, because he told them we'd worked together. And I told them I just hadn't recognized him, that I never knew him that well. I don't know if they believed me. But they gave me the information for the order of protection anyway."

Tommy let the silence go on for a moment. "And then you told me he'd been in your house. Was that a lie, too?"

"No." Lisa looked him in the eye when she said it, and Tommy wanted to believe her. "You think I used you, don't you?" said Lisa. "You think I just manipulated you into going after Joe Salerno."

"It crossed my mind."

She reached for him then, and Tommy had to respond. They held the clinch for a few seconds and Lisa put her lips near his ear and whispered, "That was for real, Tom. I could never fake that." She drew away and wiped a tear away with a finger. "That was true, what happened with us."

There was another tear at the corner of her other eye and Tommy took care of it with his thumb. "Well, I'm glad to hear that. It was a hell of a ride."

"I'm so sorry. I can't believe I was that stupid."

Tommy sat there looking at her. Don't say it, he told himself. Just leave it lay and walk away. You got an explanation, and that ought to be good enough. He said, "So the lies didn't have anything to do with the half million bucks that went missing."

The last time Tommy had seen a look like the one on Lisa's face, he'd been looking at a raw young trooper who had just been shot through the heart after standing up at the wrong time. It was a bad thing to see. Lisa held it for what seemed like forever, and then her eyes closed for a second or two. When they came open again she said, "Do the cops know about that?"

That was when Tommy knew for sure: that was the wrong question for an innocent person to ask. "I don't think so. But I don't really know. You want to tell me what really happened?"

In a second everything had changed: Lisa was a frightened woman. "Who'd you talk to?"

"One of Rocco Salerno's guys."

"Oh, Jesus." Now Lisa was starting to hyperventilate. She reached for the door handle.

Tommy put a hand on her arm. "Talk to me."

"Does Salerno know about me?" The words barely made it out of her throat.

"Not that this guy mentioned. What the hell'd you do, Lisa?"

Lisa fought to control her breathing, looking straight ahead. People went by on the sidewalk, laughing. Lisa calmed a bit, gulped in a lot of air, and turned to Tommy. "I'll split it with you, half and half."

34

Tommy could just see her in the light from outside the car. "Hold on a second. You skipped a couple of pages. You trying to tell me you got the money?"

"I hid it. I haven't touched it. Please, Tom. Help me and I'll give you half of it."

"Whoa. Just a second. You got the half million bucks?"

She nodded a few times, rapidly, and said, "Yeah. I got it. Me, little Lisa, the quiet one. Are you surprised?"

He was, and he wasn't. Tommy shook his head in wonder. "How did that happen?"

Her look hardened just a little. "Are you going to help me?"

"Help you do what?"

"What do you think? Recover it, move it, make it so we can use it. Half and half. I need your help, Tom. Please."

Tommy was looking at a different person from the one he'd thought he knew. "You gotta tell me what happened."

She froze for a second and then heaved a sigh. "I took it out of Chuck Gagliano's car. The night they came for him."

"How did you even know about it?"

"I knew what Chuck was up to. We shared an office, and all it took was a little attention to see what he was doing. He was skimming from the cash receipts. Yeah, cash. For a real estate company they handled a whole lot of cash. That was what made me start paying attention. Chuck thought he was being smart, but I figured it out. It scared me to death, because I'd heard the rumors about the guys that owned the company. But I didn't say anything to anyone. Joe Salerno was supposed to be the boss, but he was an idiot. After a while I was almost rooting for Chuck. And then I could tell he got scared. Overnight, from one day to the next. I don't know what happened, but he got scared. And then one day he got a phone call. I saw his face when he took the call, and I knew he was in trouble. He hung up the phone, looked at me for a second like I wasn't there, and then got up and went to the closet and grabbed this, like, overnight bag out of it and walked out of the office. I could see the parking lot from the window, and I saw him open the trunk, throw in the bag, and get in his car and start it. And then before he could back out, another car came and blocked him in. A couple of big guys got out and said something to him, and he got out of his car and he looked like a zombie or some-thing, and they put him in their car and they drove away. And

I almost called the cops, but I was scared to, because I was afraid they would ask how I knew he was in trouble and why I hadn't reported it before. So I didn't."

"So how did you wind up with the money?"

She stared out the windshield for a while before answering. "You have to understand, Tom. We never had any money growing up. My father was a baker, for God's sake. He worked all the time and we still never had any money. And I had thousands of dollars in student loans to pay off. Can you see why it was a temptation?"

"I'm not judging you. I'm asking what happened."

"After I saw them take him away I started thinking. When he opened the trunk to throw in his overnight bag, I had seen something else in there. He had a couple of courier bags in there, like the ones the cash came into the office in. And his car was sitting out there in the lot."

"Aw, hell, Lisa." Tommy saw it all now.

"Yeah, I did it. I worked late, waited till everyone else was gone, and when I finally left I started my car and then pulled up just behind his. I was so nervous I barely knew what I was doing. But there was nobody else there to see me. He had left his car unlocked, so I just opened the door and looked for the little lever that pops the trunk and pulled it. I didn't even check what was in the bags. I just took them out and put them in my trunk. I drove home and just went inside and tried not to think about it. It was like it had all been a dream. The next day I finally worked up the nerve to look. And the bags were full of cash. I was, like, in shock. I actually drove around with the money in there for a day or two before I figured out what to do. I put it in a storage locker in Northbrook. And then a couple of days after that they found Chuck's body and I was actually sick for a few days. And I've been too scared to go anywhere near it."

Tommy just looked at her profile for a few seconds. "And Joe Salerno figured it out."

She sighed, and nodded a couple of times. "It took him two years, like I said. I had left the company and moved and everything, and I was starting to think I was in the clear. And then he showed up. He said he knew I had to have taken the money, and he wasn't going to tell his father, but I had to cut him in on it. He wanted half of it. I denied everything, of course, but he wouldn't quit. He turned into a stalker. He said if I called the cops he would just say we'd been lovers and they wouldn't do anything. He said he knew from experience. And of course he knew I couldn't say anything about the money."

There was a silence, and Tommy said, "And then I showed up."

"Which was the best thing that ever happened to me."

Tommy couldn't believe how beautiful she was with her big sad eyes. He said, "That *was* a lie, about his being inside your apartment, wasn't it? And the note? Did you cook that up, too?"

Lisa sagged back on the seat, eyes closed. She shook a couple of times and then she was sobbing, face in her hands. "I was desperate, Tom. I was so desperate."

"You knew about my sister and you were hoping I'd go after Salerno."

"I didn't know what would happen. I just wanted somebody to protect me."

"Well, that I can understand. You didn't have to lie to me."

"I was scared. I'm still scared. I don't want to get killed, and I don't want to go to jail."

"Okay, so you can turn the money in."

"What?"

"Turn it in. Make up whatever story you want, give it to the cops so they can get it back to the rightful owners. You won't go to jail."

She had stopped sobbing and was looking at him, eyes narrowed a little. "The rightful owners? Tom, where the hell do you think that money came from?"

"Shit, you tell me."

"Gambling, mostly. That and whatever else Rocco Salerno's into. That's what Star Capital was for, to launder his cash. That's money he took off all the idiots who throw away their paychecks on the Super Bowl. How are you going to find them all? How are you going to decide who gets what? For that matter, why do they deserve to get it back? They've already written it off. If we turn it in, it'll just go to the government, and they've got enough of our money already."

Tommy wasn't going to try to argue with her. He wasn't sure he could. Lisa grabbed his hand. "But if we split it, my loans are paid off, you've got enough money to set you up in whatever you want to do, we can go off somewhere and just be together for a while."

He hadn't expected that, and it threw him. She pulled his hand to her lips and kissed it. "I know. I was ready to let you go. And maybe we're not cut out for each other in the long run. But I bet we could have a real good time in Mexico this winter. We can just love each other for a while and see where it goes."

That set Tommy back in his seat for a second. All of a sudden he could see something in his future besides strangers in California. The image stunned him. Mexico with Lisa.

Tommy saw himself on a patio, in a hammock maybe, flowers everywhere, drinks to hand, Lisa in his arms. We can just love each other for a while. He had to pass a hand over his face. "That'd be good," he said.

"So you'll help me?"

Hell yes, one of his voices said. Another one said, "I don't think it's that easy to turn sacks full of cash into paid-off loans and a winter in Mexico. You know anything about laundering money?"

"I've worked in finance long enough to have a few ideas, yeah."

Tommy waited a moment before stating the obvious. "Then you don't need me."

Her face went blank and then took on a faintly hurt look. "I need somebody to protect me, and I need help with the logistics. It's got to be a lot easier with two. I've been waiting for somebody I trust to come along."

"Why didn't you trust me enough two days ago to tell me about this?"

He'd expected that to throw her, at least a little, but it didn't. She looked calm, focused and completely frank. "I'll be honest with you. Two days ago I didn't think anybody knew about the money besides me. I didn't think it was time to go yet. Now it sounds like it's time to go. And I'll never have anybody better than you to help me. Call me fickle if you want. But if you're a realist you know things can change from one day to the next. And they have. So now I'm offering you half, offering you winter in Mexico and whatever comes after that. What about it?"

Tommy sat there and looked at it. It looked a lot better than anything else he had going at the moment, except for minor considerations like homicidal gangsters and pissed-off federal agents. "We'd be running from the law. Even if it is just found money, that's not how the law's gonna look at it. You really want to be an outlaw?"

Her eyes narrowed a little and she peered at him for a moment before saying, "You didn't seem real concerned about being an outlaw when you shot Joe Salerno."

Tommy sat there and thought about things and made a decision. Ever since shooting Joe Salerno he had been doing his damnedest not to tell outright lies, the whole way along, hard as it had been. Tommy believed in telling the truth. Now he looked Lisa in the eye and said, "I didn't shoot him. He was dead when I got there. I didn't have anything to do with it."

He watched for changes in her face but didn't see any. She just looked back at him. More people went by on the street, more snow danced on the wind. After a long time Lisa said, "I see."

"So I don't know if I really deserve to be your hero."

She took a deep breath, closed her eyes for a second, and said, "You'll always be my hero, just for standing up to him. Now, tell me if we're going to Mexico together."

Tommy had a feeling he was at what his old man used to call a turnout. Tommy's father had worked on the railroad when he was young, and instead of a fork in the road he used to talk about a turnout any time there was a decision to make. "You throw the switch the wrong way, you go places you don't want to go," he used to say. Tommy could feel the heavy lever in his hands. "Okay, let's talk about it," he said.

35

Lisa had rented a closet-sized unit at a self-storage facility and bought some file boxes at an office supply store. She had transferred the cash to the file boxes and tossed the courier bags into a Dumpster behind a shopping center in the middle of the night. She had told the manager of the storage facility she was stashing tax records and rented the unit in the name of a company she made up. She'd paid a lot of rent on the unit over the past couple of years but figured a small fraction of what was in the file boxes would cover it.

"To do it right, you take your time," said Tommy. "If you don't want people to get suspicious, you don't fly off to Mexico all of a sudden. You start talking about how you need a change, you got a better job offer somewhere else, whatever. You give notice, have your going-away party, promise to write everybody. Meanwhile, you're putting that cash into bank accounts or whatever, little by little. You want to do it right, we're talking about a few months."

"I know," said Lisa. "Believe me, I've given this some thought. They've made it a lot tougher to launder money. The bank has to report any cash deposit over ten thousand dollars. You know how long it would take to deposit half a million in ten thousand dollar units? Do the math. I don't think we have time for that. If the cops know about me and Joe, they could be looking for connections right now, and that makes me nervous. What I'm thinking is, it's probably easier to get around the currency laws down in Mexico. And nobody's going to be particularly surprised if I decide I need a vacation in Mexico around Christmas time. With you, a little romantic adventure. And then if we don't come back, well, we can tell people any story we want. We liked it down there and stayed, whatever."

"All right. What do you want to do? How do we get the money to Mexico?"

"In a suitcase. I've been to Mexico. They don't give the tourists any trouble at the airport. We fly into Acapulco with three or four bags, swimsuits on top and money underneath."

"Man, I don't know about that."

"Or we drive across the border with the money in the trunk. Believe me, simple is best. All the security is the other way, drugs and terrorists coming into the U.S. The Mexicans don't care. We're tourists. They'll wave us through. I've done it.

They check your passport and that's about it. I say we fly into Acapulco or Cancún, rent a car, take it from there."

"Okay. When?"

Lisa thought about it, looking past Tommy. "I'll need a week. One week to set it up with my boss, add some vacation time to the days I get off anyway for Christmas and New Year. He's pretty flexible about that kind of stuff. I'll make flight reservations, too. In a week we should be ready to go. We'll pick up the money, pack it there at the storage place, go straight to O'Hare. Can you hold out for a week?"

If I can stay out of jail, Tommy thought. He shrugged. "Sure. Maybe I'll go back to Kentucky for a few days, just lie low."

They traded a look: Lisa's eyes were wide. "God," she said. "I can't believe I'm finally doing it."

"Sleep on it tonight. Things might look different in the morning."

"No. It's time to do it. It'll be an adventure. You and me, the perfect team." She grabbed him again, leaning across to plant one on his lips. "You and me."

"You and me." And half a million bucks, Tommy thought.

"Tom, take me home."

Tommy's stomach was lighter than air all of a sudden, her lips next to his. "I don't have a home anymore."

"My home, then."

"I don't think so. People who know I know you are looking for me."

Lisa pulled back a little. Her eyes were gleaming. "I guess it will have to be another motel, then."

Christmas came early, Tommy thought. This was something he

hadn't foreseen that morning, sitting on the edge of the bed, watching the cold light grow. Sometimes things dropped into your lap. Tommy risked the drive in his hot Chevy, hoping the feds had better things to do than roam the streets looking for him.

They wound up at the same place on Lincoln Avenue. The same clerk greeted them like valued regular customers, and up in the room the heat, the haste, the hunger were the same. Tommy had decided while he was still parked there on Kinzie that he was going to wait until the morning to think about what the hell he was doing. He decided he didn't care if the only reason Lisa was slipping out of her panties in front of him was that she needed his help. Tonight he was willing to be used.

Afterward, with Lisa breathing against the side of his neck, Tommy knew he should be coming to his senses, thinking hard about the future, but he still wasn't ready to let go of the illusion that this beautiful girl in his arms was there for no other reason than that she liked being there. Tommy knew that sometimes illusions could keep you going for a while, like fudge brownies saved up from MREs. He'd been down that road before.

Tommy could have stood to spend the night there: he didn't have anywhere else to go. But Lisa was wide-awake and hungry at ten o'clock. They had a late supper at a Mexican place on Lincoln not too far from Lisa's apartment. There was loud mariachi music on the sound system, and Tommy was gratef ul: it meant they didn't have to talk too much. All he wanted to do was eat, drink, and gaze at her. "I hope you like this kind of food," Lisa said at one point. "We'll be having a lot of it."

"Sounds good to me."

Tommy dropped her a block from her place, just in case somebody was watching. "One week," she said, cradling his face in her hands. "One week from today. Call me the day before. I'll have flight times and all that. Okay?"

"You sure you want to do this? I'm thinking, we could find out that money's a lot heavier than we expect."

She kissed him and let go. With a serious look on her face she said, "I've done the risk-benefit analysis, Tom. That kind of money is life-changing. And I don't know about you, but my life could use a change. How about yours?"

"Not much else going on right now, that's true."

"So. You coming with me?"

Tommy nodded. He reached for her, let her brush his knuckles with a kiss. "I'll see you in a week." He watched her disappear around the corner.

Tommy still had the keys to the apartment house basement where he used to work. He just hoped the Greek hadn't changed the lock. It was close to midnight when he stashed the Chevy on Sheffield a few blocks from the place. The key to the basement worked just fine. Tommy threw himself on the cot and went to sleep.

When he woke up, his watch said it was nearly seven, and he knew he had to clear out before the new janitor, whoever that was, came in. He splashed water on his face at the laundry sink and booked. The snow that had been in the wind the night before hadn't stuck: it was a cold hard bastard of a day like Chicago gets in early winter, a day as congenial as frozen concrete, a day to make people dream of Mexican beaches. Tommy headed south down Kenmore toward his car.

He had almost reached it when a black Dodge SUV slewed to the curb just in front of him. Foss jumped out of the passenger seat, Stefanovich got out of the driver's seat, and they hustled to block Tommy's way. They'd ditched the suits in favor of dark windbreakers, but they still looked just like what they were. "Well," said Foss with a wicked smile. "Look who's up early."

Tommy wasn't going to try to outrun anyone. He pulled up in conversational range. "You guys got nothing better to do than track me around? You must have caught all the terrorists already."

"You're number one in our hearts, Tom," said Foss. "Get in the back."

Tommy ignored him. "How in the hell'd you know where I was?" Tommy pulled out his cell phone: sure enough, it was off.

Foss laughed. "Not as smart as you thought you were, huh?"

Tommy frowned for a second. "Shit," he said. "I left the batteries in, didn't I? Damn, you guys got good equipment."

"Okay," said Stefanovich. "What's the deal, Tom? You spooked Vince so bad he's refusing to cooperate anymore. Why'd you go after him?" They seemed to have forgotten about getting him in the van. They stood bracketing him on the sidewalk, Stefanovich with his arms folded, Foss with his hands on his hips in the classic position for getting in a man's face.

Tommy relaxed a little: they weren't going to arrest him. "I didn't go after him. I went looking for somebody who could tell me about Star Capital, and he was who I found."

269

"Why the interest in Star Capital?"

"Because Joe Salerno used to work there."

"So what?"

Tommy frowned. "Am I being charged with a crime here?"

Foss said, "Not yet. We're sort of mulling that over, know what I mean? Obstruction, threatening an informant, witness tampering, we'll think of something. Not to mention assault and battery, which we'd be happy to farm out to the local department. You broke Vince's shoulder."

"It was self-defense."

"That's not how he tells it."

Tommy kept his mouth shut: he figured Vince hadn't mentioned the shotgun, and that was fine with Tommy. He shrugged and said, "Why don't you guys tell me what you want?"

"First we want to know what your agenda is. An informant with an agenda bothers us. An informant who keeps switching sides bothers us. An informant who jumps into the middle of a hit attempt and breaks it up bothers us. There are a whole lot of things about you that bother us. We want to know what makes you tick, so we can decide whether we made a mistake in signing you up as an informant."

"Okay. Right now what makes me tick is trying to get out of this damn town. Ever since I got mixed up in this Salerno thing, all I wanted to do was leave."

"Right. So you went around asking questions about Star Capital. What's up with that, Tom?"

Keep your mouth shut, Tommy thought. "Salerno used to work there."

"So? So what?"

"You wanted me to be an informant. I was looking for

270

information. I figured if Salerno used to work at Star Capital, there had to be something shady about it."

"Oh, horseshit. You were playing Sam Spade, gumshoe by trade? Give me a fucking break, Tom."

Stefanovich said, "How did you know Salerno worked there?"

"The cops told me."

"The CPD?"

"That's right."

Again Stefanovich and Foss traded a look. "Those pricks," said Foss. "Who'd you talk to?"

"Why don't you go ask them? I ain't getting involved in no cat fights between agencies."

Foss made a disgusted sound. "Christ. We told you to work on Catania's crew, not Salerno's. What the hell happened there?"

"Well, I figured I blew that by saving Salerno's ass. Catania's not going to be real happy to see me again."

There was a brief silence and Stefanovich said, "You're going after the money, aren't you?"

"What money?"

"The money Vince told you about. The missing half million bucks. That's your agenda, isn't it, Tom?"

Tommy sighed. "You guys are too smart for a poor dumb hillbilly, I guess."

Foss snickered a little. "Cherchez la dough, huh? Well, well. Have we found what makes you tick?"

Tommy said, "You guys are free to think what you want. What I'd like to know right now is, what do I have to do to get the federal government off my back, now that I got both factions of this here mob pissed off at me? What do I have to give you so you'll let me leave town and get on with my life?"

Foss made a little puffing sound, a sound of contempt. "You're free to take off any time you want, Tom. Of course, in that case, we'll have to cooperate with the Salerno task force by giving them that transcript. How long do you think you can last on the run?"

"Tell you what," said Stefanovich. "You come up with that half million bucks, I'd consider that a very helpful gesture. You help the government recover proceeds from an illegal enterprise, we'd look very kindly on it. We just might consider that a fulfillment of your obligation."

"Just don't get any big ideas about trying to take off with it," said Foss. "We'll be right on your ass."

"Don't worry," said Tommy, brushing past him. "I'm all out of ideas."

36

The G-men got back in their SUV and peeled out. Tommy just sat there in his car for a couple of minutes, making sure they were gone, looking for anything that looked like a tail in his mirror. Finally he started up the Chevy and drove down to Lincoln Park. He caught a parking spot opening up at the end of Lisa's block as somebody took off for work. Tommy grabbed it. After he parked he got out of the car and went and knelt down at the rear and started feeling under the bumper. He had heard you could track a cell phone even if it was turned off, but he wasn't sure how precise that was. He thought it was more likely they'd put a tracker on his car when they'd had him in custody.

He found it in five seconds. Tommy tugged till the magnet gave way and pulled a little black box, about two by three by one inch thick, out from under his bumper. He shook his head and then turned around and put his hand under the front bumper of the car behind him and left the device there. Then he got back in his car.

He sat there and watched Lisa's doorway and thought about Joe Salerno, who had sat here watching for Lisa just as Tommy was now. Tommy had shot Joe Salerno dead and now here he was stalking her himself: Tommy had come a long way in a month. He wondered if Joe Salerno had lusted for Lisa or if he just lusted for the money. Both, probably, he decided. How could you not lust for a girl like Lisa? The thought of Joe Salerno watching Lisa made Tommy glad once again he had shot the son of a bitch.

Lisa came down the steps at seven-thirty, dressed for work, and went south, toward the Fullerton El stop. Tommy gave her a lead and then got out of the car and followed. He had to close on her a bit as they approached the station for fear of her catching the train ahead of him, but he managed to make it through the turnstiles and up onto the platform without her seeing him. He stood a hundred feet from her, shielded by the crowd, and watched her stand with her chin sunk down into her scarf, steaming breath whipped away on the wind, waiting patiently for the train.

When the train came he got in the car behind hers. At the Merchandise Mart he followed her into the vast echoing hall and let her disappear into the crowd at the elevators.

Then he found his way down to the street. He had some time to kill.

Tommy found a bookstore and looked at tourist guides to Mexico. Acapulco, Cancún, Oaxaca, Puebla, Cozumel. The pictures helped but they were still just names to Tommy. He couldn't imagine himself there. He couldn't imagine himself with Lisa.

He took the El back to Fullerton, retrieved his car, and drove back to his place once again: he couldn't seem to shake free of it. He didn't give a damn if the FBI knew where he was. He slept until midafternoon and woke up hungry. At the diner on Wilson he thought about his choices and then went upstairs to get on the El. He took it back south again, switching lines to get to the Merchandise Mart.

He waited closer to the elevators this time, making sure he would spot Lisa at quitting time. Sure enough, he saw her and let her go past him in the crowd, fifty feet away. She walked looking straight ahead, the sign of a clean conscience and an unsuspicious mind. Tommy gave her a lead and then went through the turnstiles after her and onto the northbound platform. She was in her normal spot and this time he just hung out at the other end of the platform and watched her. When the train came he moved up so he could get in the same car as she did, at the opposite end.

He had just convinced himself she was heading home as usual when she threw him a curveball. She went one stop north and got off. Tommy had to step on some toes to get off before the doors closed. He saw Lisa disappearing down the steps to Chicago Avenue.

He followed her east and then north, and when she got to

where she was going he saw she'd outsmarted him, or maybe he'd just shot himself in the foot: she walked into a Hertz car rental agency. Tommy swore and started thinking hard. He made a pass by the storefront and looked in and saw her standing at the counter. He went up to the corner and crossed the street and stood there trying to look casual, watching the Hertz place. There was a garage exit next to the office that Tommy hoped was where the rentals came out. After a long fifteen minutes a green Escort came out of the garage and turned north. It went right by Tommy and he got a good look at Lisa at the wheel, concentrating on her driving, hands in the classic ten and two position. He memorized the license number and then started sprinting for the nearest subway entrance, at Clark and Division.

The ride north was a nail-biter. Tommy ran through all the scenarios he could think of and couldn't come up with any reassuring answers as to why Lisa would be renting a car. He knew he had blown it: he was going to need some luck to pick her up now. He ran from the Wilson El stop to where he'd parked his car. When he got there his guts were hurting. Heaving, wheezing, sweating, he started up the Chevy and pointed it south.

Night was coming down again, and Tommy saw everything coming to an end. If he blew this, it was over. He would light out for parts unknown and to hell with the FBI: let them track him down.

There was always the possibility he'd misinterpreted what Lisa was doing. Tommy truly hoped so. He made a pass up her block without seeing the Escort. He circled the neighboring blocks. He didn't find it. He tried the alley that ran behind

Lisa's place, but he didn't find it there, either. He finally pulled over at a corner just to think.

There were a million things that might be going on, but only one that Tommy really wanted to prevent. Tommy figured Lisa wouldn't pay a week's worth of car rental fees just to have the thing around: if she had rented the car it was to use it, soon. For a second he thought about just letting her go: kiss her good-bye and let her see how much happiness half a million dollars in dirty cash could bring her. Then he got mad. Tommy was tired of being lied to. He'd given her too much of a head start already. Tommy put it in gear and pulled out.

He pushed out Irving toward the expressway, swearing at the traffic. He didn't even know where the hell he was going. At a red light he pulled out his cell phone, switched it on, and dialed Brian's number. He got nothing but voice mail, so he cut it off and tried Mary's. She answered as Tommy was pulling away from the light. "Can you do me a favor?" Tommy said, skipping the explanations. "I need the addresses of any self-storage places there are in Northbrook. You got the Yellow Pages there?"

He'd found a way to render her speechless: after three or four seconds Mary said, "Uh, sure. What's going on?"

Hell of a good question, Tommy thought. "I'm looking for Lisa. She wanted my help to pick up some stuff out there and we missed connections. Can you find out and call me back? I'm in my car."

The good thing about women like Mary was, they loved to be helpful. Her tone of voice went straight to Competent Mode. "I'm sitting at the computer now. Just hang on and give me a second."

By the time Tommy was negotiating the ramp onto the expressway, Mary had told him that there appeared to be only one self-storage facility in Northbrook and had given him the address along with directions for getting there. "What the heck's going on with you two?"

"Soon's I know, I'll give you a call, I promise." Tommy switched off. The expressway was still jammed even though it was past six, and it made Tommy's stomach churn to have to sit there and crawl with the rest of them. Things thinned out a little as they got out of the city, and Tommy was flying, breaking speed limits right and left, by the time he shot onto the exit ramp at Willow Road. He pushed west and in five minutes he was there.

The storage facility was a big-box structure among half a dozen others along an industrial road in the middle of nowhere, more massacred countryside. There were apartment complexes on the other side of the road for people who didn't need a view. Tommy had decided he was on a wild-goose chase to end them all. The drive had worn him out and he was starting to confront the truth: his obsession with Lisa was making him crazy. He couldn't possibly track her movements for a whole week. As for the car, there could be any number of explanations. He was wasting time, gas, and his life.

And then as he passed the gate to the storage complex he saw the Escort, parked at the side of the building in a brightly lit lot, near an entrance door in a big blank wall. Tommy wheeled into a neighboring lot and parked, shielded by another car, and cut his lights. He couldn't quite make out the license number, but how many green Escorts could there be?

Tommy let out a gentle sigh of disappointment, disgust, res-ignation: all the things he was good at. He remembered Lisa

278

talking about how they would pack up the money at the storage place and go directly to O'Hare. He remembered her saying "See you in a week," just last night. He remembered holding her, feeling her go to sleep in his arms.

I loved you, Tommy thought, I truly did. He didn't know what to do: go over there and wait for her to come out, or follow her all the way to the airport to make sure, confront her there? And what would he gain by confronting her? It would be ugly. It would be better to drive off and just have the memories.

While Tommy was sitting there feeling miserable, Lisa came out of the door in the side of the building. Tommy was startled: she wasn't alone. Two men came out with her, and Tommy recognized one of them. He swore out loud. Steve had his arm around Lisa's shoulders and they were walking like lovers. She barely came up to his armpit. Tommy couldn't make out the expression on her face, but he could see Steve was smiling. Behind them came a man Tommy hadn't seen before, pushing a hand truck with four cardboard file boxes on it. They all walked over to the Escort and the man Tommy didn't know left the hand truck to pull out a key and unlock the doors. Steve opened the rear door for Lisa and handed her in like a man being polite to his date. He stayed there at the open door, leaning on the roof of the car, saying something to her inside, while the other man went back and opened the trunk and transferred the file boxes from the cart to the trunk. Then he shoved the hand truck over by the wall of the building and got in behind the wheel. Steve got in the back seat, next to Lisa.

Tommy was so amazed by what he was seeing that when the Escort started to roll he did nothing for a moment. He watched through the fence as the Escort rolled by within fifty feet of him and turned out onto the road. You bitch, he thought. You worthless lying cheating bitch.

Tommy turned on his headlights and spun out of his parking spot. This he had to see: he wasn't going to let Lisa waltz out of his life like this. Tommy was going to have something to say about this: he was going to chase them all the way to Mexico if he had to.

37

He had given them a bit of a lead, but it wasn't too late. He caught up with them at a stoplight on Willow Road, with three cars between them. Tommy was starting to recover, starting to think again, and the first thing he thought was that nothing made sense. If Steve and Lisa were in cahoots, what the hell was Tommy doing in the picture? She had never needed him for anything. He was starting to doubt the evidence of his senses.

The Escort turned south off Willow, then went west to the tollway. Tommy concentrated on keeping them in sight in the traffic, not worrying too much about being spotted. It was night and all they would make out was his headlights among a lot of others. They took the tollway down past O'Hare where it bent west, and then the Escort slowed and put on its signal as they approached the Irving Park exit. Tommy followed them west on Irving Park and then into the left-turn lane and suddenly they were on Mannheim Road, going south. They were taking Tommy to the West Side again.

They went past endless malls, acres of parking lots, vast housing tracts. They went under highways and over railroad tracks. Tommy didn't know where the hell they were when the Escort swung right onto another multilane main road. He seemed to be in the transportation hub of the country: it was all truck depots, as far as the eye could see. After a quarter mile or so the Escort swung left into a road that led between two giant yards full of trailers, parked in rows or backed up to loading docks. Tommy saw right away that if he followed the Escort he was going to be spotted, in a heartbeat. He went on past and wheeled into a parking lot a couple of hundred yards further down. Tommy wrenched the Chevy around, poised to turn back onto the road, and waited a minute or so. Then he pulled out and went back the way he had come.

He turned into the lane the Escort had taken. It was an alley that ran slightly downhill, with rows of trailers on either side. Even at night there was activity in the yards: Tommy could see trucks moving, people on the docks. A hundred yards ahead of him, he could see railroad cars. He was scanning for the Escort and not seeing it. The lane bottomed out and he had to decide what to do: go right into the huge truck lot, left into a parking lot behind a small office building with a row of mostly dark windows, or straight ahead into the rail yard. Tommy took a guess and swung left. There were two cars parked by the shed. Neither one was the Escort. Tommy figured one more wouldn't be noticed. He parked and got out into a bitter wind, closing the door softly.

Tommy knew you could get away with a hell of a lot if you just acted like you knew what you were doing. He also knew there was a hell of a lot of theft from truck and rail depots and there tended to be police around. He was getting to the point where he didn't give a damn. Tommy pulled up the hood of his sweatshirt, opened the trunk of the Chevy and rooted under his duffel bag until he came up with the shotgun. He pulled it out, still wrapped in its blanket, and closed the trunk. He threw the gun up on his shoulder like John Henry with his hammer and started walking toward the railroad tracks.

Before him the yards opened up, stretching a half mile across in front of him and away into the distance on either hand, the vast railway universe that was the whole reason the city of Chicago was there. There were hundreds of rail cars in sight, parked on sidings or moving slowly, shifting the country's freight. Tommy spotted the Escort a hundred yards away, parked next to a GTO that looked a lot like Vince's, a few feet from a couple of odd-looking railroad cars on a siding that ended at a bumping post. They were converted boxcars, painted white, and one of them had a door and windows along the side, with fold-down steps deployed to give access to the door. Tommy recognized them. Years ago they had been used as kitchen and dining cars for work crews. Now they were old and battered, shunted up a stub track to sit and rot. But light showed in the windows and Tommy could see a power line running from the car to a nearby pole: someone had made himself a little hideaway.

Tommy looked around, trying to figure the odds he was on somebody's security TV screen right now. He decided if a Ford Escort could drive right onto the yard, he could probably get away with it. There was a line of tank cars on a track a hundred feet in front of him. It would shield him from view while he got closer to the boxcars.

Tommy strode out like he had business there and ducked between two tank cars. He took a quick look for railroad cops and then started moving up the other side of the track toward the boxcars. He still had the gun up on his shoulder, bundled up. If anyone stopped him, he was a hobo. There were still people that did it. Tommy had had a friend in the army who had ridden the rails for a while and told him a story about being stranded in the yards in Chicago for two whole days, not moving.

Tommy ducked back between two tank cars and found himself twenty feet away from the boxcar with the light coming from its windows. There was no door on this side and the windows were too high for Tommy to see into. He set the shotgun on the platform at the end of a tank car and then climbed up onto it, which put him high enough to see in the windows. He could only see a narrow slice of the room inside, but he could make out what looked like bottles behind a bar. Somebody moved through his field of vision and Tommy recognized Vince, his arm in a sling. Tommy jumped down and reached for the gun, shaking it free of the blanket. He looked up and down the track, and then he stepped out and crossed to the boxcar. He slipped underneath it and started crawling up the track toward the steps.

The sound of car tires on gravel stopped him. Headlights came sweeping over the ground and Tommy scuttled back toward the wheels and went flat, the gun underneath him. The wheel assembly shielded him as the lights swept the length of the car. The sound of the tires came very close and stopped. Tommy kept still. He heard car doors open and close, steps on the gravel. "Watch your step," somebody said.

"I ain't no fuckin' invalid," said Rocco Salerno. "Keep your hands to yourself." Tommy heard the steps creak. He heard the door come open. He heard an indistinct voice from inside. He heard the door close.

Tommy didn't know what the hell he was doing there. He didn't know what the hell Lisa was doing there, either. He remembered the way she had been walking, with Steve's arm around her shoulder. They had looked pretty friendly. But then Tommy only remembered one of them smiling. Tommy didn't know what to believe. But the more he thought about it, the more he thought he needed to get inside this railroad car and have a talk with people. He didn't give a damn about the money. He only cared about Lisa, and if she was there against her will he was going to take her out of there. After that they could talk about their future.

He was wondering what a simple knock on the door would accomplish when he heard the door come open. He shifted so he could see the base of the steps, and he watched a pair of legs come down and then walk toward the Escort. As the man drew away and came into full view, Tommy recognized Steve, walking relaxed, in no hurry. Steve stopped at the door of the Escort and lit a cigarette. He threw the match away, took a long drag, and blew it out. He stood for a moment looking in the direction of the truck depot, then he pulled keys out of his pocket and reached for the door handle of the Escort.

He started and turned at the sound of Tommy's rush but

froze in a hurry when he saw the shotgun. "Hold still," said Tommy, quietly. "I got no plans to do anybody harm. But I could change my mind."

"Christ. What the fuck are you doing here?" Tommy had never seen Steve's cool waver, but nobody liked looking at the business end of a shotgun and Tommy could see he was shaken.

"Turn around and put your hands on the car."

Steve dropped the cigarette and obeyed him, recovering enough to give him a murderous look. "You're starting to get on my fuckin' nerves, you know that?"

Tommy put the shotgun to the back of his neck. He took the car keys from his hand and put them in his pocket, then searched him. He didn't find any weapons. "You're gonna do me a big favor," he said.

"That what you think, you dumb cracker?"

"Keep your voice down. You're gonna get me into that boxcar. Is the door locked?"

"How should I know?"

"If it is, you're gonna knock. Tell 'em whatever you want, you forgot something, whatever. But get me in the door. I don't want to use the gun, but I will if I have to. I get in and out with the girl, nobody gets hurt. Understand me?"

Steve said nothing for a moment and Tommy thought he was thinking about putting up a fight. Finally he said, "Yeah, I understand."

"Okay, let's go. Fuck with me and I'll blow your balls off." Tommy pushed him toward the steps and jammed the muzzle of the shotgun in his ass, knowing that would make a man as careful as could be. Over his shoulder Steve said, "You're a fucking dead man. You know that, right?"

"Not as long as I can squeeze a trigger. Move."

Steve mounted the steps and knocked. Tommy kept the gun where it would do the most damage, but he knelt to stay below the range of vision of anyone looking out the window in the door. The shade over the window was pulled aside. Tommy couldn't see who was there. Steve said, "I forgot to tell Rocco something." Tommy heard a lock click and then the door came open. He gave Steve an encouraging jab with the gun and Steve stepped up into the light. "Rocco," said Steve. "I got some bad news for you."

Tommy went up the steps fast. He gave Steve a shove in the small of the back that put him against the opposite wall and put the muzzle of the gun a foot from the face of the man who had opened the door, who proved to be the burly young guy that had been bodyguarding Salerno at the hospital in Maywood. "Nobody panic," Tommy said in a reasonable tone of voice. "This here's just a friendly visit. You get over there with him." He motioned with the gun, sending the young guy toward where Steve had wound up. Tommy shoved the door shut with his foot. "I'm assuming some of you got weapons and I'm assuming all of you are too smart to try and use them. I don't have to be too accurate with this thing to fuck you up pretty bad. You two, move down there with the rest of them."

Tommy herded them with the gun, scanning the place. Vince was leaning on the bar with his good elbow. Next to him on a barstool was the man Tommy had seen pushing the hand truck at the storage center, a bullnecked hardass with a pitted face. Everyone looked surprised.

Somebody had done a hell of a job on the inside of the old boxcar. It was paneled in dark wood, with plenty of booze ranged behind the bar, leather-upholstered couches along the walls, warm light coming from shaded lamps on the wall. To the right of the door was the main reason the hideaway had been fixed up, a green felt-covered poker table with eight or ten places around it. It looked like a nice place to while away an evening and drop a few thousand bucks in a mob-sponsored high-stakes game. On a coffee table in front of one of the couches were the cardboard file boxes. The lid was off one of them, showing a jumble of greenbacks inside.

Tommy took it all in with a glance. What he really had eyes for was Lisa, who was sitting on a couch at the end of the car. If he had had any doubts about her, one look wiped them away: she looked like a corpse that had been propped into place. Her face was bone white and the big dark eyes were round with shock. Tommy wondered how he could ever have been taken in by the arm around the shoulders. That had been to keep her from running away screaming. Just now she looked as if she were starting to come alive again, eyes fixed on him.

Rocco Salerno had been standing in front of Lisa. Now he was looking at Tommy, hands on his hips, a frail old man with a toxic expression on his face. "Jesus H. Christ," he said. "I should have killed you when I had the chance."

"I didn't intend to pester you again. You give me what I came for and you'll never see me again."

"I told you," said Vince. "I told you he was after the money."

"I don't give a shit about the money," said Tommy. "I came here for her, and that's all I want. Let's go, Lisa." She looked at Salerno as if asking for permission, but she was already coming up off the couch, resurrected. Salerno stopped her with a hand on her arm and said, "This little girl stole a half million dollars from me, after I gave her a job as a favor to her father. She has to pay for that."

Tommy said, "You got your money back. She sure as hell ain't gonna go to the cops, and I got a feeling she's done with high finance. Once we're out of here, it's history. We on the same page?"

Salerno peered at Tommy for a while, then looked at Lisa and said, "Well, little girl, looks like you got lucky. But watch your step, 'cause I got a long memory." He let go of her arm and Lisa came running up the car, weaving a little, bouncing off barstools.

Tommy grabbed her by the arm and pulled her behind him. "All right then. We're gonna take off, and we don't want to see y'all in the mirror." Tommy swept the room with the gun again, making his point: Vince and the man with the pock-marked face at the bar, watching him intently; Salerno's body-guard and Steve standing across the car from them. Steve looked a little sick, and Tommy thought he was one of those guys that was tough only as long as things went his way. Salerno stood down at the end, shaking his head.

Somebody knocked on the door. The handle rattled. "Police," somebody yelled outside. "Open up."

38

The handle rattled again. "Jesus Christ," said Salerno. "Is that that dumb fucking Marini? How much do I have to pay that son of a bitch?"

The voice came through the door again. "This is a police operation. Open the door or we will force entry."

"Well, go ahead and open," snapped Salerno. "What are you gonna do, argue with the police?"

Tommy was closest to the door, but he wasn't going to say hello to a police officer with a sawed-off shotgun in his hand. He retreated toward the poker table, taking Lisa with him. He didn't know how this was going to play out, but he knew he had to keep the gun out of it. "Open the fucking door!" Salerno growled, and his bodyguard hustled to the door.

Tommy laid the shotgun across the arms of one of the chairs at the poker table and shoved the chair in close to the table. As he did, he caught sight of Steve's face.

Steve looked as if he were about to throw up on his shoes, and he was edging toward the bar. Tommy said, "Wait a minute."

It was too late: Salerno's guy had turned the handle. The door burst inward, knocking him off balance, and through it came a full-length shotgun in the hands of a man in a dark blue ski mask. "Hands in the air!" he yelled. He pointed the shotgun down the car toward Salerno. "Hands up, hands up!"

Behind him came a second man with a nylon stocking over his face. He had a Mac 10 submachine gun in his hands, and he locked on to Tommy and Lisa. "Don't move! Get your hands up! Now!"

Lisa screamed. Tommy whirled and grabbed her, put a hand over her mouth. "Just do like the man said."

"What the fuck?" Salerno said. "I wanna see some fucking badges." Everyone had frozen, eyes wide, hands not going up yet, everyone still trying to process the shock.

"Just get your hands up and nothin's gonna happen," said the man with the shotgun. He looked back over his shoulder at Tommy and Lisa. "Get them down here with the others."

"Let's go, move!" screamed the one with the Mac 10, motioning.

Tommy knew for damn sure these weren't cops. He knew that because he had spent a morning trying to teach them something and he had recognized them despite the masks and the stress-distorted voices. The one with the Mac 10 had to be Bobby, the loser Tommy had surprised with the boss's girlfriend on the living room floor.

Tommy wished to God he hadn't put the gun down.

"Move your ass!" Tommy had a decision to make, and he knew it had to be fast. The masks made it look like a stickup, but Tommy figured the personnel involved meant that the real idea was that Rocco Salerno wasn't going to survive. The question was whether anyone else was meant to.

"She's sick, dammit." Tommy had his back turned, one arm around Lisa, and with his free hand, shielded from view, he pinched her in the stomach, hard. Lisa cried out and sagged, giving him a bewildered look. "Let me set her down here." Tommy hooked his foot behind hers and pushed, tripping her and stumbling a little as he caught her.

"HANDS IN THE AIR, GODDAMMIT!" Bobby was running out of patience.

"Just a damn minute, okay?" Tommy pulled out the chair next to the one he'd laid the gun on and lowered Lisa onto it. "She's gonna throw up."

He looked at Bobby's squished face in the stocking and suddenly knew for sure that Salerno wasn't going to be the only one to die: Bobby was looking at payback and the only thing keeping Tommy alive right now was Lisa in his arms. "Let her," said Bobby, his voice cold now. "Just get your fuckin' hands up and move. You got three seconds."

"That ought to be plenty," said Tommy, his hand on the stock of the shotgun. He had made his decision. He flicked off the safety but didn't bother to bring the gun up. He just shifted it a little where it lay and pulled the trigger, sending a load of

292

double-aught buckshot into Bobby's crotch. Lisa screamed in his ear.

Bobby's sudden distress occupied pretty much all his attention while Tommy brought the gun up and pumped it. A third man with a clown mask over his face and a big black Glock had come into the car, and Tommy had to kill him first because he was closest: he had spun at the sound of the blast and shot Salerno's bodyguard in the chest at point-blank range, not knowing who had fired. That gave Tommy time to blow the clown mask clear off his head along with a lot of his face. Lisa was still screaming. Tommy had to move then, because he saw the third man leveling the shotgun at him, a wicked black Remington. Tommy dived to his left as Vince jumped off his barstool onto the gunman's back, letting out a ragged yell of pain and rage as he did. The gun boomed and things in Tommy's vicinity splintered. The dive put the end of the bar between him and the shotgun, which gave him time to rack the slide again. His view of what happened next was obscured, but there was the sound of a brief scuffle and when Tommy looked around the end of the bar, he saw Vince on his back on the floor with the muzzle of the Remington planted on his chest. Vince screamed, the shotgun blew a hole in his chest, and Tommy killed the gunman with his last load of buckshot, all pretty much at the same time.

Suddenly the loudest sound was Bobby's groaning. Tommy turned to look and saw him trying: as badly hurt as he was, Bobby was still trying. Kneeling in a pool of blood, he was struggling to bring the Mac 10 up.

Tommy picked up the Glock and shot Bobby through the head.

Now the loudest noise was Lisa's sobbing. She was curled up on the floor, clutching her head in her hands. The pockmarked man was throwing up, bent over with his hands on his knees. He finished puking, wiped his mouth with his sleeve, and said, "Holy shit." He staggered a little and then started running. He ran past Tommy and bounced off the door frame on his way out. He made it down the steps before three shots sounded just outside the door. Tommy rolled to the doorway and put two quick shots into the head of the man who had been lurking to the right of the steps. He hit the ground a second after the pockmarked man did. Tommy scanned for more hostiles. He didn't see anybody, and after a couple of seconds he pulled back inside.

Lisa was still crying, curled up in a fetal position. Salerno was slumped on the couch at the end of the car, a hand on his chest. Steve was at the far end of the bar, leaning on it, shaking his head.

Tommy stalked up the car, stepping over bodies. He went past the table where the money sat, flecked with blood. He stood over Rocco Salerno and said, "That's twice I saved your life. All I want in return is, I was never here. The girl and I were never here. Make up any story you want. But we were never here. Agreed?"

"Jesus H. Christ. I think I'm having a heart attack."

"Agreed?"

"Yeah, yeah. Sure. Jesus, we gotta get out of here."

"I need a drink." Steve moved behind the bar.

Tommy pointed the Glock at him. "You go back there, I'll kill you."

Steve froze: after what he'd just seen, he had to take that very, very seriously. "What the fuck."

"Mr. Salerno, did Steve know you were going to the hospital that day?"

"Huh? What?" The penny dropped. "Bullshit. Stevie? I've known Stevie since he was a kid. Stevie's my boy."

Steve said nothing, but his look told Tommy he was right. Tommy was backpedaling, the Glock still trained on Steve. "You keep a gun behind the bar, Mr. Salerno?"

"Fuck, I don't know. Vince ran the goddam place. Help me up, we gotta get our asses out of here before the cops show for real."

"He's going for the gun, Salerno." Tommy stooped and picked up the Remington. He went back and handed it to the old man. "He sold you out to Catania. He set you up at the hospital, he set you up here. You let him get behind that bar, he'll get that gun and kill you. I'd keep this on him if I were you."

Tommy started backing away again, both men's eyes on him. When they looked at each other, Tommy turned and ran. He went to where Lisa was just rising to a sitting position, looking like a sleepwalker. Tommy grabbed her arm and pulled her to her feet. He practically threw her down the steps, jumped down after her, helped her up and dragged her to the Escort. He had the key out and the driver's side door open when the shot boomed out inside the boxcar behind them.

Tommy drove the Escort the short distance to where the Chevy was parked. He went around to the passenger side and pulled Lisa out and gave her a wicked slap. "You together enough to drive? I hope so, 'cause otherwise you're walking."

Tommy watched her struggle for focus. "All right," she said, but she didn't look it. He shoved her toward the driver's side and ran for the Chevy. He got in and drove the hell out of there, Lisa following in the Escort.

Tommy had no guarantee they hadn't been seen and all he could hope was that nobody got a plate number. He went east and north, looking for flashing lights behind them. Lisa seemed to be in control of the Escort. When Tommy was sure they were clear he pulled out his cell phone and drove one-handed and one-eyed while he punched in the contact number he'd memorized for the FBI.

When a neutral male voice answered, Tommy said, "Listen good. Catania's guys are gonna hit Rocco Salerno some time tonight and take the half million bucks. If you move fast you can scoop them all up and get the money to boot. Salerno's camped out in the rail yards on the West Side, near Mannheim and Lake, in a converted rail car behind the truck depot."

There was a brief silence. "Identify yourself properly, please."

Tommy'd had it with the feds; they were worse than army brass. "I'm Eliot Fucking Ness, who do you think it is? Tell Foss and the other guy, what's his name. They wanted me to give them Catania, I'm giving them him and the money. Now get your ass in gear. You don't have a lot of time." Tommy switched off the phone.

"They were waiting for me when I got home with the car. They'd broken in through the back door." Lisa had finally recovered enough to talk. They were at her place, after a long drive. Lisa was under the covers, shivering, while Tommy sat on the edge of the bed with his back to her. He had showered, washed the blood off his boots, and was drinking bourbon he'd bought in a 7-Eleven out of the bottle.

"That was my fault," said Tommy. "Vince must have done some thinking after I talked to him. They knew about you but they'd never made the connection with Star Capital."

In a faint strangled voice she said, "Oh, God, what an idiot I was."

"I ain't gonna contradict you there."

"I don't know what came over me, Tom. I just panicked, I couldn't wait a week. I would have contacted you, you know I would."

"Yeah."

She covered her face with her hands again, the horror taking her. "I keep seeing it. I'm sick."

Tommy took a drink of whiskey. "Yeah, you are. That's what it is. And you'll be sick for a while. But you'll get over it."

After a while she took her hands away from her face. "I was so sure I was going to die. Oh God, I was so scared."

Tommy couldn't say anything for a moment. He could feel the rage inside, pushing at the walls. "Now you know how my sister felt."

That shut her up for a minute or so, and then she was sobbing again. "Tom. I'm so sorry."

Tommy couldn't help himself. He twisted to look at her. "For what? For lying to me? For trying to cheat me? Forget it. I got to fuck you, so I got nothing to complain about, right?"

She cried some more while Tommy drank. He could hear her composing herself before she said, "All I can say is, the money like . . . made me crazy. Try to understand. I grew up poor."

"Yeah, and I grew up in a fuckin' castle."

"Don't go cold on me, Tom, please. Whatever I did, that's all gone. I was an idiot. I did bad things. But tonight changed me. I'll never be the same. And I need you. God, I need you. Please. I didn't know how much I needed you before, but now I do." She was babbling through tears.

Tommy had had enough. He reached back and grabbed her by the hair. She squealed as he pulled her face close to his. "You know what happens when you lie to people? After a while they don't believe you anymore. That's what happens. It takes some people a while, but they learn." Tommy let go of her and got up off the bed. He grabbed his coat and put the pint in a pocket. "I saved your life tonight, for real. The best way to thank me is to keep your mouth shut about it, till the day you die. And tomorrow, you go get on that plane to Mexico. You don't want to be around for a while."

"Don't leave me." She was screaming it, sitting up in the bed, when he closed the door on her. "*Don't leave me!*"

39

Tommy jumped in the car and went. He found a gas station near an entrance to the expressway and pulled in to fill up. From where he stood at the pump he could hear the roar of the traffic. In a little while he could be heading west, with two thousand miles to go before he hit the Pacific. He knew this was the time. He figured if he got on the road and kept driving, Chicago cops and FBI special agents would be hard-pressed to ever find him. He was through.

So why was he standing here by his car with his hands in his pockets, letting the wind chill suck the life out of him?

Tommy wasn't sure. All he knew was, there was nothing ahead of him but a lot of road in the dark.

Tommy was still seeing the firefight, watching his shots blow people apart, hearing Lisa screaming. It was bad, but what bothered him most was how little it bothered him. Tommy had gotten really good at shooting people. He had gotten really good at shutting down.

It was something else, and he was having trouble putting his finger on it. Part of it was all that road ahead. He'd been waiting for days for a chance to leave the city behind but now it felt like he was leaving behind the only life he had, the good parts along with the bad. There wasn't anything for him in California except starting all over again.

But that would be a hell of a lot better than doing jail time in Illinois. Wouldn't it? Tommy was confused. He wanted to go somewhere and finish that pint of bourbon. He wanted to go back and grab Lisa and hold her till she stopped crying. He wanted to hear her say she needed him and he wanted to believe her.

Tommy wanted all kinds of things he couldn't have. That was his life on this earth. Most of all right now he wanted to figure out what the hell was keeping him from getting on the interstate and flooring it.

He leaned on the roof of his car, chin on his folded arms. Tommy was starting to see that all the miles of highway in the United States of America weren't going to be enough to leave Joe Salerno behind him. Shooting Joe Salerno had been the first turnout, the big mistake. It wasn't that he felt bad for Joe Salerno, or for any of the other lowlifes that had gotten themselves shot afterward.

No, what really bothered Tommy was that whether he had

lied outright or not, he had never been able to look a policeman in the eye and tell him exactly what had happened in that bar that night. Tommy had been lying to himself about the whole thing. He'd gone there that night looking to kill Salerno, from the start. And lying to himself about that had forced him into a lot of other lies, for now and for years to come.

If his father had been standing in front of him, Tommy would have been ashamed to tell him. Tommy remembered his father telling him that a clean conscience was the most precious thing a person could have. Tommy didn't have that anymore. He had lost a big part of his integrity.

Tommy could only think of one way to get it back.

A newspaper lay on the counter, the headline screaming *Mob figure Salerno only survivor of bloodbath.* A subhead said *Cops seeking rival Catania.* Tommy had looked at the papers earlier: they were full of breathless speculation. It was the biggest gangland shootout since the St. Valentine's Day Massacre, and all bets were off. The Outfit was up for grabs. The police and the FBI were playing it close to the vest. A photo had shown body bags on the ground by the railroad car.

Tommy had drunk too much coffee and his stomach was bothering him. He had been up all night thinking about doing jail time. He figured with extenuating circumstances there had to be some kind of deal he could cut: it couldn't be first-degree murder. He thought he could maybe hack up to five years and still have a life left afterward. But he didn't know how realistic that was. Even with a good lawyer he was looking at some hard times ahead, harder than the army. He wondered what he could hang on to to get him through it.

He paid his check and went out into a dirty cold Chicago day. The hard part was figuring out who to confess to. Strictly speaking, the case belonged to the Maywood Park department, but Tommy wasn't going to give those crooked sons of bitches anything: they'd sold him out to Rocco Salerno. That left the joint task force. All Tommy could think of to do was go to Belmont and Western and ask for the detectives who had grilled him there after he'd been picked up on the stop order. The only problem was, he couldn't remember their names.

In the end, Tommy figured the best thing to do was just to drive out to the rail yards and look for somebody he knew. He figured that was where all the task force detectives would be today.

When he turned off Mannheim Road he saw he was going to have a hard time getting anywhere near the rail yards. The alley he'd gone down the night before was blocked off by a state police car. There were TV vans from all the channels in town parked along the road, along with police vehicles from a grab bag of departments, city and suburbs and the Cook County Sheriff. It looked like the circus had come to town.

Tommy parked on a side street and hiked back. He was coming up on the circus when the black Dodge SUV went past him and then abruptly swerved over to the curb just ahead. "Shit," Tommy said out loud.

Foss jumped out of the passenger seat in his dark blue FBI windbreaker and called to him. The look on Foss's face was strange: amazed, like he couldn't believe Tommy was in front of him. "Where in the hell did you come from?"

Tommy kept walking; there was no place to run to. "Kentucky," he said. "You guys ever get my message last night?"

"We got it," said Foss, opening the back door. "Hop in."

"Am I under arrest?"

Foss threw up his hands. "Give me a break, would you? You're working for us, remember? Now get in, for Christ's sake. We got some catching up to do before we pin that medal on your chest."

Tommy didn't like the sound of that, but he could see there was no way to avoid talking to them. He got in the SUV. Stepanovich was behind the wheel, and he had the same strange look on his face, like somebody had just given him a surprise present. "Are you all right?" he said.

"Why in the hell wouldn't I be all right?" Tommy said.

Foss jumped onto the passenger seat and slammed the door. "Because half the cops in the city are looking for your body today. What the fuck happened to you?"

Tommy just looked at them. Stepanovich pulled away from the curb and accelerated, going on past the crowd at the entrance to the rail yards. "What do you mean, what happened? I followed a couple of Salerno's guys here and then I called you. You didn't get here in time, did you?"

"We didn't miss it by much. Were you around for the shooting?"

Tommy was tired of editing everything he said, but these weren't the guys he wanted to confess to. "Are you kidding me? I hauled ass out of here as soon as I figured out what was happening."

Stepanovich said, "Okay, so how did your army ID wind up covered in blood and in a pocket on one of those corpses back there?"

Tommy gave it a second and then he laughed. "Is that why they're looking for my body?"

"Of course it is. The cops think you're victim number nine. So did we. We thought you must have run out of luck just after you called us. That's why the cops are checking the sewers for you."

"Well, the card was just a trick I played on Salerno, to try and make him think I was dead. I don't think it worked."

"Well, it worked on us. We actually felt bad about you, especially after Salerno cleared you."

Tommy wasn't sure he'd heard right. "What do you mean?"

Foss threw him a look over his shoulder. "Salerno confessed to shooting his son."

Tommy felt light-headed all of a sudden. "Say what?"

Foss and Stepanovich traded a look. Foss said, "Salerno's in the hospital, in a coma. When we showed up last night, the railroad cops had a hold of him. He was like, delirious, having another heart attack. We went with him to the hospital and before he went into the coma we talked to him. And all he could say was, he killed his son. He just kept repeating that, over and over—'I killed the only son I ever had.' We asked him about the eight dead guys, but we didn't get anything else out of him before he went under. The docs don't think he's gonna survive."

Tommy just there paralyzed. He knew who Salerno was talking about. He also knew he'd been handed a great big free pass, the biggest of his life. What it was going to do to his conscience he didn't know, but the last thing he was going to do right now was open his mouth. "No shit."

"No shit. The cops don't give a damn about the Joe Salerno case now anyway, what with this pile of bodies they got on their hands. It's just a footnote. But we did pass on what Rocco said to the task force dicks. If they do find out you're still alive,

I don't think you're gonna have any more problems with them. And we won't tell them if you don't want us to. We can get you in the program and get you set up far away if you want."

Tommy said, "You must have got the money, huh?"

"We'll get it when it's not part of a crime scene anymore. We'll have to fight the local guys for it, probably, but I think we'll wind up with it."

"You're the government," Tommy said.

"Yes, we are. And we got Catania, too. We got him on tape saying 'All they had to do was kill the old fart. How could they fuck it up?' or words to that effect. I think we're gonna nail him this time."

Tommy looked straight ahead out the windshield for a moment. "So are you done with me?"

"Well, we're gonna need to debrief you. And depending on what you know and how you found out, we may want you to testify when Catania comes to trial."

Tommy saw he wasn't out of the woods yet. He thought for a minute and said, "Nothing I could tell you could be used in court."

They traded a look and Foss said, "Why is that, Tom?"

"You don't want to know. But I ain't testifying. You wouldn't want me to."

Tommy hoped that was convincing. There was silence in the front seat for a little while. Stepanovich said, "You know, what Rocco said still doesn't explain that bit on the tape about you having to tell about doing Joey. You want to clarify that?"

Tommy had to think about it all then: whether any purpose would be served by going through with his confession, what the whole thing was going to do to his conscience. Finally he decided he was through lying but he wasn't obliged to give anyone any extra help. "I got nothing to hide," he said. "You want to tell the cops I'm still breathing, be my guest. If we're done talking here you can drop me off back at my car."

Stepanovich pulled over to the side of the road. He and Foss traded another look and then they both turned to look at Tommy. Foss sat there shaking his head for a minute. He said, "You did it for the old man, huh? How much did he pay you to whack his son?"

Tommy had to keep a tight grip on himself then, because he saw that if that was the story, nobody would ever be able to prove it. He kept his face a blank and said, "You guys got it all wrong." It was good to be able to tell the truth.

Foss said, "You know, Tom, sooner or later this unhealthy lifestyle of yours is gonna catch up with you."

"Get the fuck out of my car," said Stepanovich.

Tommy sighed and reached for the door handle. He was going to have quite a hike back to the Chevy.

Tommy drove out and parked by the lake at Montrose Harbor. He got out of the car and stood in the harsh wind, watching the whitecaps roll in to break on the rocks, one after another. He was a free man, the odds were he was going to stay that way, and his life was what he was looking at: cold and gray and endless. He wasn't going to do jail time, but he was going to have to carry Joe Salerno on his conscience, along with a few other things. He was going to have to find a way to atone. Tommy had read about people who had devoted their lives to good works to make up for things they'd done wrong. Tommy figured he had his work cut out for him.

The hard part was going to be facing that road. It had gotten harder for him to be alone. He remembered Lisa telling him he looked dangerous, and he wondered if everything he had done had changed him too much. Maybe that was all anybody would see when they looked at him; maybe it was too late for anybody to love him.

That made Tommy quake with fear.

"Well shit, Tom. It's been real." Brian shook his hand. "I ain't gonna say it was all fun, but it sure as hell was interesting."

Tommy stood at the door of the Chevy, ready to get in. "I owe you, brother."

"Nah. Just put me up in L.A. next time I'm out there."

"You got it." Tommy was anxious to get going. He had a lot of road ahead of him. He gave Brian a wave and got in.

He almost ran over Mary at the corner: she came running out of the side street and almost into his path. He braked and honked at her. When she saw who it was she put a hand over her heart, made a face and came around to the driver's side window.

"I'm glad I caught you," she said, panting. "I wanted to say good-bye."

"Yeah, well. Good-bye." Tommy didn't know what to say: this was Lisa's best friend.

Mary just looked at him while she caught her breath. "Lisa called from Florida. She sounded better. She was kind of mysterious, but she did say not to blame you. She said she'd been heading for a breakdown for a long time. God, like who knew? Lisa, of all people. But she did say, 'none of it is Tom's fault.'"

"That's good to know." Tommy wondered how long this was going to go on. He wanted to get on the road.

307

Mary dug in a pocket and pulled out a small gift-wrapped package. "I got you a going-away present," she said, handing it to him.

All Tommy could do was look at her, standing there with her hair blowing in the wind, her usual cheerful look strained by the cold. "Now why would you do a thing like that?" he said, forcing a smile.

Mary opened her mouth, hesitated, and said, "Because I've been in love with you since I first laid eyes on you. Since you first walked into my house."

Tommy gaped at her. "Well hell, Mary." He gaped at her some more and she smiled. Tommy couldn't believe he'd never noticed how nice her smile was. "Hop in," he said. "Let's go for a ride."